the initiation of
ms. holly

k d grace

Published by Sourcebooks Casablanca, an imprint of Sourcebooks, Inc., in conjunction with Xcite Books.
P.O. Box 4410, Naperville, Illinois 60567-4410
(630) 961-3900
Fax: (630) 961-2168
www.sourcebooks.com

Originally published in 2010 by Xcite Books, London.

Library of Congress Cataloging-in-Publication data is on file with the publisher.

Printed and bound in the United States of America.
VP 10 9 8 7 6 5 4 3 2 1

This book is dedicated to sex and romance and love
and all the other good things the world could use more of.

Chapter One

HE PRACTICALLY FELL ON top of Rita, his hand grazing her left breast in the complete darkness. She yelped and grabbed him to keep from losing her balance.

"God, I'm sorry!" He gasped. "Bloody nuisance, this, isn't it?" His voice was warm, melodious, by far the most pleasant thing that had happened to Rita since she left Paris. "Oh dear. You're trembling. Are you all right?"

"I'm claustrophobic." Her words were thin and shaky, as though she didn't fully trust herself to let them out. "It wouldn't be so bad if I didn't know where we are." For an embarrassing moment, she realized she was still clinging to him, but the embarrassment passed, and suddenly she didn't care. If they were going to die trapped in a train in the Eurostar tunnel, buried beneath a gazillion gallons of water, she'd just as soon not do it alone.

He either understood, or was too polite to leave her in such distress. He wrapped his arms around her, engulfing her in a muscular embrace, the scent of which was maleness barely masked by deodorant and some spicy cologne, both fading at the end of a day much longer than either of them had anticipated. "Don't worry." In the darkness, he misjudged the distance between them and his lips brushed her earlobe. "It's just an electrical malfunction. Anyway, we're better off down here than in the snowstorm up above. Sounds like all London is shut down. Who'd have expected snow this late in the spring? Never mind that, where else do you get the chance to cuddle strangers in the dark?"

He pressed a little closer to her, and she was relieved to find other thoughts, thoughts more welcome than those of their predicament, pushing their way into her head. He felt good, broad-shouldered and tall, easy to lean on.

"Why are you huddled here in the corner rather than hunkered down in your seat?"

She concentrated on his warm breath pressing against the top of her ear. "I was on my way back from the loo when the lights went out and…"

"And this is as far as you got."

She nodded against his chest, honing in on the reassuring sound of his heartbeat.

"Shall I help you back to your seat then?"

The train lurched forward, and she yelped again, tightening her grip around his neck. "No, please. It's better if I just don't move."

There was a long pause. "Do you want me to stay with you?"

She realized the poor man had little choice, clenched in her strangle hold, as he was. "I don't want to be any trouble," she lied.

He readjusted his stance and tightened his embrace. "No trouble at all. I can't think of a better way to pass the time than in the arms of a beautiful woman. You are beautiful, aren't you?"

In spite of the stress she felt, she forced a laugh. "Gorgeous, actually. Too bad you can't see for yourself."

He ran a hand down the contour of her spine to rest low on the small of her back. "I don't have to see you to admire you."

The thought that the man was rather cheeky barely crossed her mind before he lifted her fingers to his lips and planted a warm kiss across the back of her knuckles. "I'm Edward. I'm from London. Clearly you're not."

"Rita," she replied. "I'm from Seattle, but I live in London now."

"Well Rita, from Seattle, we've established that you're an exotic beauty. Perhaps you'd like to return the favor." He lifted her hand to his face and guided it gently over the slight stubble of his cheek. As her hand cupped his well-formed chin, he pulled her middle finger into his mouth and nibbled it, teasing the pad of it with his tongue. Suddenly her struggle to breathe had nothing to do with being claustrophobic.

"Well?" He asked pulling her hand away to massage her fingers. "What do you think? Am I acceptable?"

If he was cheeky, she was downright brazen. She stopped his words with her mouth, amazed at how easily she had found the mark in total darkness. Perhaps it was the darkness that made her so bold, but, whatever it was, he didn't disappoint. His mouth was warm, opening eagerly to the probing of her tongue, responding in kind, caressing her hard palate, nipping at the fullness of her lower lip before pulling away just enough to speak.

"There, you see? It's not so bad being in the dark, is it? The other senses are too often overlooked, which is very sad, since they offer such exquisite delights." His hand moved up to cup her cheek, and he raked a thumb across her still-parted lips. "Taste, for example. Few pleasures exceed that of the tongue."

She heard him fumbling in the darkness, then she heard the rattling of foil. "Open your mouth," he whispered. "I have something that'll make you feel better, guaranteed. Oh don't worry, it's nothing illegal."

Reluctantly she opened her mouth, which he primed with a wet kiss, then slipped a chocolate truffle between her lips. It was covered liberally in cocoa and warmed exquisitely, almost, but not quite, to the steamy melting point of his body temperature, which only enhanced the sharp, edgy flavor that separates expensive chocolate from the cheap stuff.

She gasped her surprise, then moaned softly at the intensity of the taste.

"Don't bite." He kissed her jaw, then her throat. "Savor it, roll it around in your mouth. There are places on the tongue that taste only sweet and places that taste only bitter or salt, or sour. Chocolate can have all those flavors. Caress it in your mouth like you're making love to it, and you'll be amazed at what you taste."

She cheeked the truffle, slurring her words as she spoke. "I thought I was tasting you."

He chuckled softly. "Everything tastes better with chocolate." Without another word, he took her mouth, plunging his tongue deep against the melting truffle, whirling it, lapping at it, sighing with the pleasure of it. The more liquid and heated the truffle became, the more liquid and heated Rita became.

"The taste buds can distinguish wonderfully subtle flavors," he said between tongue dances. In the meantime he slipped his hand under her skirt, stopping to caress a garter belt. Rita had always hated pantyhose, and sexy or not, she preferred garter belts and stockings, which she found much less confining.

Still sharing the truffle in her mouth, he shoved aside the crotch of her panties and plunged a finger between her swollen labia, moaning his satisfaction at finding her so slippery and receptive.

She ground herself against his fingers. Wriggling and squirming until she was practically sitting on his palm, the heel of it rubbing deliciously against her clit, while they savored the taste of the truffle.

He smeared chocolate against her lips as he whispered, "It's amazing how closely linked scent and taste are." Then he pulled his hand from her panties, and she caught the salty-sweet scent of herself just before he plunged a wet finger into her mouth, allowing her to suckle her own juices.

"You see? The taste is completely different when you add your own flavor." He pulled his fingers away to taste for himself, then plunged his tongue back into her mouth.

"What about your flavor," she gasped when they came up for air, dribbling chocolate and saliva down their chins.

She didn't have to ask twice. Suddenly they were tugging and pulling at his trousers and struggling to get them open enough to extricate his enthusiastic erection. When the warmth of it, the heavy shape of it, pressed against her hand, she dropped into a squat and took it into her mouth, finding him thick and smooth and slightly salty with a warm, yeasty scent not unlike new-made bread, like *pain au chocolat*, she thought.

He curled his fingers in the waves of her hair and shifted his hips. She adjusted, nearly gagging in her efforts to take more of him into her mouth and still hang on to the last taste of chocolate as long as possible.

It was inevitable that her hand, the one not stroking Edward's distended balls, would find its way between her legs.

But her fingers weren't enough. She stood quickly, nearly bumping him in the chin with her head. "I want more than a taste," she gasped, already shoving her skirt up and turning her bottom to him, guiding his cock toward its goal. The thought crossed her mind that, if the lights came back on, they would very much be caught in the act. But when Edward spread her lips with warm fingers and slipped inside her, she forgot all about the risk and thrust back against him.

Surely people around them—even in the total darkness—could figure out what was going on. Who knew? Maybe some of them had also slipped hands in trousers or under skirts for some pleasurable relief from the stress of the situation.

She could tell by Edward's bruising grip on her hips that he was about to come, and she was riding the edge of her own orgasm, just barely managing to hold back, just a little longer, just a few more seconds.

It hit with such force that for a moment she thought her worst fears had been realized, and there had been an explosion on the train. But there were no screams, though she was desperately trying to keep from screaming herself. That must surely mean that the explosion was personal.

In the midst of the intense pleasure hurtling through her, Edward grunted in her ear, "You still want to taste me? Let me come in your mouth."

As she pulled off him, and they fumbled to switch positions, from somewhere he produced another truffle and shoved it into her mouth, followed in short succession by his engorged cock.

Quickly she cheeked the chocolate to make room for his penis, which she took as deep into her throat as she could, trying to savor both truffle and thrusting cock without choking on either.

The curl of his fingers in her hair tightened as he pulled her mouth further on to him with each thrust until, at last, he grunted the first spurt of semen into her mouth, which blended with the chocolate in an earthy richness that made her pussy twitch again. Chocolate and sex, chocolate and come. The taste alone catapulted her to another orgasm.

As his grip lessened on her hair, she knew exactly what to do next. Holding the last of his come in her cheek next to the truffle, she stood, took his face between her hands, and teased his lips apart, drizzling the blending of maleness and chocolate onto his tongue.

They were still gobbling hungrily at each other's mouths when the conductor's voice came over the intercom. "Ladies and gentlemen, a train has just arrived to tow us into Ashford. Upon our arrival, another train will be waiting for those of you who wish to continue on to London St. Pancras. For those of you who would prefer, arrangements have been made to put you up at a hotel in Ashford for the night and get you safely on your way in the morning. Once again, we apologize for the inconvenience."

The car erupted in a buzz of conversation as people discussed their options and their relief that at least something was finally happening.

"What will you do?" he asked. She heard him zip his fly, then she felt him carefully wiping between her pussy lips with what must have been his handkerchief.

"I'll stay," she said, opening her legs to his ministerings, almost wishing the conductor had kept his mouth shut long enough for round two. "With all the snow, I can't get home even if I do get to London. You?"

"I have to go." He pressed a lingering kiss to the inside of her thigh just above where the stocking was attached to the garter belt. "Business. It would have been lovely to continue the fun in a hotel room. But I can't. Not this time. Come on. Let me help you back to your seat."

When they arrived in her car, by the light of his mobile, she found her place much more quickly than she would have liked. "Give me your phone," he said once she was seated.

She did as he asked. He keyed in something and handed it back. "Now you have my number. Text me." Then he gave her a brain-searing kiss and left as the train lurched forward and gathered speed. She hadn't even seen his face.

Chapter Two

"OH FOR FUCK'S SAKE, just text the man already." From where she sprawled on the sofa, Rita's friend, Kate, stretched to check if the lacquer she had just applied to her toenails was dry. "He did ask you to."

Rita refilled their wine glasses and flopped back into the recliner. "I keep wondering if I imagined the whole incident, with the stress of being trapped in the dark under the channel, you know, the fear of dying without getting laid. I mean it's been so long."

"Not so long any more, you lucky cow."

"And that's another thing. What if he thinks I'm a slut, I mean I did kiss him first."

Kate rolled her eyes. "Honestly, you Americans are so squeamish about sex. You're never going to know what he thinks if you don't text him." Kate grabbed Rita's mobile from where it lay on the coffee table and pulled up the directory. "You see? Look. Says right here *Edward*, the only Edward you know, isn't it? Edward with no last name."

"Christ! That's right. I don't even know his last name. I don't even know what he looks like." Rita lunged for her phone, but Kate pulled it away with a giggle.

"You definitely know what he feels like, hon, and what he tastes like. I'll be riding my rabbit to fantasies of jizz and expensive chocolate for months to come, thanks to you."

"What are you doing? Kate? Kate, give me back my phone."

With a wicked laugh, Rita's friend leaped off the sofa just out of her reach, texting frantically, and as Rita was about to tackle her, she tossed the phone back, barely missing her wine glass.

Rita fumbled to catch it. "What the hell did you do?" But being familiar with Kate's naughty little mind, she already knew the answer. On screen the text message read:

Sun nite was gr8. Would luv 2 do it again. R.

The message had been sent.

"Kate! Damn it, how could you? Now for sure he'll think I'm a slut and—"

Her reprimand was interrupted by the beep of an incoming text. She nearly dropped the phone. Kate was instantly at her side.

"Well? Is it from him? What'd he say?" She shoved in close and looked over Rita's shoulder at the text that read:

Me 2. Drinks and din @ The Mount. 8:30 Sat? E.

"The Mount!" Kate practically squealed in her ear. "Even God can't get rezzies at The Mount. And even if he could, he couldn't afford to actually go there. The bloke must be rolling in dosh." She danced a little jig in front of the sofa. "Find out if he has a friend."

—⁓—

Saturday night, Rita arrived by taxi at the reclaimed warehouse along the Thames that was The Mount. But for the Jags and Porsches arriving as fast as the valets could drive them away, no one would have guessed it was a favorite hangout of people with money.

Suddenly a sleek white limo pulled up in front of the awning protecting The Mount's customers from inclement weather. A liveried driver opened the door with military precision. The woman who stepped out had to be the perfect female. Her full, high breasts were well displayed in a simple silver gown. The low back hugged the exquisite narrowing line of her long spine, culminating in an elegantly small waist, which blossomed into the swell of her hips and rounded hillocks of her bottom. Her ripe wheat hair was caught up in a simple chignon exposing the elegant arch of her neck and shoulders.

The woman lingered to shake hands with a few adoring worshippers, then glided into The Mount as though her feet never touched the ground. "I can't believe it," the taxi driver breathed. "That's Vivienne."

"I know." Rita said. Kate would never believe she'd seen the goddess herself in person.

"In all the times I've dropped people here, this is the first time I've ever actually seen her," the driver said.

Rita swallowed her nerves and stepped out of the cab. Granted, she wasn't Vivienne, but, she reassured herself, she knew how to dress for success. The midnight blue sheath caressed her curves almost like Edward had, and the double spaghetti straps offered her full breasts just enough support to get by with the braless plunge that displayed her abundant cleavage without being too slutty. Twin slits up the sides of her gown gave tantalizing glimpses of her thighs as she walked. The matching stilettos were not quite fuck-me shoes, but they could definitely be classified as make-love-to-me-naughtily shoes.

Inside she found herself in a lounge paneled in mahogany and filled with richly upholstered chairs and sofas strategically placed to offer an atmosphere of intimacy. The room was decorated in leather, wood, and wealth. Several couples and small groups, dressed to kill, talked softly, nursing their drinks in quiet nooks and crannies while waiting for their tables. But Vivienne was not among them.

"May I help you?"

With a start, Rita turned to find herself face to face with a woman swathed in black, caressing a martini. The parts of her anatomy that weren't being fondled by designer silk were dripping in pearls and diamonds, which Rita had no doubt were real. In fact, she was sure any one item of the woman's stunning ensemble would have maxed out her credit card and cost her firstborn, if she ever had one. Intimidation hit like a slap in the face, and she would have happily slipped back out the door and made a run for it if she hadn't been caught in the act, or at least that's how she felt. She stepped forward and offered a weak smile. "Yes. I'm here to meet Edward." She hoped no last name was required.

The woman did not smile back. "Of course. You must be Rita. Edward's expecting you. Come with me."

She was led through a restaurant full of sleek diners who spoke quietly over the tinkle of fine crystal and silver, then past a dance floor, where couples moved to a big band medley. Up above the dining room on a cast iron catwalk, no doubt a remnant of the original warehouse, stood the exquisite Vivienne gazing out over the diners below like a queen overlooking her realm. That was pretty much what she was, Rita thought. By her side, and slightly in the shadow, stood a man bending to whisper in her ear. She didn't seem pleased with whatever he was telling her.

The woman in black hurried Rita past the queen of The Mount and her consort, down a long hallway that opened on to several private dining rooms, most with private dance floors surrounded by dark, intimate booths.

"The Mount is a dance club," the woman said, noticing Rita's curiosity. "Mostly ballroom and Latin. It was once an old wool warehouse. Restoring it was quite a risk, but you'd be surprised at the number of people who love to dance." Rita wondered what planet this woman thought she was from that she needed to tell her the obvious. Everyone in London knew the guidebook history of The Mount. But it was what the guidebooks didn't say that intrigued everyone.

In one of the more intimate dining rooms, the woman guided

her to a lushly upholstered booth near the back, away from the dance floor and the few other diners who occupied the room.

"Edward will join you shortly." With that, the woman turned on you-could-only-afford-to-fuck-me-in-your-dreams stilettos and retreated back through the maze of rooms.

Before she was out of sight, a server approached Rita's table with two glasses and a bottle of Moët et Chandon on ice. "I'm Aurora." She sat her burden down on the table. "Edward has instructed me to apologize for his small delay." It was only her name and a slight feminine pout which assured Rita that Aurora was actually a woman. Her androgynous features were accentuated by white-blond hair cropped short. She was dressed in a black suit, waistcoat and tie, completely camouflaging the swell of her small breasts. When she spoke, even her voice was deep, and gravelly. "There is one other thing Edward asked me to give you." From her pocket, the waitress produced a black velvet blindfold. "He asks that you wear this. He said you would understand."

A frisson of anticipation laced with the tiniest hint of fear ran up Rita's spine and accumulated at the tips of her nipples as the waitress stepped behind her and secured the blindfold. That done, she filled a glass and placed it in Rita's hand. "Enjoy the fizz," she said. Then she left.

The scent of oregano and basil and other more subtle seasonings blended with the smell of expensive perfume. Glasses clinked, people laughed, and somewhere in the background the melodic strains of "A String of Pearls" wafted on the air. She had only just tasted the champagne when a warm body scooted into the booth next to her. She recognized Edward's scent a split second before his hand cupped her cheek and his mouth covered hers, familiar territory, she thought, as her tongue became reacquainted with his.

"I hope you don't mind the blindfold," he said when he came up for air. He slid warm fingers under the spaghetti straps and caressed her left shoulder. "Being in the dark was so much fun last time."

She ran a hand over his cheek, raking a thumb lightly over a fluttering eyelid. "What about you? You're not wearing a blindfold. That's hardly fair."

He chuckled, and she felt his warm breath against her earlobe. "I never said I play fair. I was right though. You are exquisite, but I wouldn't have imagined your hair to be chestnut." He caressed her tresses, pushing a strand back behind her shoulders to fondle her nape. "For some reason I was certain that cascade of silk would be strawberry blond." He ran his other hand up the outside of her thigh, toying with the exposed edge of her garter belt, making her squirm. "Guess in some cases, there's just no substitute for the sense of sight."

"But I want to see you too. I want to know what you look like."

"You will in good time. That is if you want to play my little game. Of course you could take off the blindfold. I can't stop you, but admit it, it's fun not knowing. A bit of an adventure, an initiation almost."

"An initiation?"

"Yeah, you know, at the beginning, when a man and a woman are just getting to know each other, it's like an initiation, don't you think?"

"I never thought of it like that, kind of like a hazing?"

He chuckled. "Can be. Could be, if you want it to be." He nipped her earlobe, "Or maybe like an induction into some secret cult with secret rituals of wild, kinky sex."

"Mmm. Sounds good. Where do I sign up?"

Another chuckle. "All you have to do is keep the blindfold on until I say you can take it off. Let your other senses do the work." His finger slipped beneath the garter belt to stroke her thigh, making concentration next to impossible.

"I've always wanted to be a member of a secret sex cult." Breathing was becoming more of an effort as his touch became more insistent. "OK then. I'm in. Have your way with me."

There was a long moment of silence, and for a split second Rita wondered if she had said something wrong, if she been too forward, too quick with her answer. But just when she was about to backtrack, he leaned in and kissed her softly on the mouth. She could almost hear his heart beating in his words when at last he spoke. "Then welcome to your new playground." His hand slipped underneath the spaghetti straps to cup her breast and stroke her engorged areola. "Expensive dress?"

"What?" Intimidation knotted her stomach. "Does it matter?"

"Not really." She could hear him filling the champagne flute. "I'll buy you a new one." He lifted the glass to her lips. Just as the taste hit her tongue he pulled it away and she felt a cold wet splash over her left breast. She stifled a yelp, but not before his lips clamped down tight on her drenched nipple, and the friction of tongue and teeth on wet silk caused delicious shock waves down her belly all the way to her cunt.

"You know," he said between sucklings, "at the command of Louis 15th, the original champagne glass was said to have been shaped like the breasts of his mistress, Madame Pompadour. I can understand why. Once you've suckled champagne from a beautiful breast, champagne alone, no matter how expensive, isn't nearly as nice."

Another cold splash across both breasts and down her cleavage. She gasped and held him to her as he shoved down the spaghetti straps and freed her into his hungry mouth. "What if people are watching?" she whispered.

"Don't worry. I know the owner." Another drizzle of fizz, but this time over her belly, dripping down icily against her mound. She squirmed and ground her hips against the seat. "Open your legs for me," he whispered. "There's one cup even more perfect than Louis's design."

She did as he asked, wriggling and lifting her butt, her pussy clenching in anticipation. In one fluid motion, he shoved the dress up over her hips and pulled her panties down and off over her shoes. She wasn't sure how he had managed it, but he maneuvered himself onto the floor beneath the table. Before she could figure it out, cold liquid bubbles tickled her clit and dribbled down between her labia, chased by the white-hot lavishings of his tongue.

She moaned and everything inside her tensed with the surprise of it, the tantalizing, bracing shock of it, just before everything went molten and she slid down in the booth until her bottom was practically off the seat. His hands kneaded her buttocks, thumbs spreading her folds open to the explorations of his mouth. "The perfect cocktail," he spoke against her pussy. "Champagne and lady juices."

The music changed to a Latin beat, and behind her blindfolded eyes, bright flashes of color burst and exploded like fireworks as she rocked and thrust, concentrating only on his mouth and her pussy and the sweet, tart scent of champagne bubbling against her slit. She was so focused that she nearly slid off the seat when he pulled away, and she heard scrambling under the table.

"What's wrong," she gasped. "What is it?"

"Excuse me, but might I have this dance?"

The voice near her ear at the side of the booth startled her and she jumped. It wasn't Edward's!

"I love Latin dancing, don't you?"

"What? Dance?" She gasped. "Now's not a good time. Who are you? Edward? What's going on?"

There was the familiar whisper in her other ear. "Go with Alex, Rita. Trust me, now's a very good time."

Before she could protest further, she was half dragged, half tangoed on to the floor. "How can I dance," she panted, "when I can't even see?"

There was a humid chuckle close to her nape. "What? You don't trust me to lead you?"

"Not when my brain's in my knickers." She struggled to catch her breath.

"You're not wearing any." The words were pressed to her ear in a warm kiss, followed by a sigh of resignation. "Oh all right." He pulled off the blindfold, and she found herself squinting at a lovely face in a halo of blond curls. A well-muscled man with a dancer's body pulled her into an intimate tango. She was so close that she could feel the bulge in his trousers and wondered how the hell he could still move so gracefully. Heat flared with the driving pulse of the percussion, and his groin rubbed deliciously against her mound with each shifting beat of the music.

Without warning, he lowered her into a heart-pounding dip, and she yelped out loud, causing several dancers to glance in their direction. As he pulled her back to him, she spoke between clenched teeth. "Is this some kind of a joke, Edward gets me all excited then hands me over to someone else? That is if I was with Edward at all. How the hell would I know?"

"Shshshs." Alex covered her mouth with a kiss. "Relax. Of course you were with Edward, still are. I'm his gift to you. When you're done with me, I'll take you back to him."

"When I'm done with you? What's that supposed to mean?" She shot a glance into the darkness at the edge of the dance floor, but to no avail. She was blindfolded when Alex led her from the table. She had no idea where Edward was.

Once more he lowered her into a dip, this time pulling her up slowly, lingering to kiss the mounds of her breasts, nipples chilled stiff and clearly visible through the champagne-soaked fabric. Her pussy clenched with a wave of sensation that reminded her just how close to orgasm she had been when Edward had handed her over. "What do you mean you're his gift to me?"

"Edward's a bit of a voyeur, and he wants to watch your pleasure."

"What? And have a wank? Oh that's just great."

Alex chuckled, and she realized his hand was working its way beneath the slit of her dress. "Hardly. Edward isn't exactly what I'd call a wanker. Trust me, he'll be more than ready for you when you're finished with me." He shoved the hem of her dress aside until her bare pussy pressed against the bulge in his trousers, then he flicked a finger into her pout so quickly she wouldn't have been sure it happened if not for the rush of pleasure and wetness. He pulled her still closer. "You need to come. Use me. That's what I'm here for."

"I thought that was Edward's job."

Another chuckle. "I promise you, Edward won't disappoint." He thrust hard against her. "Do you want me?"

"What do you think? You just fingered my cunt."

Another dip, this time slow and serpentine. With a deft hand, he freed his cock. She didn't know how he'd managed it, but there, in plain sight with moves that would have made a magician jealous, he slipped his substantial erection between her legs, then he lifted her onto him. With one thrust and a grunt she was completely penetrated. All she could do was wrap her legs around him and hang on, marveling that with each thrust he never missed a beat of the music. In fact, he continued the dance as though nothing out of the ordinary was happening, hands cupped supportively under her arse, dancing amid the few other couples who moved beneath the sparkle of the disco ball. Were they blind? Could they not see that Alex was slinking around the dance floor, hammering her cunt with each pulse of the tango?

And she didn't care. It was totally insane, but she didn't care. They were thrusting and swaying with the music, and somewhere in the darkness Edward was watching with his cock aching to be inside her. She wondered if he were touching himself. She wondered if his balls felt close to bursting. She certainly hoped so. She wondered if, when she returned, he would take her right there in the booth, her pussy still wet from her erotic dance with Alex. She imagined her fizz-soaked cunt swallowing up Edward's penis in hungry gulps.

That did it. Suddenly it was as though champagne had been uncorked inside her. She gave a startled little cry as her orgasm exploded up through her, rocking her from head to toe with its impact.

When the aftershocks subsided and the music stopped, Alex

danced her off the floor to a discreet nook near a linen cabinet and helped her dismount. Then with a heavy grunt, he spurted his wad into a handkerchief he'd extricated from his pocket. When he finished wiping his cock, he said, "It wouldn't be polite for me to come inside you when you're with Edward."

The sense of excitement she felt at Alex's words was visceral. And surprising. She'd just had totally hot sex with him, and in truth she wouldn't know Edward if she saw him, but still it was Edward she wanted. Maybe their time together on the train had somehow bonded them. It was certainly a relief knowing that he hadn't pawned her off, even on such a good lover as Alex.

While Alex tucked himself in, Rita had time for a quick glance around the room. Her eyes now accustomed to the light, she could see only one booth occupied by a single diner. And though that booth was in shadow, she could still make out the shape of a tall muscular man seated, watching.

"There, now I'm presentable again." Alex held the blindfold up for Rita. "I'll just slip this on and take you back to Edward."

"Wait." She ran a hand through her disheveled hair and smoothed down the front of her wet dress. "I'm sure I look a mess. Can I just nip to the ladies' room and freshen up a bit before you take me back? I'd feel so much better."

He nodded to the restrooms on the other side of the linen closet, then handed her the blindfold. "I'll wait here."

She locked herself in the stall and plopped down on the throne to plan her next move. Though she had agreed to the blindfold, suddenly she wanted desperately to see Edward, to know what he looked like. And, in all fairness, it would serve him right to wait with a raging hard-on while she took her time in the loo. After all, he had handed her off to Alex just when things were getting hot. She would sneak up behind, put the blindfold on him, then she would be the one in control, and what fun she would have.

Chapter Three

"RITA HOLLY. COME WITH US."

She had just stepped out of the ladies' room and was sneaking around behind the linen closet. To her relief, Alex was gone, and the coast was clear to Edward—at least it had been until the two tank-sized security guards in Armani suits appeared out of nowhere, flanking her and herding her back down the hall toward the main restaurant.

"What's this all about?" she asked. "I was just heading back to my table and—"

"We know what you were doing, Ms. Holly. Alex gave us the heads-up. You're not very good at following rules, are you?"

"Excuse me?" The smaller of the two grabbed the blindfold away from her and held it up. "Oh that. Edward said the blindfold was—"

The guard held up his hand. "Rules are rules."

They marched her down the hall and through the main restaurant, where she was suddenly, painfully aware of her disheveled appearance and how it must look, her being escorted by two glorified bouncers.

"I haven't done anything wrong. You can't treat me like this." In spite of her best efforts to remain calm, she couldn't shake the feeling that everyone in the restaurant was looking on in disapproval.

As they turned down another hallway, the big bouncer opened the first door they came to and motioned her inside. Her heart jumped in her throat as the door slammed behind her.

There was a gravelly laugh. "You're not a prisoner if that's what you think."

She turned with a start and found herself face to face with Aurora, the waitress, who offered her a feline smile. "You're free to go whenever you like. Shall I call you a cab?"

"Where's Edward? I want to see him." Aurora's gaze took in Rita's wet top nearly bursting with her heavy nipples, then followed the line of her body down to where her thighs came together and the dress clung to her champagne-soaked mound, leaving little to the imagination.

"You enjoyed Alex, I assume."

"Is that what this is all about? I was tricked. I had a date with Edward, but I've never seen his face, then Alex asked me—"

"Enough!" Aurora raised her hand, and for a frightening moment, Rita thought she was going to slap her. "I know all about you and Edward. We tried to tell him you didn't belong here, that it would be a mistake to bring you, but he wouldn't listen, would he?"

"What the hell are you talking about? It was a date. That's all, a date!"

Aurora slid off her jacket and hung it carefully over a cedar hanger on the back of the door. "Edward doesn't date, and if he did, he certainly wouldn't do it here."

"I want to see him." Jesus, what was she thinking? She should get the hell out of this nuthouse. It might be the place for bored rich people, but it was no place for her, and yet…"I want to see Edward." If nothing else, she wanted to give him a good piece of her mind. Who did he think he was, humiliating her like this?

Aurora stepped nose to nose with her and ran a heavy hand down her cheek to rest on her throat, thumb caressing one side, fingers producing just enough pressure along the other to make it slightly uncomfortable. "You broke the rules, the rules you agreed to."

Rita shoved her hand away and stepped back. "You mean with the blindfold? It was only a game, and it was just between us."

"We take games very seriously here at The Mount. You can't

change the rules. It's Edward's game, his rules to make. I'll call you a cab, then the game's over, and you lose."

Take the fucking cab. That's the smart thing to do, a part of Rita's brain screamed. And yet she heard herself saying, "If I don't want to lose? If I want to see Edward?"

The woman offered her a contemptuous grunt. "Then you have to pay the penalty for breaking the rules, and Edward has to agree to continue the game. Personally, I think he's wasting his time. There are better people for him to play with, but Edward always has been stubborn. So what's it going to be? Are you going to take the penalty?" She jerked open to the door. "Or go home where you belong?"

Suddenly all the evening's humiliation and manipulation bubbled into rage just beneath Rita's sternum, and being bullied by a butched-up waitress was the final straw. She moved to the door, gaze locked on Aurora, who stepped aside.

But instead of leaving, she gave the door an explosive slam that made even Aurora jump. "I'm staying. I'm staying until I see Edward."

The words were barely out before Aurora grabbed her by the hair and yanked her head back against her muscular shoulder. "Breaking the rules in the middle of a game is serious." Her hand still wound tightly in Rita's hair, she half dragged, half guided her to a leather upholstered settee and shoved her down on it. "I can't punish you without Edward witnessing. It's his game." The sculpted contempt on Aurora's face was the last thing Rita saw before another blindfold ensconced her in darkness.

"You punish me? What the hell do you have to do with this?" She reached for the blindfold, but the waitress wrenched her hand away none too gently. "I'm the enforcer. It's my job to make sure the rules aren't broken and to punish those who do break them."

"This is insane. I want to—"

Her protest died in her throat with a little gasp as the other woman's hand slid between her legs and probed her pantyless cunt, then she heard her suckle her fingers. "I see Edward's shown you the best way to enjoy champagne, though you probably didn't deserve it. Now wait here, and don't move, or you'll make your punishment even worse." This time Rita heard the click of the lock as Aurora left.

She had no way of judging how long she waited. And now, thanks to her stupidity, she had cut off her only way of escape. But Aurora said she would return with Edward. And Rita definitely wanted to have a few words with him. If it meant being roughed up a bit by Butch Woman, well she could handle that. She was not about to let Edward get away with treating her this way.

She reached down to stroke the wet spot low on her belly, and the anger was subsumed into something a little more intriguing. Her pussy quivered when she thought about Edward lapping champagne from her cunt and Edward watching her and Alex on the dance floor. And Alex refusing to come inside her out of deference to Edward. There was an awful lot of deference to Edward, and for some mind-less reason, that made her feel proud, in spite of the desire to strangle him with his own blindfold.

But what if Edward was just the gang leader, like some kind of mafia boss, and what if she never saw the light of day again. She'd heard all kinds of rumors about the mysterious Mount. Where the hell was her sense of self-preservation? Was her wounded pride worth her going along with this insanity—insanity that might be very dangerous?

She was seriously contemplating yanking off the blindfold and making a run for it when the door burst open and Edward called her name. Suddenly she was engulfed in his arms, and her mouth was consumed with his kisses. He pulled away just enough to speak, his breath coming in fast, tense gulps against her parted lips. "Are you all right, Rita?"

"How the hell do you think I am? Dinner and drinks, you said. You didn't mention humiliating me in front of half of London's rich and powerful. I don't understand any of this. I thought you were just teasing me with the blindfold, and then there was Alex. I just wanted to see what you look like." She felt dangerously close to tears, which made her even more angry. She swallowed back the lump in her throat. "Then these bouncers came and Aurora pulled my hair and—"

He stopped her words with another kiss. "And yet you chose to stay and play the game with me." He cradled her close to his hammering heart and stroked her hair. "I'm so proud of you. I knew I wasn't wrong in choosing you. I promise you won't regret it." His hand came to rest low on her belly, his thumb stroking her mound through the dampness of the dress.

"Get away from her, Edward." Aurora commanded. "You know the rules. You can't have her until I've exacted punishment."

He caressed Rita's cheek. "Listen very carefully, darling. In order for the game to continue, in order for us to be together, I must let Aurora punish you, and I have to watch without interfering. Do you understand?"

"But—"

"I'm sorry, Rita, but I can't explain anything until that happens. Are you OK with that?" She nodded, and in spite of her best efforts she felt tears seeping into the blindfold.

"That's my brave girl. If you take your punishment, I promise you, the game will be so worth it. You'll see."

"And if I win?" Her voice sounded loud in the sudden quiet of the room. "What's my reward, if I win?" She heard the click of Aurora's heals and smelled her perfume. "What you get," she said, taking Edward's place next to her, "is membership."

"Membership?"

To her surprise, Aurora pulled off the blindfold and held her chin in a vice grip. "Membership into The Mount, which is more than you deserve."

"What?" The resounding slap across her face stung like fire and made her eyes water, but the gasp she heard wasn't her own. As her eyes focused through the tears she saw a man sitting stiff-backed on the edge of a wooden chair. His face was concealed in an expressionless golden mask, which covered all but the bow of his lips. Otherwise he could have passed for any of the male diners at The Mount that night. "Edward?" She half whispered, rubbing her stinging cheek. There was a slight nod of his head before Aurora vice-gripped her chin again.

"You give me your undivided attention, or I'll call you a cab whether you want it or not." Aurora slapped her again. "Are we clear?"

"We're clear," Rita breathed.

Aurora pulled off her tie, then yanked Rita's hands behind her back and bound them with it. While Rita watched, she leisurely removed the waistcoat and shirt until she stood before them stripped to the waist except for a black leather bra displaying small firm tits and supple ropey muscles that might have belonged to a female body-builder. "Good, then let's just see what's so special about you that Edward would risk everything for."

"Shut up, Aurora." Edward's back stiffened against the chair. "Your job is to punish, nothing more."

"Then stop interrupting me and let me do my job." Aurora grabbed both spaghetti straps and yanked them down, exposing Rita's goose-fleshed breasts. "Couldn't be these that won Edward over." She slapped Rita's tits in turn, then pinched her nipples until she gasped at the pain that went straight to her pussy, where it was amazingly transformed to pleasure. "Edward can have all the nice tits he wants, including mine." She grabbed Rita's right hand and shoved it inside the plunge of her bra and over the muscular dome of her breast until her pointing nipple pressed into Rita's palm.

Rita held her breath. Was this punishment, fondling another woman's tits? Surely not. It felt too good.

"Can't be this." Still holding Rita's fingers against her breast, Aurora slid her other hand under Rita's dress. "No matter how much

Moët et Chandon he pours into it, it's still just a cunt, and there are plenty of cunts aching to ride Edward's cock." She ran her open palm between Rita's legs, spreading her labia, pressing against her clit, then giving it a sharp slap, chuckling as Rita flinched.

"Doesn't matter. I'm just here to punish you for breaking the rules." She grabbed the front of Rita's dress between the side slits and yanked it as though it were a leash. Rita followed, feeling cool air on her exposed pussy.

Standing in front of a straight-back chair upholstered in chintz, Aurora undid her trousers and slid them off to reveal garter belts and black net stockings framing her shaved, panty-less mound. Then she sat down, wriggling and squirming her bottom against the chair until she was comfortable. "Edward, be a dear, and give me your knife."

Rita's pulse quickened, as Edward retrieved a large Vitronox from his pocket, which he handed to Aurora, the golden mask completely disguising any emotions her request might have elicited.

Aurora opened the knife expertly. "Turn around," she ordered.

But Rita stood frozen to the floor unable to move.

There was a hard slap across her breasts. "I said turn around."

"Do as she says, Rita." Edward moved behind her, placed his hands on her shoulders, and gently turned her to face him. "It'll be all right." He pulled her into his arms and held her while Aurora grabbed the back of her dress and slit the side seams to just above her bottom, laughing softly as Rita cringed. Then she gathered the fabric into her hand and sliced smoothly across so all that remained of the back of Rita's dress was a thin strip high across her hips and lower spine.

"There, that's better." Aurora tossed the cut fabric aside and handed the knife back to Edward. "Now help me with her." She patted her bare thighs and nodded.

He pocketed the knife and guided Rita to bend over the punisher's lap. "Just get it over with, Aurora." The edge in his voice was nearly as sharp as the Vitronox.

"Relax, Edward." Aurora stroked Rita's arse cheeks almost tenderly. "Some things can't be rushed."

He didn't return to the chair, but instead knelt on the floor stroking Rita's hair and the nape of her neck. His touch was so comforting that, even though she knew what was coming, the first hard thwack against her exposed bottom made her cry out in surprise.

"You broke the rules," Aurora scolded as her hand came down again, this time on the other buttock so that they both stung equally. "Rule breakers must be punished." With the next hard thwack, Rita flinched and bit the inside of her lip, tasting blood.

Edward lowered his face and took her mouth, gently suckling away the thin ribbon of red before the next smack came. "Shshshsh," he whispered. "Relax. It'll be over soon, and we can be together." He kissed her again, then ran his hand down to caress her breasts as he lifted his head to watch Aurora's efforts. For the first time, Rita noticed he had thick auburn hair that smelled almost like moist earth after a storm.

From her awkward position across her punisher's lap, Rita's gaze took in the tightly stretched front of Edward's trousers. When the next smack stung her bottom, the pain blossomed into something hot and burning low in her belly, and suddenly she knew she would gladly take her punishment to be able to see Edward's erection, even through his trousers.

Aurora was ranting about the rules, about the reputation of The Mount and of Edward, about ignorant usurpers or some such, but Rita had stopped listening. Edward was fondling her breasts where they were uncomfortably squished over Aurora's lap. With each kneading, and with each smack, she found herself grinding against Aurora's bare thigh.

Edward opened his trousers and took his cock in a firm grip, positioning himself in front of her. But just as she was about to take him into her mouth, Aurora stopped spanking and with a powerful backhand, knocked Edward onto his haunches.

"I said leave her alone, Edward, or you'll not have her at all. Now back off."

Cursing under his breath, he returned to his chair, not bothering to tuck his cock back into his trousers, though he probably couldn't have if he'd wanted to.

Aurora returned her attention to Rita. "Look at this. You've soaked my leg with your cunt juices. I should punish you more for that. Stand up."

Rita did as she was told. Aurora grabbed the front flap of her mutilated dress and yanked it tight between Rita's legs, wedging it into her slit and tugging on it until Rita stood on her toes in an effort to relieve the pressure from the bind of fabric rubbing almost, but not quite, pleasurably against her clit.

"It's all right if you like punishment," her tormentor's voice was suddenly honeyed and sweet. "See? Spanking you made my pussy wet too." She opened her legs, and Rita was greeted with an exquisite view of Aurora's dark, swollen pout glistening with moisture. The enforcer gave the fabric leash a hard tug, causing Rita to gasp. "Here's the real punishment, chick. If you ever want to ride his cock again," she threw a nod at Edward, whose hand was wrapped around his erection while the other cupped his balls, "then you'd better make me come, and come good." With a quick flick of her wrist, she untied Rita's hands, then yanked on the bodice of what remained of her gown, bringing her to her knees only a nose length away from the woman's fragrant, warm pussy.

Rita had never touched another woman's cunt before, let alone tasted one. Of course she had fantasized about what it would be like, but she never imagined she'd ever actually be commanded to make another woman come. She reached out a trembling hand and stroked the incredible softness of Aurora's shaved mound, and Aurora let out a shuddering sigh, spreading her legs even further and leaning back in the chair. She curled her fingers roughly in Rita's hair and pulled her forward, but Rita pulled back.

"Wait. I want to look."

"You can't make me come with your eyes, bitch."

"Come on," Rita struggled to keep her voice calm. "You can't honestly expect me to believe you don't like to have your cunt admired."

For a brief second, she thought Aurora would hit her again, but instead she chuckled softly and shifted until not only could Rita see the whole of her engorged vulva, but also the dark pucker of her anus, which clenched and relaxed each time Rita caressed and stroked between her folds.

She breathed in the high-tide scent of pussy that wasn't hers, a scent that made her own pussy itch to be full, a scent that made her feel deliciously naughty. While she caressed Aurora's heavy pout, she shifted and raised her hips, giving Edward a good view of her own slit. He was, after all, the reason she was in this position, her bottom stinging from a brisk spanking, doing things she'd only secretly fantasized. As she fingered the creamy juices beading in the tiny cup at the bottom of Aurora's cunt, she thought of the champagne Edward had poured in her own pussy-cup, and the urge to taste was overwhelming.

There was a trio of sighs, all in unison, at her first tentative taste of cunt. And suddenly she couldn't for the life of her understand how even expensive champagne could enhance the flavor of such ambrosia. She slipped her hands under Aurora's tight arse cheeks and pulled her close, burying her face deep in the woman's slippery femaleness, feeling her moans of pleasure vibrate all the way through her body down to Rita's probing tongue.

"I must be getting soft," Aurora grunted. "You seem to be enjoying your punishment way too much." She lifted her stiletto-clad feet onto Rita's bare shoulders to better position herself, but Rita barely noticed the digging of the heels into her clavicle. She stroked and caressed Aurora's swollen labia with her thumbs, while she lapped and nibbled the valley in between, saliva and pussy juice dribbling down her chin, over Aurora's dark bottom hole and onto the upholstery of the chair.

Rita couldn't resist. She nipped Aurora's clit just enough to make her clench and open, then she wriggled a wet thumb none too gently into the woman's tight back grip, feeling an immense surge through her own pussy and anus as Aurora cried out and bucked against her. She could see the woman's pussy convulse and quiver with orgasm. A woman might be able to fool a man, but she could never fool another woman. With a mirror, Rita had watched herself come, and she knew. She knew the heavy convulsion, the internal clamping down of everything followed by the little shock waves that made all those lovely pouting slippery muscles tremble and quake. Just watching was almost enough to bring her. Almost.

Suddenly Edward was on his hands and knees behind her, his fingers spreading her folds, his cock pressing against the inside of her thigh. But just as she was about to ease back onto his erection, Aurora shoved her away, then grabbed her by her hair and pulled her to her feet.

"Damn it, Edward! She's being punished. She doesn't get any satisfaction. If you have to empty your balls," she gave herself a rough stroke, "do it here, or have a wank, but leave her alone. You're the one who got her into this mess." She turned her attention to Rita, who she still had in an uncomfortable grip. She dragged her to a wardrobe and shoved a calf-length black leather coat at her. "Put this on." Then she grabbed the phone. "Bruce, have the limo brought round, now. I said put the coat on," she barked at Rita. "And get out of here."

"But what about my punishment? What about Edward?"

Rita barely got the words out before the door swung open and the bigger of the two bouncers took her firmly by the arm. She was able only to catch a glimpse of Edward before the door slammed between them and the bouncers escorted her away from the main restaurant and out a side exit into an alley. There, the smaller one opened the door to a waiting limo and shoved her inside.

In all the insanity and the incredible confusion of feelings racing through her, Rita barely noticed the tears until she tried to tell the limo driver where to take her. He simply raised a hand. "I know where you need to go, luv." Just then his mobile rang. He listened briefly, then hung up, and pulled out of the alley.

Rita was too miserable to enjoy the plush interior of a limo that was clearly designed for decadence. Any other time it would have been a wonderful story with which to tantalize Kate. Instead, she sat in silence, staring out into the darkened streets wondering why any of this mattered. It had been good sex, fabulous sex, and nasty, yummy experiences she'd only ever fantasized about, and who cared if she got humiliated in front of a lot of rich people, who cared if they sniggered about her in the morning over coffee. She'd never see any of them again, nor they her. And yet she hadn't been with Edward. Why did she care? She'd never even seen his face. She knew nothing about him, and what little she did know made her angry, made her wonder if perhaps she was better off not knowing him.

Try though she might, she didn't understand why she had not been considered worthy to play the game. The worst part was that Monday morning she would wake up, go about her job, go about her ordinary boring routine, and all this would be nothing more than a memory.

Rita's brooding was interrupted when the limo pulled to a stop, a man jumped in and slammed the door behind him. With a flip of some hidden switch, shades descended and the privacy window snapped shut. "You're not leaving before I make love to you."

Her heart leaped to her throat. There was no denying Edward's voice, nor his touch as he undid the belt of the leather coat and covered her breasts and belly in kisses. The driver pulled away from the curve, and Rita found herself cocooned in soft velvety darkness. What had once been her enemy was now her friend as Edward kissed the inside of her thighs. One hand stroked and caressed her heavy pout while the other fumbled to free his cock. "I have no more patience," he grunted as he shoved into her. "I've waited all night, I've waited all week, to be inside you."

There was a groan of pleasure, then he pulled her close, engulfing her in his strong arms, flooding her senses with the scent of rampant maleness. With each thrust the base of his penis rubbed maddeningly against her clit. Her breasts bounced each time they pushed and shoved and humped. It didn't take long. His balls were full and heavy as they slapped against her bottom, and his whole body was tense with the need he had been containing for hours. He was hard all over, brittle, barely able to keep from shattering as he growled and grunted. She clawed and dug her heels in, riding him until there was no breath left in either of them, until there was nothing but gnawing, clambering need, which ignited like a spark and exploded through both of them as they came together, and the limo was filled with the humid scent of sex.

For a long moment they lay, arms and legs entwined, catching their breath. Then the limo stopped in front of her flat, and Edward pulled away. "I can't stay," he said, buttoning the coat around her. "If they find out I was with you before the initiation it'll go hard for both of us," he cupped her cheek in the darkness, "but I couldn't wait. I just couldn't."

"I thought they kicked me out. I thought the game was over."

"The game's just beginning. That is if you still want to play." He opened the door and helped her out with a long, lingering kiss. "Oh, and if you do still want to play, it would make things easier for both of us if you'd keep what happened tonight a secret."

"Yeah, of course. Who would believe me anyway?"

He chuckled softly. "Who indeed? I'll text you." He gave her one last kiss, then got into the limo and was gone again just as she realized she still hadn't properly seen his face.

Chapter Four

Sending limo. Can't w8 2 C U. E.

THAT WAS ALL THE text said. She received it only seconds before the doorbell rang, and a man in a black suit stood in front of her. "I'm ordered to bring you to The Mount, Ms. Holly."

Rita's heart was still somersaulting from the text. She still held the mobile in her hand. "I can't go like this." Her hair was caught up in a careless ponytail. She wore a faded blue sweat suit with pink flip-flops accessorizing her can't-be-arsed fashion statement. "Just let me change and get my bag."

"You're to come immediately and as you are," came the curt reply. "You won't need your bag, or that." He nodded to her mobile.

"But I—"

The man offered a seen-everything sigh. "Ms. Holly, I promise you, there's nothing in your possession that you'll need tonight. Now if you please. It's not wise to keep the Mistress waiting."

"The Mistress?" She locked the door behind her, feeling naked without her usual accoutrements, and followed. "I thought I was going to see Edward."

"I'm not at liberty to answer any questions."

Inside the limo, she tried to avoid her reflection in the tinted glass. She wore no make-up and no bra, neither of which she considered helpful in her efforts to put together the story proposal she would present to her boss tomorrow, efforts which hadn't been going well.

It had been nearly two weeks since Edward had made love to her in the limo and promised he would text. She moped about for over a week, jumping to attention every time she got a text, hoping against hope that every knock on the door might be him. Not that she would have known if it had been. Just when she had surrounded the soft spot at her center with a hard shell of indignant anger at the way Edward had used her, here was the long-awaited text. The shell had cracked like an egg exposing tender, squishy feelings she was pretty sure it was a mistake to allow herself.

She made excuses whenever Kate questioned her about her evening at The Mount, excuses that had caused friction between the two friends. But, in all honesty, she hardly knew where to begin, even if Edward hadn't asked her to keep it secret.

They were at The Mount almost before she knew it, and, for a horrifying moment, she thought the limo driver would drop her right at the front door. Instead, he pulled discreetly around behind the building, helped her out of the car, then led her inside and left her in the room where Aurora had punished her.

Now the space looked like nothing but the expensive office of someone with good taste. She stared for a long time at the chair where Aurora had spanked her bare bottom and Edward had fondled her. Then she turned to pace. Why was she putting herself through this? Yes, the sex had been amazing, but so was the humiliation and the abuse.

It was damn cheeky of Edward to assume he could summon her at his will to play more games with her. She should leave. She should just get a cab and leave. But she had no money. She had no phone. She had nothing. Nothing! These people could do whatever they wanted with her and just drop her body in the Thames. Or worse, sell her off to the highest bidder, and she could end up in Bumfuck Who-knows-where-istan doing who knows what with who knows whom!

The door burst open and she let out a yelp of surprise as Aurora walked in, this time wearing no waitress costume to cover the PVC and metal that she wore so well. She gave Rita the once-over, but made no comment on her appearance. "Come with me." She turned on her heels as if it never entered her mind that Rita might not follow.

Rita followed.

At the end of the long hall, Aurora stopped in front of the linen closet where Rita had been with Alex and opened the door. "You have five minutes." At first Rita thought the waitress was talking to her. "Don't use your cock. If you do, you know she'll find out. My arse is already on the line. I'm warning you, if I have to I'll pry you off her with a crow bar." Then she shoved Rita inside and shut the door.

In total darkness, Rita stumbled backward, then strong arms embraced her, and warm breath bathed her neck. "I couldn't let you go before the High Council without seeing you first." Edward pulled her into a hungry kiss, even in the thick darkness finding her mouth effortlessly, deeply. At the same time his hands cupped and fondled their way over more of her body than she would have thought possible in such a short few seconds. He didn't bother coming up for air, but spoke between gulps of her mouth. "It's been ten long days. I didn't think I'd survive."

"You could have at least texted, and—"

He stopped her words with a deep probe of his tongue. "She took my mobile, and I couldn't come to you without nullifying your right to initiation."

She reached for his fly, but he pushed her away. "You heard what Aurora said. Trust me, she's right. You don't want to go before the High Council smelling of my semen." He took her face in her hands and kissed her hard. "I just had to reassure you that you can do this. Don't let the council intimidate you. Remember, that's what they're supposed to do. It's an initiation." He pulled her into a bone-crunching embrace, then released her. "It would be bad for both of us if anyone knew I'd seen you."

"What difference does it make if we see each other? Why do we have to do this?" She grabbed his hand as he turned to go. "And who took your mobile? What right do they have? I don't understand."

He gave her another toe-curling kiss, then pulled free. "I know you don't, Rita, but you will in time. You have to trust me that all this, the punishment, the separation, the waiting, all of it is so we can be together. I'll understand, darling, if you don't go through with this. Believe me, no one will understand better than I, but I'm hoping with all my heart that you'll see it through, that you'll give me the chance to prove to you that it's worth it." He shoved open the door and left her standing alone in the dark, wet, trembling, and frustrated.

Before she could decide if she was touched that he'd made such an effort, or furious that he offered only excuses, Aurora jerked the door open.

"Come on. It's time."

The waitress led her through what looked like another linen closet at the end of the hall, then down a winding staircase that felt like it descended forever. The air around them no longer smelled of leather and silk and wealth, but more like she remembered her grandmother's garden smelling when she had dug among the rows of herbs.

When they finally reached the bottom, Aurora took a deep breath and squared her shoulders before she flung open the double doors.

At first the bright light was dazzling, then Rita realized it wasn't bright at all, just much brighter than the darkness she had grown accustomed to in the closet and on the barely lit stairs. If she'd had to describe it, she would have said it was bedroom light.

Aurora took her by the arm and led her into the middle of a large stone chamber—not exactly a dungeon, though Rita had no trouble imagining it might be used as such. On a raised dais complete with velvet curtains, sat seven elaborate chairs, almost like thrones. Five of them were occupied.

Rita could hardly believe her eyes, but, sure enough, there at the center on the most elaborate chair, dressed in a red gown that was only slightly less than transparent, was the elusive Vivienne Arlington Page. In the overwhelming presence of a legend, Rita could have stared at her for hours, but she forced her gaze to the other members of the High Council.

To either side of Vivienne was an empty chair. To the left sat a tall man with a neatly trimmed beard. He was dressed in khakis and held a pith helmet in his lap, as though he were about to go on safari. Next to him, Rita recognized Alex, who was dressed as though he had just come from a tango competition, black spandex trousers hugging his package suggestively.

Beyond the empty chair on the other side of Vivienne sat the woman who had led Rita to wait for Edward when she first came to The Mount. This time she wore plain black silk dressed up with emeralds. Lots of emeralds. Next to her sat a caramel-skinned man of mixed race, and it was a lovely mix. His blue-black hair was pulled back in a ponytail, revealing the sculpture-perfect lines of his face. He wore three silver hoops of graduating size in his left ear. His left arm and the left side of his exquisite bare chest and torso were tattooed like leopard skin, a tattoo that disappeared into the front of low-slung black jeans, which were tucked into leather boots. Something about his demeanor made Rita think he'd gladly let her follow the trail of leopard spots into his tight-fitting jeans.

When she was sure she had everyone's attention, Aurora addressed Vivienne. "I've brought the candidate for initiation, as you've commanded." Surely Rita was just imagining the slight tremor in Aurora's voice.

Vivienne paid no attention to Rita. Instead, she patted the chair next to her. Two muscle men dressed in the Armani uniform of The Mount's bouncers came to stand on either side of Rita, then Aurora joined the council, taking the seat at Vivienne's left.

For a long moment everyone simply stared at Rita, who tried to act as though she wasn't staring back. At last Vivienne spoke. "Where's Edward? He knows we can't begin without him, since it's upon his petition we meet."

"Don't worry," a voice Rita recognized as Edward's spoke from behind the curtain, then the man in the golden mask, dressed in black tie and jacket, stepped forward and took his place in the chair to the right of Vivienne. "I wouldn't miss the opportunity to present Rita to you for the world."

For the first time, Vivienne's amber gaze came to rest fully on Rita, who suddenly had that bug-under-glass feeling. She did her best not to squirm. At last, Vivienne offered a light chuckle and took Edward's hand from where it rested on the arm of the chair. "Really, darling, couldn't you at least clean her up before you brought her before us?"

Rita felt as though she had been slapped, but the indignant temptation to turn and walk out was thwarted by the bouncer-blokes who flanked her.

"Why should I?" Edward responded. "She needs no tarting up." He paused before the last statement, his eyes coming to rest on Vivienne, and even Rita could see the prickle run up the woman's spine.

But the prickle ended in a deep-throated kiss that nearly unseated Edward and had the rest of the council gasping. "We all need a little tarting up, Edward dear." Vivienne said when she came up for air. She ran a slender hand over the edge of the golden mask. "Look at you, trying so to hide the monster beneath from Cinderella or Red Riding Hood or whoever you've imagined this chick to be in your deluded fantasies."

Vivienne turned her attention back to Rita, who was struggling now to keep from making a break for the door. "Girl, do you want initiation into The Mount?" She threw back her lovely head and laughed. "Of course you do. Everyone does. Our job is to judge your worthiness. I already know my opinion on that, but the High Council has the final say and I shall defer to their wisdom."

"I'm not sure that I do, actually." Rita knew immediately that she had said the wrong thing.

"Oh?" Vivienne rose from her throne and came to stand in front of her, so close Rita could smell the rich, musky perfume she didn't recognize. "That's strange, since my enforcer tells me you took your punishment, shall we say, more than willingly, in order to continue your little game with Edward."

"Yeah, well I get enough abuse at work. I really don't need more."

Vivienne took a step closer until Rita could feel her warm breath. "Ah, but I'll wager you don't get rewarded for that abuse at work like you do here." Without warning, she grabbed Rita by the disheveled ponytail and pulled her close. Somehow in one petty, insulting kiss, the bitch managed to make every part of Rita's body ache with the want of her.

As she pulled away, Vivienne didn't release the ponytail, but wound it around her fingers until there was barely lip distance between her and Rita, and, even this close, the woman was flawless. "I think you like abuse just fine, girl. In fact, I think it makes you wet. I think if I pinch your tits and slap your bottom and pull your hair until it hurts, you just might come right here in front of the whole council." She reached to unzip the front of Rita's hoodie.

"Vivienne, stop it," came Edward's voice from behind the mask. The silky chuckle was so close that Rita could almost taste it. "You're right, of course, Edward. As head of the High Council, it's hardly my place to pleasure chavs." While everyone watched, she returned to her seat on the dais, taking her time, smoothing her dress as it swirled around her, shaking her hair back over her shoulders. Then she spoke.

"Bruce."

"Yes, Mistress Vivienne." The bodyguard to Rita's right snapped to attention.

"Make her come."

Both the guard and Rita, along with the rest of the council, gasped their surprise simultaneously.

"Pardon?" Bruce said.

"You heard me. Make her come. I know you've had fantasies about participating in what goes on in here. Now's your chance. I don't care how you do it. Just make her come."

"Vivienne, this is insane. Stop it," Edward growled.

Vivienne ran a hand up the inside of his thigh in a sinuous caress. "OK, let's make it more interesting. Bruce, put your hand in her panties and feel her pussy. If she's not wet, then I'll write it off to opening night nerves, but if she is wet, then I'll assume she's in need of a good orgasm. An initiate must be able to focus, and we all know how hard it is to focus when one needs to come. That will be your job, Bruce, to make our little initiate come."

Her face suddenly became sympathetic, and her gaze came to rest on Rita. "Of course, if you consider my methods too abusive, Rita dear, you can leave without Bruce ever touching you. I'll even send you home in a nice limo. Would you like that?"

The woman's condescension felt like ground glass in Rita's stomach, but in spite of her best efforts to be indignant, she suspected the bitch might be right. The thought of the big bouncer checking out her state of arousal with those large, beefy fingers didn't exactly turn her off. And better yet, she was pretty sure seeing her so played with would make Edward very hard.

"I could save you the trouble, Bruce." She shot a quick glance at Edward as she unzipped her hoodie and let it drop off her shoulders to reveal her braless breasts pressing hard against a thin gray tank top. "But I won't."

The bouncer seemed deliciously embarrassed by the whole situation. She wasn't certain, but she thought she heard a collective gasp from the dais as she took Bruce by the wrist and guided his hand down into the elastic front of her yoga pants.

He stepped closer and his big hand moved awkwardly inside the opening she had provided. He lifted an eyebrow at the discovery that she wore no knickers. "Now you know my little secret," she said, catching her breath as his fingers grazed her tightly trimmed curls. She shifted her stance to offer him easy access. As he gave an upward thrust with his middle finger, her slick hole practically sucked him in. Then it was his turn to catch his breath.

"Well?" Vivienne's voice broke into the moment.

"She's wet, Mistress." In spite of the bright flush rising on the bouncer's cheeks and neck, even expensive Armani couldn't hide his growing erection.

"Then make her come."

For an awkward moment Bruce only stood there with his hand in Rita's bottoms.

Vivienne cleared her throat loudly. "Come on, Bruce, surely you know how to make a woman come, or do you prefer men?" She nodded to the other bouncer still standing stoically at Rita's left. Both men blushed heroically, but at last Bruce found his voice. "Here? Like this?"

"Granted, it's not the bedroom or the back seat of a limo, but surely you can improvise. Have Gavin there help you. I'm sure he's willing. I can see his hard-on from here. Take off her top, Gavin, go on. I know you want to see her tits. We all want to see her tits."

Gavin wasn't nearly as shy as Bruce. He peeled off Rita's top, making sure to get a good grope as he did so, which she barely noticed in the sudden realization that all eyes were now on her tits. Everyone was leaning forward as though it were opening night at the theater, and the curtain had just risen.

The swishing of cloth drew her attention back to Gavin, who had shed his jacket and tie and was working on his buttons with one hand while pinching her nipples alternately with the other. But poor Bruce was a rabbit in the headlights, just standing there with a finger in her pussy. Strangely, that excited her.

She slid her hand inside her sweat bottoms on top of his and smiled encouragement. "Here, let me show you what I like. There, that's better," she sighed, shifting her hips to get him right where she needed him. "Now put another finger in. Oh, that's nice." She began to rock against his hand. "Now use your thumb on my clit, mmm, yes, like that."

"Come on, Bruce." Gavin's husky voice brushed her neck. "Undress her. I want to see her cunt."

It was then that she looked up and caught Edward's gaze locked on her. He sat on the edge of his chair, white knuckling the arms. Holding his gaze, she pulled away long enough to step out of her yoga pants. This time there was a definite gasp of approval from the dais. She heard the sound of a zipper behind her and turned to find Gavin with his substantial cock in his hand.

"She's the initiate, not you, Gavin." Vivienne's voice broke into the sound of heavy breathing. "I said you were to help Bruce make her come. On your hands and knees."

Gavin stopped mid-stroke and stared up at her blankly.

"Go on. Get down on your hands and knees. Can't you see the girl needs a place to sit while Bruce licks her pussy?" Once Gavin was in position, Bruce guided Rita down until her bare bottom was firmly planted on Gavin's back, as though he were a park bench. She gave him a good slicking of pussy juice as she got comfortable. Then Bruce dropped to his knees, pushed her legs apart, and buried his face between her thighs.

Suddenly the man was no longer awkward. He nibbled and suckled her clit until it was a tight cherry pressing against his lips.

His long tongue was muscular and agile as it snaked deep between her folds, making her buck and grind against poor Gavin, who made a valiant effort to support her on three limbs while he attempted to yank on his cock. The effort nearly sent them all tumbling before he groaned his frustration and restabilized them on all fours.

In her peripheral vision, through the haze of heavy arousal, she saw that the man with the leopard spots had opened his trousers and sat handling his own hefty cock. Aurora and Khaki Man were getting touchy feely with each other and Alex and Emerald Lady were getting touchy feely with themselves. Only Edward and Vivienne sat unmoving, watching Rita and the two bouncers. Then, without warning, Vivienne dropped to her knees in front of Edward and suddenly his cock was in her mouth. He shifted uncomfortably in the chair, as he wound his fingers in her exquisite hair and pistoned into her accommodating lips. But his eyes never left Rita.

So she decided to give him something to look at. She pushed Bruce away and stood to the shocked groans of the council. "I believe in reciprocity," she said. She lay back against Gavin's spine, bringing both feet to rest on his shoulders. Then she motioned Bruce to move behind him. From where she lay flat on her back, she released Bruce's thick erection and guided it into her mouth. He caught on quickly and arched over her in a stylized sixty-nine, just the perfect height to continue his tongue worship of her pussy while she sucked his cock.

When they had got used to the new position, and she was sure what she had imagined in her head could actually be accomplished by human bodies, she reached underneath Gavin and began pumping his jutting erection first with one hand, then with the other, feeling his muscles tense and strain beneath her as he drew near ejaculation. Her head bounced rhythmically against his thrusting buttocks. Bruce had gone into hyper-hump in her mouth until she had to place one hand on his hip to keep him from gagging her.

Performing for Edward only intensified the imminent orgasm that was building low in her belly.

The strange threesome strained and writhed, displayed as they were, in front of the High Council. She could feel Gavin's buildup beneath her and Bruce's in her mouth, while catching glimpses of the peripheral orgy that was happening on the dais, all against a sound-track of grunts and moans. Gavin bucked beneath her as his semen gushed over her hand and onto the floor. That was enough to send her, stiffening and arching, digging her heels into Gavin's shoulders, trying not to sink her teeth in as Bruce followed suit and filled her mouth with his load, just as they all collapsed onto the floor.

The post-orgasmic bliss, however, was short lived as she rolled off Gavin and found herself gazing at Vivienne, wiping her mouth like the cat who ate the cream, while Edward hastily tucked his cock back into his trousers. Before she could completely decipher the upwelling of feelings that threatened to explode her chest, Vivienne stood, smoothed her dress, and chuckled. "I wager Bruce and Gavin didn't expect to be so rewarded this evening." She dismissed them with a wave of her hand, and they both left the room, their arms loaded down with crumpled Armani.

As Rita stooped to put on her clothes, Vivienne shook her head. "Don't bother. We have other business to tend to before you get dressed." She seated herself on her throne and made a point of smoothing her hair and applying fresh lippy. The room was silent except for the zipping of flies and the rustling of expensive clothing as everyone tucked and tidied.

"Now," Vivienne said, heaving a satisfied sigh. "Time to vote. Do we, the High Council of The Mount, believe this girl deserves an opportunity to undergo initiation into our honorable institution?" She shifted in her chair and crossed her legs. "As for my part, I can see the type of display we've witnessed tonight on any number of Internet porn sites. I can't imagine what this girl would add, nor can

I understand your fascination with her, Edward. That being the case, I vote no. And we already know Edward's vote."

As though everyone knew their role, first the man in khaki spoke up. "I also vote no." He said nothing else, and his face remained neutral.

"Thank you, Leo," Vivienne said. "I can always count on you to see sense."

"I vote yes." Alex said, holding Rita in a meaningful gaze.

"She's really that good a fuck, is she?" Vivienne commented.

"I also vote yes," Aurora said.

"Rory, dear, if you just need someone new to lick your pussy, you should have told me. I'm not without resources. I could have got you the best, the most expensive, even one with—"

"Vivienne, that's enough," Edward interrupted. "I don't see how your running commentary is relevant to this vote. In his voice, there was no post-coital fondness toward the woman who had just sucked his cock.

Vivienne only shrugged. "Lorelei, what about you? How do you vote?"

The Emerald Lady held the same look of cool disregard she had on the night Rita had first met her. It came as no surprise when she voted no.

Leopard Man would offer the deciding vote, and Rita was outraged at herself that she cared, that she wanted him to vote yes, in spite of what Vivienne had just put her through, the thought of which still sent aftershocks through her pussy. And that made her even angrier.

For a long moment Leopard Man held her in his brown sugar gaze until she felt a blush crawl up her breasts and over her throat. Everyone in the room shifted uncomfortably.

"Well? Morgan? I've got more important things to attend to," Vivienne scolded. "Do you mind hurrying it up."

The lovely mocha face broke into a pussy-creaming smile, which was completely reserved for Rita. "I vote definitely." There was no denying the American accent.

The sexy smile was counteracted by Vivienne's glare that would have wilted thistle. "So, we have an initiate. I can't say I'm pleased, but then I'm not surprised. This is what happens when I let Edward go slumming." She stood and Edward stood next to her. He took her hand and escorted her to stand in front of Rita.

God, Rita wished he'd lose the damn mask. She wanted to at least have the chance to read the emotions on his face. But the bitch had taken even that away from her.

Vivienne stepped closer and pushed a loose strand of hair away from Rita's face. "Did you enjoy your orgasm, darling? I certainly hope so because it's the last one you'll be having for a while." She snapped her fingers, and two men dressed like medieval dungeon guards appeared from the wings carrying a black velvet box, which one held and the other opened before Vivienne.

"I have a little gift for you, Rita. Something to keep your slutti-ness under control until I think you're a little less skittish and a little more docile. Aurora," she turned her attention to the enforcer, "this is your domain. Would you do the honors?"

Aurora joined them in front of Rita, and from the box she took a black leather chastity belt. Rita felt a chill run down her spine. The unforgiving edges of the metal crotch glinted in the light as Aurora held it up for inspection.

Vivienne watched happily. "This was especially designed for you, Rita. Aurora's explorations of your cunt combined with her photographic memory and access to the best chastity belt–maker in Europe, means that it will fit you and only you."

The urge to run would have overwhelmed her if Rita hadn't been trembling so hard that even standing was a struggle.

One of the dungeon guards produced a warm wash cloth that smelled of fresh herbs and handed it to Edward, who knelt in front of her and gently cleaned her pussy. To her horror, she found herself crying. Aurora placed an arm around her for support. Once Edward was finished cleaning her, he carefully fitted the thick belt around her waist, and she fought back panic as its confining grip closed in on her. Then he knelt again and pulled the strap between her legs, tightening it until the metal plate pressed against her labia, making penetration of even a finger impossible.

"Don't forget this." Vivienne handed him a secondary metal plate.

"Is that really necessary, Vivienne?" He growled. "She's done everything you've demanded of her and more. Do you really think she'll cheat?"

"She has powerful urges, Edward. You above all people should know that. Now put it on."

"I'm sorry, Rita," he half whispered, as he knelt once again in front of her and reached between her legs.

She hated that she couldn't be seriously angry without tears. But anger wasn't all she felt, not nearly all. As she stood in front of the High Council, with Edward attaching the metal plate, all she really wanted was to be left alone.

Once the secondary plate was attached, Edward stood and handed her the key.

"You can remove the belt whenever you want," Vivienne said. "The key is in your keeping. But once you've removed it, it's been designed so it can't be put back on. That will be an indication that you're not a worthy candidate."

"You'll wear the chastity belt until I decide you can take it off. That's the first part of your initiation. Perhaps you think membership into The Mount is one giant orgy, but I can assure you, girl, sex is nothing without control, without discipline, without trust. And when I'm convinced you can control yourself, then you'll be ready for the next level."

"Oh, and don't think I'm stupid, Rita. I know why you're here."

Vivienne shot Edward an acid glance. "And that's why I think you're unfit to be an initiate. Your motives are too personal, and that's why you'll fail." She heaved a sigh. "Nonetheless, I've been outvoted, so we'll continue with this farce.

"Since I know your motives, it's my duty to keep temptation from you. The best way I know to do that is to set certain ground rules. First of all, you are not to see Edward's face until you've completed your initiation and are accepted as a full-fledged member of The Mount."

Rita felt herself reeling. Suddenly there were wings hammering in her ears.

Vivienne continued. "Secondly, you are not to have intercourse with Edward again until you've successfully completed your initiation." She raised her hand before Rita could protest. "Oh don't worry, darling, once I've removed the chastity belt, we'll make sure your little pussy is well satisfied during the interim. Believe me, you won't have time to miss Edward."

The chastity belt bit into the tops of her inner thighs and the heavy leather of the waist band cut off all possibility of a truly deep breath. She felt claustrophobic in a way she would have never dreamed possible.

Even a claustrophobic week or two in the chastity belt she would have been willing to endure, but the whole point of going through all this was to be with Edward. She thought he wanted to be with her. Or did he? After all, he had just had a good come in the mouth of the most beautiful woman Rita had ever seen while he watched her play the slut in front of the whole High Council. Perhaps he just saw her as another diversion for the rich and bored. Her stomach felt like stone, and her eyes stung. God, she wanted out of this place, and fast.

"Oh, and one more thing, dear," Vivienne said. "The chastity belt is your little secret. If anyone finds out for any reason, and believe me, if they do, we'll know. Game's over, and your initiation is nullified."

Vivienne snapped her fingers and the dungeon guards left. It was Edward who knelt to help her into her yoga pants, then he slipped the tank top over her head, dressing her as though she were a helpless child, and indeed that was how she felt. As he leaned forward to zip her hoodie, he whispered very softly against her ear. "You were magnificent. I'm so proud of you." He cupped her face in his hand and thumbed away the tears. "I'll text you as soon as I can."

Once again, Vivienne snapped her fingers and Aurora escorted Rita back up the stairs without a word and out behind The Mount to a limo waiting to take her back home. There she still had a proposal to finish for tomorrow's meeting, all to be made more complicated by the biting and binding of the damned chastity belt.

Chapter Five

"THAT'S IT?" THE CORNER of Owen Frank's upper lip twitched double-time, which was never a good sign. "You want to do a story on an allotment run by homeless people? Look at the sign on the door, luv." He jammed his finger in the general direction of the outer office. "It says *Talkabout Magazine*, not *Gardener's World*, not *Big Issue*."

He slapped the edge of his desk so hard that his tea mug jumped, threatening to spill the contents. "Damn it, Rita, I hired you because your work is edgy, quirky. And so far all you've given me is generic." He stood and walked behind her, surreptitiously checking out his Majorca-tanned reflection in the plate-glass window. He always looked like he'd just had a date with an airbrush. "You're not in Kansas anymore, Dorothy." He laid solicitous hands on her shoulders and gave them a knead.

She would have squirmed out of groping range, but the chastity belt pinched when she squirmed, so she sat still. He was used to having his way with women. She'd known that when she took the position, but she had naïvely believed her work spoke for itself, a belief that had definitely detoured her advancement at *Talkabout*. "Seattle," she said.

"What?"

"I'm from Seattle, not Kansas."

"Whatever. My point is being in London is a big change and it's enough to make anyone nervous. I know that, really I do. I'm a small-town boy myself. But hon, it isn't going to get any easier. You'll have to buck up."

He moved to pace back and forth in front of her, giving her the opportunity to admire his pretty-boy physique. She had to admit his choreography was always flawless. "I know you've got it in you, Rita. I've seen the good stuff you've written. You've just not written any of it for me. And frankly," he turned to face her so she could admire the front-on effect, "I'm really struggling to find a good reason to keep you here when I can get anyone to write generic. I want you, really I do. But I have to answer to the owners, don't I?" His gaze flitted to her breasts, then back to her face so quickly that anyone who was less familiar with the man might have missed the subtext. If she wanted her story in his magazine, she'd have to pony up.

Her eyes stung from lack of sleep. She rubbed the corners to avoid smearing her make-up. At the moment, there'd be no ponying of any sort, even if she wanted to, and she sure as hell did not. There must be something else she could offer to get him off her back, but Jesus, it was hard to concentrate on anything but getting enough breath in her lungs and keeping her tender bits from being pinched.

She was such an idiot. She could have been chastity-belt-free by now. Last night, in the wee hours as she struggled to finish the proposal, she'd had three calls from her mother on the landline, calls she didn't answer. Her number was supposed to be unlisted. Fat lot of good that did. The woman knew she was in London now. That worried her.

Somewhere between the awful itching of the belt and her efforts to master peeing through a sieve, she had made up her mind. She would suffer no more humiliation. She never wanted to be a member of The Mount in the first place. She didn't even know what the hell that meant. And as for Edward, well if he was truly interested in her, he'd be interested whether she played Vivienne's stupid game or not.

Then his text had come.

I no the nite was hard, but itl b so worth it. Plse trust me. I miss
u terribly. Exx.

The "*Exx*" had kept her hanging on. Enduring Owen's abuse in
a chastity belt—surely that must be the definition of hell. It wasn't
Edward in the chastity belt, was it? Oh no, he was too busy being
sucked off by Vivienne, and who knew what else they got up to after
Rita had provided the evening's entertainment. That was it! When
Owen finished ranting, she'd go home and remove the chastity belt.
Then she'd masturbate her pussy raw, and mail the key back to
Vivienne specifically telling her what she could do with it.

Owen had got around to groping her shoulders again, in the
form of a friendly massage. "I'd hoped to mentor you, Rita," he said,
enjoying the view down the front of her blouse. "But somehow I've
failed you. If you could just give me something, something to make
me believe you're up for this job."

The words just came out. "What if I could get you an inside
exclusive on The Mount?" The minute she'd said it, she felt guilty.
Thoughts of making love to Edward flashed through her head.

Owen nearly busted himself in a fit of laughter that came out in
hot little puffs against the top of her head. "Honey, if you could get an
inside exclusive on The Mount, you'd get a Pulitzer. Hell, you could
have my job, or anyone else's. Your career would be made, wouldn't
it?" He heaved a sigh that ended in an avuncular chuckle. "I know
your situation seems desperate, darling, but there's no need to promise
what you can't deliver. I'm sure we can work something out."

Suddenly she could think of nothing she'd love more than to
expose that bitch Vivienne to massive media humiliation. Visions of
the woman kneeling in front of Edward with his cock in her mouth
went a long way to assuage the guilt she felt at betraying him. Once
the Vivienne-hate stopped making her feel like her chest might
explode, she ignored Owen's continuing rant, as the realization

K D Grace

suddenly sunk in. The gift horse had been given to her. Here was the story of a lifetime all wrapped up with a bow and a chastity belt, an exclusive that no one else in the whole world could get. And it was all hers. She was an insider. She was an initiate. All she had to do was endure, and she was good at enduring.

"I've been there," she said softly.

Owen stopped mid-rant. "You what?"

"I said I've been there, to The Mount. Twice."

"Bloody hell!" He stumbled back to his desk and downed the rest of his tea in one burning gulp. "Are you serious? You can't be serious? How could *you* have got into The Mount?"

She shifted in the chair to scoot forward, then thought better of it when the belt gave her a good pinch in the crotch. "Let's just say I have friends there, and that chances are extremely good I'll be invited back. Soon."

For a long moment, he studied her hard. She could just make out the flutter of his pulse against his throat. Then he leaned over his desk. "Can you get me in?" His words were little more than a breathy rasp. She was certain the rumors about The Mount's orgies and sex parties were not nearly as arousing to him as what being seen there would do for his reputation.

"I can try." True enough. She could try. But she wouldn't, not even if hell froze over.

He drummed his fingers. "Mind you, I'm still not convinced you were ever there in the first place. I mean, people do strange things when their jobs are on the line."

She said nothing. She held the winning hand, and he knew it.

"Of course," he added quickly, "if you could get me a story, even just an insider's account of an evening there, readers would eat it up. If you can do that, well, like I said, you're on your way up, honey."

"Oh, I can do that." She leaned forward and felt the pinch. "I can do that and a whole lot more."

———

Once Owen was convinced that Rita had actually been to The Mount, and hints had been dropped that she'd try to get him a reservation, her escape from the office was easy enough. After all, she was an investigative reporter, and as such she now had a plan of action, something to concentrate on other than the constant feeling of suffocation.

It was unusually hot in the flat for early spring, so she stripped down to the dratted belt and a thin tank top and began to write, in as much detail as she could remember, the events that had led to her acceptance as an initiate into The Mount. What did it actually mean to be a member of The Mount? Did it just ensure she could get reservations for the table of her choice and free dance lessons whenever she wanted? She stroked the metal crotch of the chastity belt. Somehow she seriously doubted it.

Most of the online information about The Mount was purely speculative, a lot of it from gossip rags that claimed to know somebody who knew somebody who had an acquaintance who got reservations. Still Rita hoped to uncover something new.

There were claims that The Mount taught the dirtiest of dirty dancing, the kind that ended in the horizontal mambo. There were claims that the place was really a restaurant where rich epicureans paid massively to sample rare species of animal. There were claims of orgies and devil worship and money laundering and white slavery.

Amid all the rumors, there was one actual restaurant review from a *Guardian* journalist who wrote that he'd seen nothing more exotic on the menu than locally farmed ostrich meat, though he had eaten the steak Diane, and it was superb. He had added as a post-script that he had not found the dancing dirty in the least, and that it had been rather subdued the night he was there.

Later, rumors went out that the whole interview had been

orchestrated, that the journalist had never actually been to The Mount, but had been hired by The Mount to take some of the heat off. This was outrageous in light of the fact that the more wild the rumors, the harder people tried to get reservations and the longer the queues were in front of the entrance every night.

Everyone knew that Vivienne Arlington Page managed The Mount, but no one seemed to know who owned it. No one knew anything beyond the fact that the empty Victorian wool warehouse had been bought up and renovated and *voila*! The Mount burst fully formed into the world.

The sleepless night and the stress of the past twenty-four hours made concentration hard. Rita finally turned off the computer to take a nap. She usually slept in the nude, which made the chastity belt even more of a pain, but with a heavy sigh she slipped out of her tank top and pulled back the duvet.

As she did so, she caught a glimpse of her reflection in the mirror, and a flash of blinding light reflected off the metal plate that cupped her pubis in a tight caress. She hadn't noticed that the plate below the locking mechanism was shaped like a cupping palm, as though someone had reached between her legs and rested a protective hand against her pubic bone. Still concentrating on the detail of the plate, she pulled a chair in front of the mirror and sat down, cursing under her breath at the pinch.

The pinch was always followed by an unsatisfied sense of anticipation. Sometimes when she masturbated she pinched herself down there until it almost hurt. And when she was right on the threshold between pain and something much nicer, she often had her best orgasms. Perhaps if she concentrated on the almost pleasure the pinch could provide, she'd forget about how trapped it made her feel. She opened her legs wide, and in spite of the tightness at her waist and the chafing at the tops of her thighs, she had to admire the workmanship.

She ran a hand down over the openings for her urethra and anus. She had heard somewhere, or maybe read in some nasty piece of porn on a rainy day when there was nothing better to do but curl up with her Rabbit, that some chastity belts could have butt plugs and dildos attached to them. With a sudden rush of pleasure, she imagined what it would be like if Edward were the one in control of what attachments should fill her holes. She imagined his hand pressed against her pubis like the metal plate. She imagined his fingers, or maybe even his teeth pinching her, like the plate against her vulva pinched.

Her focus, which had until now been only on the intricacies of the chastity belt, took in the entirety of her body. Her legs were splayed at either edge of the chair. Her waist looked slimmer, longer, and porcelain-delicate beneath unforgiving black leather and polished metal. Above it all her full breasts seemed even fuller, crowned urgently with heavy, aching nipples that made them look like decadent twin desserts waiting to be devoured.

And the one man she wanted desperately to enjoy them was off-limits. A flash of guilt tightened her chest. She had put herself through all this for him, and now she would betray him. But if she mattered so much, then why didn't he just tell Vivienne, with all her Mount rules, to go fuck herself.

Granted, she wasn't nearly as pretty as Vivienne. But she knew things, things Vivienne didn't. She cupped her breasts and stroked her nipples with her thumbs, then very carefully began to rock against the chair.

At first the pinch was shocking, making her wince and gasp. But after a little practice, she learned to rock just enough to keep the pinch stimulating without being agonizing. She did that by letting her arse cheeks do most of the moving while she squeezed from the inside, tightening those exquisite muscles designed to grasp an erect penis in that amazing internal massage that caused such pleasure.

With careful focus, she managed just enough rocking so that the pinch stimulated her vulva. With the tensing and relaxing of her girlie muscles, she imagined Edward unlocking her and filling her with his distended cock. Tense and relax, tense and relax. Edward riding her so hard. Tense and relax. And her ripping the golden mask away, tense and relax, just in time to see his face when he came. The view in the mirror drifted out of focus, the edges burnished by the afternoon sun and the encroaching tremors of imminent orgasm. At last, in a yelp of pleasure and pain, she came, trembling and convulsing against the metal plates covering her pussy, slickening them with her juices.

Vivienne didn't know everything. If she did, she would have known a chastity belt, even one with triple metal plating, couldn't keep Rita from coming. She was an expert at stealth orgasms. She'd been having them since she was ten, under the watchful eyes of unwitting adults, in restaurants, in classrooms, on buses. No one ever suspected just how well she'd mastered the use of her secret girlie muscles. She smiled at her flushed face shining in the mirror, then crawled into bed and slept.

—~~—

"So what's up with you and Edward?" Kate called from the kitchen.

Rita pretended she hadn't heard the question.

"Lots of rumpy pumpy, I'm guessing."

Her voice was closer this time, and Rita looked up to find her friend standing over her with two cups of coffee. "Well?"

Rita returned her attention to her laptop, feigning noninterest. "I get a text occasionally."

"Come on, Ree. I don't believe you for a second. You're walking around like you've been riding a big one all night. You only walk like that for one reason, and it's a good one."

Actually there were two reasons, Rita thought, and the second wasn't so good. Almost as a reminder, the metal plate pinched her sharply on the pussy and she gritted her teeth. Just then her phone signaled a text, and Kate, who was deliciously free of the constraints of a chastity belt, grabbed it before Rita could.

"Mmm, yummy. Very sexy."

"Give me that." Enduring another hard pinch, Rita grabbed the phone away and read.

Less than 3 daz & I cn hardly bear it. I no how uncomfortable u must b. M damned uncomfortable myself evry time I think of u. Evry 2nd is agony. Hope u r not 2 sore. Promise I'll make it worth every ache. EXX

Rita could feel the blush crawling up her cheek and the muscles tensing deep in her cunt. But damn, his timing couldn't be worse.

Her friend tapped her foot on the carpeted floor and glared at her. "So why have you been holding out on me? Do I ever keep my love life from you? Granted there isn't much to tell, but when there is, don't I tell all?"

Rita tried to heave a sigh, but as with most efforts to breathe these days, it was rather unsatisfying. "Look, Kate, I would share all if I could, but Edward's a very secretive person, and I'd feel like I was betraying his trust if I told. Surely you can understand."

"Married, is he?"

"No! No he's not married." At least she hoped he wasn't, but she really didn't know, did she? "He just feels like what goes on between two people should stay between two people."

"You sure he's not married?"

"Of course I'm sure," she lied. The more she thought of the goings-on between him and Vivienne, the more the doubt niggled her.

When Kate went back to the kitchen for biscuits, she quickly texted.

R U married 2 Vivienne?

The reply came back almost instantly.

Edward: God no! Y wuld U thnk that?
Rita: U 2 cm close.
Edward: Bleev me, we r not.
Rita: Sorry. Evrythng so strange.
Edward: No need 2 dout me, Darling. I promise.

Perhaps there wasn't. But she was the one wearing the chastity belt, and Edward was the one wearing the mask.

Kate returned with biscuits and settled in her traditional position cross-legged on the sofa. She stuffed a Jaffa Cake in her mouth and spoke around it. "Since you won't tell me anything, I've been doing my own research on The Mount, and you'd be amazed at what I've found."

Rita burned her tongue on her coffee. "Oh? Like what?"

Just then Rita's mobile rang and both women nearly jumped off their seats. Rita hoped it would be Edward, but it was her boss. Why the hell was he calling on a Saturday afternoon?

"Rita, darling, you're an angel," came Owen's breathless voice on the phone. "I don't know how you did it, and even a limo to take us there. I have to say, I had my doubts, but you came through for me. You really did."

"Owen?"

The man was on a roll. "When you said you could get reservations at The Mount, I should have believed you, though how you did it so quickly's beyond me, and for the two of us." He chuckled suggestively.

"I'm just calling to double check. The limo will pick you up first, then me at eight. Is that right? Ressies for eight thirty, drinks and dinner, maybe a little tripping the light fantastic?"

Rita suddenly felt nauseated. Was this a part of her initiation? Did Vivienne know her plan to write an exposé? Who else could have pulled this off? It didn't matter who had done it, she had no choice. She hung up and made her excuses to Kate. She'd have to pick her friend's brain for new information concerning The Mount some other time.

Chapter Six

"SHE LOOKS GOOD IN that color, don't you think? Rose makes her skin look like she's had a little sun." Vivienne chuckled wickedly. "And oh, the cleavage. I can see why she's so willing to display it, and he's certainly more than willing to look.

"They look good together, don't they? Her boss is positively edible. He is her boss, you know? Lorelei heard him mention expensing the evening." She and Edward stood on the shadowy rise of the wrought-iron catwalk, nearly invisible to everyone below, but interested only in their initiate and her date.

When Edward made no response, Vivienne added, "Journalists? *Talkabout* magazine?"

"So?"

"So? Why do you think a budding journalist would bring her boss here? She smells an exposé, surely you can see that, Edward?"

"If she wanted an exposé, her boss would be the last person she'd bring here. Besides, Rita wouldn't do that." Edward tugged uncomfortably on the front of his jacket, feeling a strange mix of desire and jealousy at seeing Rita here in his domain with someone he hadn't approved. And the dress, my God, all he could think about was ripping it off of her and devouring her inch by inch, a thought he couldn't afford to be having. "What I'm wondering is how she managed reservations in the first place."

Vivienne brushed an invisible speck from his cuff and smoothed his hair, which didn't need smoothing. "She's a journalist. And if she's a good one, she'll find a way. I'm sure Aurora would find her a table if it would get her pussy licked again. You know what a slut Rory is, and our dear Rita certainly gives Alex quite a hard-on."

"Neither of them could get her reservations even if they wanted to, Vivienne. You know that."

The woman shrugged as though the whole situation bored her and looked out over the restaurant below. "Where there's a will, there's a way, and getting the story of a lifetime is definitely high motivation for a starving journalist, wouldn't you say?"

Edward looked down to where the two sat, heads together in deep conversation, and his stomach clenched.

"Rita wouldn't do that," he repeated. "Rita would never do that."

Vivienne offered a throaty chuckle. "My poor Edward. You're so naïve. So trusting. I'd have thought you'd have learned by now."

"That's right, I am trusting. I trust her completely." Still, why the hell did she have to look so hot for the man? Why did she bring him at all? None of it made any sense. He white-knuckled the rail as he watched Rita's boss possessively push aside a lock of her hair, silky hair that he knew smelled vaguely of coconut. Was she trying to torture him because he couldn't have her just yet, because he was being forced to wait? God, if she only knew how difficult all this was for him.

Vivienne leaned in close and kissed Edward's earlobe. "She'll betray us before the month is out. Surely you can see this. She's only using you, using all of us to get a story."

Edward jerked away. "That's not true. She wouldn't."

She leaned in again and bit his ear, playfully. "Want to bet?"

This time he pushed her away and stepped back, his eyes still locked on the couple below. "What bet? What are you talking about?"

"You know, a wager. Don't act so innocent, Edward, darling. You know all about wagers, don't you?"

He froze, his heart pounding in his chest. How dare she bring up such a thing here and now? But she continued as though she were merely discussing the weather.

"I'll wager that before her initiation is over, *Talkabout* magazine will run a front-page exposé on The Mount. I can see the headlines now." She lifted a hand in front of them as though she were placing the headline on a billboard. "Restaurant and Dance Club exposed as Secret Sex Cult." She giggled. "I like that, don't you? Secret sex cult. It has a nice ring to it."

"That's not going to happen."

She held his gaze, the humor gone from her eyes. "Want to bet? I'll give you a chance to win back what you've lost." Suddenly it was difficult to breathe, more difficult than it had been watching the woman he wanted to be with making nicey-nice with another man. It was true, he trusted Rita completely. He didn't know why. He barely knew her, and yet there had been that moment on the train in the dark, before he ever saw her face, before he ever knew how outrageous she was, how well she could play the game. He just knew. He swallowed hard. "All right. I'll bet you. I'll bet that not only will Rita Holly not betray us, but I'll bet she wins the respect of every member of The Mount and passes the initiation with flying colors. That's what I'll bet."

The humor returned to her eyes. She held his gaze with that half-smile look she often gave him when she was scheming something. "That's all very nice, darling, but remember, you have nothing to wager." The smile slipped from her lips, and she studied him. In spite of the music and laughter and the tinkling of cutlery and crystal from below, suddenly everything seemed bathed in cottony silence, and all he could hear was the hammering of his heart in his ears. Then, after what seemed like forever came the response he would have never expected. "All right, Edward. I'll spot you on this one. I've been rather generous with the terms of the last bet you lost. But this time, if you lose, I promise I'll find new and exciting ways to make you pay."

—ww—

"There's something to be said for expensive wine. Go on, try it." Owen drank deeply. But Rita barely touched hers. She couldn't afford to lose her wits to the wine when she suspected Vivienne of treachery.

"You look tired, Rita." He studied her for a long moment over the top of his wine glass, then he heaved a sigh like he'd just solved a daunting problem. "I'm concerned that this story might be too much for you, I mean, you really do look tired, no offense, Rita, but wow!" He sat his glass down and leaned over the table toward her, offering her his best concerned-boss face, then he continued very softly. "No one would argue that you're an excellent journalist, but you're new, and let's face it, honey, you're way out of your league here. You might want to consider letting me help you with this one."

She forced a smile around her gritted teeth. "Thanks, Owen. But I can handle it just fine."

He lifted his hands in a back-off gesture. "Just a thought. Keep it in mind in case the burden gets too heavy. You know I'm always here for you." Before she could respond, he changed the subject. "The woman with all the sapphires, do you know her?"

"Lorelei? I've been introduced. Yes."

"She really fancies me."

Rita nearly choked on her water.

He gave a self-satisfied chuckle. "She is a bit cheeky, though, don't you think? I mean, the complimentary bottle of vino, the lovely show of cleavage, and me here with another woman. I hope you weren't too upset. Is she seeing anyone?"

Rita mentally rolled her eyes. "It didn't come up in the conversation."

"When she said dinner and drinks are on the house. What do you think she meant by that?" Rita tried to heave a sigh and felt the pinch. "I think she meant you won't have to expense the evening."

She thought it was very decent of Vivienne not to make *Talkabout* pay for her vicious little scheme.

But Owen wasn't listening. "Surely she's more than just a hostess, dressed like that. She is, isn't she? She's somebody. I'm sure I've seen her before, maybe at L'Escargot. Yes, I'm sure I must have. I think she might have recognized me too. Maybe that's why the special treatment."

"Afraid you'll just have to ask her," Rita said. She watched Owen mentally inventory the room for who could do him the most good. And at the moment, most of the people who were anybody were on the dance floor.

He drained his wine glass and stood. "We should dance." He took her hand and practically dragged her from the booth. Fortunately the music covered her little grunt of pain, and with him eyeing the who's who on the dance floor, he didn't notice how stiffly she moved to get up. "You do dance, don't you, Rita?"

He didn't wait for an answer. He half led, half pulled her onto the dance floor, where he promptly stepped on her foot twice as they attempted a simple fox-trot. Keeping the beat seemed to be a foreign concept to him. The new discomfort growing in the pit of Rita's stomach had nothing to do with the chastity belt. If Owen couldn't dance—and it was eminently clear that he couldn't—no way in hell would he be dragged onto the dance floor in a place as important to him as The Mount.

Alarm bells jangled in Rita's head as Owen stumbled against her and grabbed at her for support. He hadn't drunk enough wine to cause coordination problems, and it was well known that the man could hold his alcohol. He stepped on her foot again and bumped into her. "Owen? Are you all right?"

"Never better." He laughed too loud and several couples glanced in their direction as he pulled her so close that what little breath she did have was forced from her lungs. "God, you smell good,

Rita. I'm not talkin' 'bout your perfume." He chuckled suggestively against her ear, and one hand slid down to grope her arse, pulling her close enough so that there was no ignoring the enormous hard-on straining against his expensively clothed crotch. "I can smell when a woman wants it, 'n' honey, I'm surprised you didn't rip my clothes off 'n ride me in the limo."

His slurred speech and sudden lack of inhibitions alarmed her even further. A quick look around assured her everyone was pretending not to notice. "Owen," she whispered urgently. "I don't know what's going on, but this isn't appropriate." He swung her around awkwardly and groped her breast, then made a frightening attempt at a dip.

It was then, in her peripheral vision, she saw movement on the catwalk, a man and a woman, but before she could get a better look, Owen jerked her back to him and shoved his tongue halfway down her throat. "My God, Rita," he grunted as he came up for air, oblivious to her efforts to push him away. "This place makes me so horny. No wonder you come here. Musbe somethin' in the air." He shoved her toward the edge of the dance floor, practically dry-humping her with every step.

"What's that idiot doing?" Edward leaned over the rail so far that Vivienne grabbed the tail of his jacket and pulled him back.

She chuckled softly. "It's called dancing, Edward. Some people are better at it than others."

"That's not dancing. Can't you see he's hurting her?"

"Hurting her? Oh, you mean the chastity belt?"

He pushed her hand away. "I can see it, even if you can't. Look at the way she moves, the way she winces."

"Poor empathetic Edward. I'm so sorry you feel her pain."

"You could have at least let her wear something underneath."

"She's an initiate, Edward. Initiates don't get silk knickers with their chastity belts."

He leaned over the rail, alarm rising in his chest. "What the hell is going on? He's practically attacking her."

"Oh don't worry. It's just a little fun, that's all." He felt ice in his stomach as the man stumbled and groped, then roared with laughter. "This is your scheming, isn't it? You got the reservation. He's here because of you isn't he? Dear God, Vivienne, please tell me you didn't give him something."

She shrugged and smoothed the front of her dress, suddenly very interested in the beading. "Not me. *I* didn't."

"Owen Frank is way too concerned about impressions to grope his employee on the dance floor of The Mount. Now what the fuck is going on?" He pulled his mobile from his pocket and texted rapidly.

"Oh come on, darling. It's just a little fun."

"At the expense of Rita's initiation? At the expense of a man's dignity?"

"What would you know about dignity," she pouted. He texted.

Alex, get Rita out of there. Now! My suite.
Rory, take care of Owen Frank. He's drugged.

Then he turned and fled, ignoring Vivienne, who called after him. No doubt she'd make him pay for that offense later.

———

"Owen, what the hell are you doing? Stop it!" Rita had managed to maneuver him back to the booth, but once there, he was practically on top of her. It was becoming more and more difficult to avoid the groping that might give away her secret. She squirmed and twisted to regain control and keep from making a spectacle, ignoring the pinch and squeeze of the belt, which bordered on full-blown pain. Something was definitely wrong. Owen might be a twat, but he would never attack her like some horny baboon. She shoved him aside long enough to grab a water glass. "Here, drink this, and breathe deeply."

He knocked the water out of her hand and spilled it down the front of her dress, which drew his attention immediately to her chilled nipples. She had only just redirected his attempt to grab her tit when his other hand found its way up the inside of her thigh. "Owen, stop it!" Alarm spiked in her chest. If this was Vivienne's doing, there would be no help for her. She was on her own.

The more she tried to disentangle herself, the more the belt pinched. Owen was frighteningly strong. She was about to take drastic measures and bash him with the wine bottle, when Alex appeared out of nowhere and pulled her away with such force that it took her breath. "So sorry, but, Ms. Holly, you have an urgent phone call. If you would follow me."

Almost before she was out of the way, Aurora, clothed in a sexy black mini dress, stepped in and pulled Owen from the booth. "You're Owen Frank, aren't you?" Her voice sounded breathy, girlish. "I've heard so much about you, and I love *Talkabout* magazine. I've been dying to meet you." She rubbed up against him. "I'm such a fan." She offered him a coy pout, which accentuated her full bottom lip. "I know someplace where we can talk, privately, that is, if you're interested." She offered her hand, and he followed without protest, barely aware that his date was being escorted away by one of the dancers.

Chapter Seven

BEFORE RITA REALIZED WHAT was happening, Alex escorted her to an elevator hidden behind stacks of spare tables and chairs near the kitchen.

Inside, she broke into a cold sweat and would have found it difficult to stand if not for Alex's supporting arm. She always took the stairs, which was great for the cardiovascular system, and cut way down on embarrassing incidents of hyperventilation in tight spaces.

She vice-gripped Alex's arm and tried to focus. "Owen's been drugged."

"I know. It wasn't supposed to happen." He mistook her distress for concern. "He'll be all right. Don't worry. Aurora will take good care of him."

"Vivienne did this." Alex didn't answer, but the muscles twitched and knotted along his jawbone. Just as the elevator opened into blessed space, he slipped his arm tighter around her and guided her down a carpeted hallway with doors on either side. If Rita hadn't known better, she could have easily mistaken the place for an expensive hotel. Near the end of the hall, he punched a coded security lock and the door opened into a dimly lit suite of smoked glass and chrome.

He had barely closed the door behind them when it burst open again, and Edward appeared in his golden mask. He pulled her into a bone-crushing embrace. "Are you all right? You didn't drink the wine, did you?"

She shook her head and viciously blinked back tears. She wouldn't give him the satisfaction.

"God, I was so worried." He pulled away so violently that for a second she thought he was angry.

"Take the dress off," he commanded. "Alex help her. Get it off her now." Rita made no attempt to protest as Alex stripped her until she stood in nothing but a small lacy bra, stockings and garter belts, and the horrid chastity belt.

Edward stood for a long moment taking in the sight of her. Once again the golden mask hid any emotions he might be feeling. At last, he spoke, "Do you have the key?"

She shook her head. "It's at home. I thought if I brought it I might be tempted to—"

"To what? Fuck your boss?"

With a move that surprised even her, she slapped him hard enough that it stung her hand, hard enough that it knocked the mask askew. If she had been a little less angry and he a little slower, she might have caught a glimpse of his face.

"I'm claustrophobic, you bastard. Remember? And my claustrophobia's not limited to small dark rooms. I was afraid if I brought the key, I'd be tempted just to take the damn thing off."

He cursed under his breath. From his pocket he pulled the Vitronox knife and opened it.

"What are you doing? What's that for? Edward, what's going on?" Panic rose in her throat. She stepped back, but found her way blocked by Alex.

"I'm getting the belt off you, that's what I'm doing." Edward reached for the waist band with one hand, but she pushed him away.

"No! Vivienne said if I take it off, I fail. Leave it alone. You'll risk everything!" She tried to push back farther, but Alex was like a solid wall behind her, grabbing her arms to keep her from struggling.

She kicked hard, and her left foot made contact with the muscle of Edward's calf. He grunted and cursed, then pushed in closer and took her face in one hand. "Damn it, Rita! Hold still. This is no longer a part of the initiation. Vivienne broke the rules by bringing Owen into the picture and drugging him. Your task for her is now void. For God sake, let me get it off of you, sweetheart. OK?"

Edward grasped the top of the belt and with a quick downward motion that a surgeon would have envied, slit the leather, allowing air to rush back into her lungs. He knelt to help her step out of the cursed belt. Then his hands were on her, examining the chafed places, caressing her pubis with a feather touch. "I'm sorry," he whispered. His breath was cool and soothing against her burning skin. "I'm so sorry." He pulled her close, kissing her navel, cupping and kneading her buttocks. She curled her fingers in his hair and held him to her, dizzy with a cocktail of feelings she figured would take her until next Christmas to sort out.

Then Alex spoiled it all. He laid a hand on Edward's shoulder. "I'm sorry, Edward, but the initiation's not over."

The sigh she felt against her belly sounded almost painful. "You're right. It's not." Edward stood and kissed her until her knees were weak and her head was buzzing, along with all the rest of her. Then he disentangled her arms from around his neck and offered her hand to Alex.

"Take her, Alex." His voice was rough, as though every word abraded his throat. "Make her feel better." She felt as though she'd been slapped.

"Are you sure?"

Alex held Edward's gaze as he took Rita's hand.

"I'm sure."

"Edward?" The panic was back, fear that Edward would leave. It was a stupid fear. He always left, and she never really got to see him, not really.

"It's all right, darling." It was as though he'd read her mind. "I'm not leaving until I'm sure you're OK."

She let Alex lead her into the bedroom. Edward followed close behind. There were candles lit around the room, and the bed in the middle was big enough for an orgy. Rita imagined it had probably been the venue for more than a few. Standing in front of the bed, Alex turned to face her. He stroked her cheek and kissed her ear, but she felt cold inside. As though he sensed it, he moved closer. "Rita, the initiation is not meant to be without pleasure or comfort." One hand traced the contours of her torso, down her hip, sliding a finger under the edge of the garter belt. "That's what I'm here for, and you're so desirable, so exquisite. Use me." He kissed her, lips parted just enough for a flick of the tongue. His breath was warm and tasted slightly of wine. "Edward will tell me exactly what to do, and you can pretend I'm him. Please. Let me make you feel better."

It shouldn't have happened, not after the trauma of the evening, not after everything she had been through this week. And yet she felt the tightening low in her belly, the bearing down, the beginnings of need that had been kindled when Edward came into her life. It was a need she could have never imagined to be so powerful, so brazen, and yet here she was about to allow herself to be fucked vicariously.

Edward nodded his approval, looking as neutral as ever from beneath the mask. He sat down in a chair close to the bed and unbuttoned his jacket.

For a few moments he simply watched while Alex reacquainted himself with Rita's mouth, each kiss deeper and more demanding than the one before, awakening her more fully to her hunger and to the delicious fact that Edward was watching. Once again, she was performing for him. No matter how angry that made her, it was still irresistibly arousing.

"Take off her bra, Alex. I want to see her breasts," Edward said.

With his mouth still deliciously engaged in the tongue dance, Alex slid his hands around her, deftly unhooked her bra, then slipped the straps off her shoulders and let it slide to the floor. She thought she heard a duet of sighs as her breasts were suddenly freed, nipples pointing insistently for their share of attention.

"That's good, that's perfect," Edward whispered. "Now touch them, Alex. You've never felt breasts so exquisite. And her nipples are so responsive. Pinch them. That's right. See how her areolae mound and pucker, how her nipples swell and get so big. Oh God, so big."

It was touching, and yet disconcerting just how well Edward knew her body, so well that he could tell someone else what she liked and how she would respond. They'd not been together that often, and much of that time had been in total darkness.

"Take off your shirt," Edward commanded.

Alex obeyed.

"That's good. Now feel the way her breasts press against your chest. Incredible, isn't it?"

Alex groaned his pleasure, and rocked his hips against her naked pubis. "You're hard, aren't you?" Edward said. "Of course you are. How could you not be? Rita, stroke his cock through his trousers. Pretend it's my cock you're about to undress."

Alex caught his breath in a gasp as she gave him a hard stroke she knew was almost painful. She had to remind herself, Alex wasn't Edward. He didn't deserve her anger. As she eased her stroking, Alex grabbed her wrist and held her tightly against him. "It's all right if you want to hurt me. I know you're angry. You have a right to be. I promise I can take it," he whispered.

She shot Edward a quick glance where he sat unmoving, distant, untouchable behind his golden mask. If he was aroused, he wasn't showing it, and that made her even more angry. The concoction of feelings erupted like a volcano, and she was suddenly tearing and ripping at Alex's trousers, growling like an angry panther. "Get them off. Get out of them now." She shoved him onto the bed and clambered on top of him just as he kicked the trousers and boxers off. "Put your cock in me. Fuck me. I'm tired of this bullshit. I'm tired of waiting." She settled onto his cock with a hard shove, so hard that she forced the breath from his lungs, and he grabbed her hips for self-preservation. "Once again, I'm the entertainment, Edward. Seems like I'm always just the entertainment."

"Rita, stop it!" Alex bundled her to him, still fully impaled, and rolled with her until she was underneath him, spread-eagled on the bed with her wrists pinned over her head. "You're talking about things you don't understand, now leave it." He ground into her hard, returning a bit of her anger, and she took it willingly. She wrapped her legs around him and matched him thrust for thrust, until she was holding her breath, bordering on orgasm.

"Bring her here." Edward's voice sounded strangled and tight amid the chorus of grunts and moans.

With Rita still wrapped around him like a straitjacket and his cock buried to the hilt, Alex lifted her, hands under her bottom for support, and brought her before Edward, who stood and moved to sandwich her between the two men. Still fully clothed, he caressed her breasts, then traced the cleft between her buttocks, lingering to fondle her anus, his finger sinking into her tight pucker each time she thrust back. His mouth found the sensitive place along the back of her neck. Kisses became nibbles, and nibbles became bites until she thrust and bucked and squirmed in a wild frenzy, feeling like her pussy and back hole would burst into flame.

"That's it, Rita, pretend it's me, pretend your initiation is over and you can use me any way you see fit. I think about that all the time. Just imagine," Edward whispered against her ear, shoving his middle finger fully into her anus, biting and nibbling between words. "I'll be yours wholly and unreservedly."

She came, howling and raging. Edward stepped back quickly and practically fell into the chair with a harsh grunt. Alex dropped her onto the bed with a hard bounce and pulled out just in time to turn and send a viscous arch of ejaculate into the air to land at

Edward's feet. Then he dropped to both knees on the hardwood floor, gasping for breath.

For a long moment, the room was silent except for their joint struggles for breath. When the world came back into focus, Edward still sat stiffly on the chair and Alex still knelt in front of him as though he were offering fealty to his king.

At last, Edward spoke, his voice once again neutral. "Get dressed, Alex. Take her home. Make sure she's OK."

Then, just like that, he stood and left the room as though he were sleepwalking. Rita felt the burn of the anger in her stomach rekindle as she struggled back into her clothes, more determined than ever to see this bloody initiation through and get her story, though she couldn't help wondering who would actually believe her.

<center>~~~</center>

A tiny Asian woman, dressed only in a string of pearls and an enormous strap-on, opened the door and ushered Edward into Vivienne's suite. She led him down the hall to the gray marble bathroom.

"I assume you've been comforting your little darling?" Vivienne sat naked on the edge of the giant marble tub, which he had often shared with her. Her legs trailed in a froth of scented bubbles. Kneeling in the tub between her thighs was an equally naked Lorelei, carefully shaving Vivienne's pussy. The Asian woman sat down on the edge of the tub and watched the intimate ritual while stroking her strap-on.

"You removed her chastity belt, did you? Never mind. Of course you did. You're such a spoilsport." Vivienne opened her legs further while Lorelei painted thick soap from a lilac porcelain cup onto her mound and over the tops of her thighs next to the pillowed swell of her vulva. She squirmed and wriggled, adjusting her bottom until he could see the whole of her gash along with an occasional glimpse of her anus. Then she ground herself against the marble and moaned softly, pressing forward to meet the razor as Lorelei delicately scraped the blade along the edge of her thigh, holding the pouting folds of her labia first to one side then the other with perfect precision.

Vivienne loved to have her pussy shaved. Edward had done it for her often enough, and then he had fucked her until neither of them could walk straight the next morning. It was a pretty safe bet that wasn't going to happen tonight.

She curled her fingers in Lorelei's hair, then absently reached to stroke her own heavy breasts. The Asian woman trailed her hand in the water, then sat forward to finger her anus with the wet hand while stroking the strap-on more enthusiastically.

"I'll see that Alex and Rory are duly punished for helping you out." She shifted and Lorelei inserted two fingers into her pussy, while carefully drawing the razor over the taut mound of Vivienne's pubis, then she laid down the razor and leaned forward, placing a lingering kiss on the newly shaven skin. Edward knew how smooth it was, how soft to the touch. With her fingers still in Vivienne's cunt, Lorelei produced a thick terry wash cloth and slowly, as though the act were deeply fascinating, washed away the remaining soap and examined her work.

"You can't punish them for enforcing the rules. Rules that you made, then broke." He tried not to watch what was going on too closely. It would do him no good to get worked up.

"Party poopers." She bent and gave Lorelei a long lingering kiss, then sat back and opened her legs wide, wriggling her bottom until her pout was within easy reach of her bather. Lorelei lowered her mouth to suckle each of Vivienne's swollen lips in turn, slurping and licking as though she were having her favorite dessert.

"You involved an outsider, Vivienne. Do you know how danger- ous that is? How stupid?"

"Stupid?" She grunted and bore down against Lorelei's mouth. "I doubt if the man has ever had as much fun, and all at The Mount.

How he'll brag to his friends and superiors." She curled her fingers in Lorelei's hair again and pulled her closer. "I'm sure Rory gave him the ride of a lifetime. It's a win-win situation." With a flick of her wrist, she motioned the Asian in, and as if on cue, Lorelei lifted her arse out of the water so the strap-on could slide easily into her soapy cunt.

He could tell by the tension in Vivienne's thighs and stomach and by the way her areolae rose like they were caressing her engorged nipples that she was about to come. The woman could come endlessly, and with a sense of resignation brought on by the painful tug in his crotch, he figured that was exactly what she planned to do. It was going to be a very long night.

With a little whimper and a gasp, Vivienne orgasmed, and rewarded Lorelei with a kiss before she motioned the Asian woman to her and began to stroke the strap-on while Lorelei moved to the rear to examine the woman's pout and finger her sensitive anus, already gripping and relaxing from her auto-stimulation.

Vivienne took the strap-on into her mouth and began to deep-throat it. Then, as though she had suddenly remembered he was still there, she pulled away and looked up at him. "Of course you're right, darling. Rory and Alex were just doing their job, but," she heaved a deep-chested sigh and turned her back to him, bending over and opening her pussy for the strap-on, "you I can punish, and I will. You're off to bed without any pussy."

By bed, she meant her bed, a place to which the party was more than likely to migrate relatively soon. A place where he would have to ignore the fact that everyone was coming but him. They would all make certain he was very aware of that fact.

He left the room with some relief, though not much. If he had not gone to Rita's rescue tonight, he would have been the one rewarded with Vivienne's full attention. That was something that he craved much less since he met Rita Holly, and, though he tried to hide it, Vivienne was not easily fooled.

Stiffly, he slipped out of his clothes to the wet sounds of pleasure coming from the next room. He tried to ignore his reflection in the mirrored walls, not an easy task since Vivienne loved to watch herself, whether she was fucking or not. As he eased his boxers down over his hips, the metal of his chastity belt flashed in the soft lamp light and reflected in the mirror.

He ran his hand over the tight weave of metal that caged his aching penis. It had been a long time since his punishments had involved the wearing of the blasted thing. And he wouldn't have had to now if he'd been able to hide his desire for Rita a little better. Vivienne didn't care who he fucked. It had never mattered until now. But then he had never been so bold as to bring a lover to The Mount, as to want that lover to be a part of more than just one night of his life. He stroked the metal again. Yes, he would pay dearly. Vivienne would make sure of it. But he hoped that if he took his punishment and kept his head low for a while, she would let him off the leash.

Carefully, he sat back against the head board and folded his legs into a full lotus position. It wasn't the most comfortable thing to do in a chastity belt, but necessary, nonetheless, as he prepared himself for the meditation he used when he had to sublimate his desire, when he knew there would be no release. As he settled into position and tried to breathe deeply, his heart suddenly skipped a beat as he remembered how Rita had fought to keep him from cutting her chastity belt off, how she had refused to give in because she was determined to successfully complete her initiation. And if she did... He dared not hope what that might mean for either of them.

"Oh God, oh God, I'm coming," Lorelei shouted from the bathroom over a wave of giggles and groans. It was definitely going to be a long night. But if Rita could endure, so could he. They would endure together, and that thought eased his discomfort considerably.

Chapter Eight

"I still think he's married."

"What?" Rita looked up at Kate, forgetting the chunk of bread in her hand and the swans and Canada geese pressing in all around. The two had decided to enjoy a spring walk through St. James's Park and get a little sun while there was some to get.

"Edward. I think he's married. I mean, look how secretive it all is. He sends a limo and whisks you off to The Mount. Then you're back the next day as moody as a bear, and you won't tell me anything." Kate raised her hand. "Don't get me wrong. I'm not being judgmental or anything. I just don't want you to get hurt."

Rita pulled her jacket around her against a sharp spring breeze and continued feeding the geese. She wished she could tell her friend everything. She really could use someone to talk to. "He says he's not. Married, I mean."

"Yeah well blokes will say anything to get shagged, won't they?"

If only it were that simple. Since Alex had returned her to her flat after the Owen incident, she'd not heard from Edward. Owen was strutting around the office bragging about his night at The Mount, so she assumed Aurora had convinced him he'd had a wonderful time. Trying to imagine Owen and Aurora together served to remind her just how indebted she was to the woman.

No one from The Mount had made any effort to explain what had happened, and she knew no more now than she did when she was in the thick of it. Anger and frustration drove her research, but so far, every angle she had tried was a dead end. As an initiate, she was no better off than anyone else in London. She had to wait to be invited, and since Vivienne had drugged Owen there had been no invites. Perhaps it didn't matter that Vivienne had broken the rules. Perhaps Vivienne was as good as her word, and when Edward had removed Rita's chastity belt, the initiation was over. If that were true, she would at least like to know.

She dusted the bread crumbs from her jacket and walked on. "You said you found some interesting things about The Mount?"

"Possibly. I've been researching Victorian England, mostly the sexual mores of the time. You know, for the novel." Before Rita could respond, she continued. "I know, I know, I've been research-ing the novel for ages, but your secret encounters at The Mount inspired me."

The novel was just a hobby. Kate made a decent, and happy, living tutoring rich foreign students in English and freelancing for trade journals.

"What does any of that have to do with The Mount?" Rita asked.

"Secret societies."

"What?"

"You know, there's a secret society for everything, the Masons, the Knights Templar. I figured if it worked for Dan Brown it might work for me too. Anyway, I started researching, and I came across this, well it appears to be a secret sex cult. Mind you, it's Victorian, but I get the feeling it might be even older. I know it sounds insane, but the coincidences are amazing."

The butterflies in Rita's stomach were doing the tango. If she'd had to describe her experience at The Mount so far, based on what was nearly a total lack of knowledge, a secret sex cult would sum it up pretty well. "Why do you think it has anything to do with The Mount?"

Kate shrugged and turned her face to the sun. "I don't know, probably just read too many wild rumors in the gossip rags, you know, about all the shagging and sex rituals that supposedly go on there. Still, it's an interesting premise, don't you think? Wouldn't that be something if there was a lot more to The Mount than just a trendy hangout for the rich and secretive?"

"Yeah. That would be something all right. I'd like to read what you found. I mean, since I've been there and all, it's sort of interesting to me."

Kate shivered and pulled her jacket tighter. "Come on, I'm freezing. Let's have a cuppa and warm up. Liz is off to Russia, so I have the place to myself." Kate's flatmate was an airy-fairy massage therapist who believed she was a Siberian shaman in a previous incarnation.

When they arrived, Kate made tea and booted up her laptop on the coffee table. The two looked on side by side, sitting cross-legged on the floor in front of the couch.

"You've got to be kidding," Rita said, as Kate pulled up a vintage erotica site.

"No, seriously. Look at this." With a few key strokes they found themselves looking at erotic pen and ink drawings from the early Victorian age, drawings detailed enough to make Rita's pussy clench, and to make her blush at sharing such intimacy with her best friend. She scooted closer and squinted at the screen. "Are they all from Greek mythology?"

"Some," Kate replied. "Some are modern, well as modern as Victorian stuff can be. Didn't you say you know Latin?"

"I can stumble through, yes. Why?"

"Well, look at this." A few more key strokes and they were viewing elegant copperplate script beneath a drawing in which Mars, with his armor strewn haphazardly around him, was about to sink a very impressive erection into Venus's exposed vulva. The script was small and smudged, but Rita could still catch the gist, and it made her pulse race in her throat. "It says something like, *Sex is the depth of our animal nature and the highest mount of our divinity. It is our inheritance, our birthright.*" She squinted closer. "Something about joy, sorrow, and magic. *It is the life force we carry within us and pass on. It is a force too powerful to be regulated by rulers or governments, or religious institutions.*" The last words were smudged and cramped, but Rita stumbled on with the help of a magnifying glass. "*We proclaim this in secret and practice it amongst ourselves. But we look to the day when we may share it with the world.*"

Kate was practically on top of her. "I was right then, that is what it says. The highest mount of our divinity. The Mount, get it?"

"I get it." Rita was finding breathing almost as difficult as she had when she wore the chastity belt. "It's probably just a coincidence." Surely it must be a coincidence. How could it possibly be that this motto, or creed, or whatever it was, could have anything to do with The Mount? The two were separated by at least a hundred years. It was only a stab in the dark. It meant nothing, so why did she find it so exciting. "Is there more?"

"Lots more." Kate sipped her tea, then moved to the next page. "I've tried to find out who owns the collection these drawings belong to, but I've had no joy. Anyway, pretty intriguing, the idea of a secret sex cult, don't you think? It's just exactly what I need for my novel. There. You see." She lifted her cup in salute. "I told you, you inspired me."

Back home Rita spent several hours poring over the site Kate had found, but no matter how she tried, she could find no actual connection between Victorian erotica and The Mount. As for the Latin inscription, she double- and triple-checked her translation and racked her brain to recall anything written in Latin in the Presence Chamber of The Mount, or anything similar in English. She'd only briefly glanced at a menu when she was there with Owen, and though she was concentrating on other things at the time, she recalled nothing unusual about it. After several hours of frustrating effort, she turned her attention back to the exquisite drawings.

She'd done a fair bit of browsing Internet porn sites, but none of them had ever made her wet like this site did. She didn't know why. It was full of old drawings, and yet those drawings felt alive, almost hypnotic, pulling her into the action. She became Venus about to be impaled by Mars, she became a young Victorian maid about to have her pussy licked by a mustached gentleman, she became Leda being seduced by the swan.

She studied the drawings with one hand in her panties, completely forgetting the reason for her research, enjoying the silken feel of herself, a thing that had intrigued her since childhood. Her breasts, her pussy, the rounded cheeks of her bottom, always, almost like magic, responded to her touch, offering endless pleasure and comfort.

Whoever had done the drawings understood that desire to stroke, to pleasure, to revel in what it is that drives humans to sex— with someone or alone. She didn't know why, but the drawings seemed familiar.

With the images coming to life in her imagination, she shut down the computer and adjourned to the bedroom, where she stripped in front of the mirror, inspecting herself, admiring the dark swell of her labia, the anxious press of her clit, peeking from under its hood as she stroked. Then she settled onto the bed, legs splayed, hips rocking against the friction of her fingers in her pout. It was just getting really good when the phone rang.

"Hello, darling. Are you all right?"

Everything inside her trembled and warmed at the sound of Edward's voice, and she forgot how angry she had been. "I'm OK. You?"

"I'm missing you terribly. Sorry I haven't called. I didn't dare after what happened."

"I thought…" She clenched the phone and fought back a lump in her throat.

"You thought what, love?"

"I thought that it was all over, that Vivienne had decided not to let me continue with the initiation, and that you'd…"

"That I'd what?"

"That you'd had enough."

His laughter came as a surprise. "First of all, the decision of whether you continue your initiation is not Vivienne's to make. And secondly, how can I possibly have had enough when I'm as helpless to get to you as you are to me." He groaned. "God, Rita, it's almost beyond endurance when I want you so badly."

He wanted her. He really did want her. She was still lost in that thought when he spoke again.

"What are you doing?"

She looked down at her slippery fingers still nestled between her labia. "Masturbating."

"What a coincidence. I've got my cock in my hand right now. Knowing you're on the other end of the phone, I couldn't put it back in my trousers if I had to."

She pressed the button to put him on speaker phone so her hands were free. "With us, it's always fucking in the dark. I never see your face, and now I can't touch you either."

He chuckled. "There are other senses besides touch and sight and smell and taste."

Suddenly she was fighting back tears. "This is all that's left to us."

"For now, darling. And for now, we'll make it be enough."

"Are you a monster, Edward?" She didn't know where the question came from, but once it was out there was no taking it back. "Is what Vivienne said the night I stood before the council true? Is there a monster behind the mask?"

There was such a long silence, she feared she had offended him and he had hung up, but at last he spoke. "Vivienne's right. I am a monster, driven by my urges, by my libido, by my cock, and if I had you here with me now, if it wouldn't jeopardize your initiation, I would devour you in ways you can't imagine."

It was her turn to be silent as the weight of his words pressed in on her, making her heart race with more than a tinge of fear, but making her pussy ache for just such a devouring. "I told you I would understand if you didn't want to go through with the initiation. The monster in me knew, knew from the beginning that we couldn't be together unless you were willing to do this. But I wanted you so badly that I kept…things from you. I'm sorry."

"Maybe I'm a monster too." She buried two fingers to the hilt in her slippery cunt and stroked the growing nub of her clit with her thumb. "I never imagined I would do what I've done and fantasize about doing it again and more. I thought it was just to get to you. But…"

"But that's not all you want, is it?"

She didn't answer, only listened to the acceleration of his breath on the other end of the line. "Rita, it's all right that you liked fucking Alex. What's not to like? I like fucking Alex."

"You've fucked Alex?" His laugh was a breathless grunt. "That turns you on, doesn't it? You'd like to see me fucking Alex, wouldn't you?"

She shoved a third finger into her cunt as the mental image of Edward drilling Alex like a jack hammer translated into raw heat.

He continued. "You'd like to supervise the whole event, hmm? Maybe with Aurora's riding crop just to make sure our fucking is up to your standards. My balls ache at the thought of being bent over your knee, Mistress Rita."

"Mmm, and I would spank your bottom so hard for being such a naughty boy, for teasing me like you have." There was no hiding her breathlessness as her cunt sucked at her fingers, nor did she try.

"Are you humping a dildo?" he asked.

"My hand. Three, no four fingers," she grunted, shoving another one in until her hand cupped her cunt from the inside, her thumb still assaulting her clit at full tilt. "A dildo won't do it when I'm thinking about you. Nothing will properly fill my pussy until I can have your cock. Where are you?"

"A car park near Brixton. No one else is around, just you and me and the phone."

"And Vivienne?"

"She wasn't invited." By the uneven jerking of his voice, she could tell he was tugging his cock pretty hard.

"Uncomfortable, are you?" she asked.

"You have no idea. I've not had my balls properly emptied since you did the honors in the back of the limo."

"In Vivienne's mouth the other night. That must have been nice."

"I was fantasizing about your mouth, on the train," he gasped. "About you sucking my cock, getting it sticky with chocolate while you cupped my balls and played with your pussy. Oh God, Rita, I feel like I'm gonna burst."

"It serves you right. I've made a complete slut out of myself for want of your cock, you bastard. And when this initiation is over, oh what I'm going to do to you." She thrust and pumped until her arm hurt. She tugged on her nipples until they were engorged and aching. A desperate whimper escaped her throat. "Edward, I need you to fuck me, I need you bad, and I intend to have you."

On the other end of the phone, all she heard was a grunt and a strangled gasp as he came, and that was enough to send her. When the world stopped juddering, she lay curled around the phone listening to him breathe. "I'm doing OK then? With the initiation, I mean."

"You're doing fantastically, darling. Vivienne didn't win herself any points by trying to sabotage you like she did. Your next test is being arranged now. You can expect it any time after I hang up."

Her stomach turned to ice. "What is it, Edward? Will Vivienne—"

"Shshsh, darling. It's OK. This test is out of Vivienne's hands. Can you get off work for a few days?"

The question did little to settle her nerves. "Owen owes me big time. I can't see there being a problem."

"Good. I think you'll find this part of your initiation considerably more interesting. I have to go, darling, but I'll check in on you. Leo won't mind if I visit."

"Leo? Wait, Edward. Please tell me—"

"Don't worry, Rita. It'll be OK. I promise. Now I have to go."

The line went dead. Rita lay for a long time with the phone next to her on the pillow, drifting in and out of sleep, dreaming of Edward and what she would do to him when the initiation was over, and she could see his face. Then, as though someone had poured cold water over her, she remembered, Edward probably wouldn't like her very much after the initiation, after her story came out. And her story would come out. She was a journalist. It was her job. People wanted to know.

There was no going back to sleep with that thought niggling at her conscience. She had just got up and rebooted the computer when there was a loud knock at the door.

Chapter Nine

IN SPITE OF WHAT Edward had said, Rita didn't trust Vivienne. Preparing for the worst, she swallowed frayed nerves and opened the door to find two men in blue coveralls. Their breast pockets sported bright green logos with a stylized leopard stretched atop italic script that read *The Zoo*.

One looked down at the clipboard and read off a check list. "Female, Caucasian, five feet ten inches tall, chestnut hair, curvy build, answers to the name of Rita?"

"Yes?"

"You're to come with us. Leo's expecting you." He lifted a hand to halt her words. "Number one rule, pets don't talk. Number two rule, pets don't wear clothes."

As she slipped out of her robe, he took it from her, folded it with military precision, and placed it on the credenza near the door. The other man helped her into an oversized trench coat. She was surprised that it no longer bothered her when people she didn't know saw her naked. These days it was almost routine. The man with the clipboard nodded in satisfaction. "All right then. Come on."

She followed the men to a white van, where a third man waited inside by a pet carrier. He took back the trench coat and her pink flip-flops. "Get in," he said, nodding to the cage. When she balked, he brought a leather riding crop down with a crisp snap against her bare bottom. She yelped. The demanding gape of the pet carrier, way too small for her comfort, seemed to be sucking the oxygen out of the van. Her palms were icy. Her chest and forehead were suddenly bathed in cold sweat.

The second lash across her bottom was more serious. The sting would no doubt leave a welt. "I said get in," the man ordered. "Trust me, you don't want to displease the Zoo Keeper."

With her bottom stinging and her heart doing a drum roll, she did as she was told, trying to breathe deeply, willing herself not to panic. The hair on the back of her neck rose with a prickle as the lock clicked behind her and the man stuck the key in his pocket. That was the last thing she saw before the carrier was covered with a heavy black cloth, and she was left in close darkness.

———————

After what seemed like an eternity, the van stopped. She was briefly jostled about in the carrier, then there was an angry voice from the void. "What have you done to her?" She recognized an Eastern European accent. "I cannot accept this. She was to be treated with the utmost care."

"We did exactly what you said, Leo," came clipboard man's nervous reply. "Just like always."

She scrabbled to stabilize herself as the pet carrier was jostled from the van. In the cool glow of moonlight, she could see Leo, dressed in safari garb, shaking the heavy cloth that had been thrown over her cage at the van men. "She is claustrophobic, you imbeciles! The journey must have been nightmare for the poor thing. Get her out of there. Forget it. I will do. Give me the key."

Clipboard man fumbled the key, and Leo jerked it away from him, opened the cage, and with careful hands, helped her out. Her feet had barely touched terra firma before Leo scooped her into his arms, as though she were a child, and carried her away from the cage. She hadn't realized just what a big man he was, or how strong. She didn't mind. She wasn't sure she could trust her own legs just yet.

He spoke words she couldn't understand, something Slavic, she thought. She could feel their comforting rumble deep in his chest. He had voted against her initiation, she reminded herself. Best not trust any comfort coming from him.

"She didn't tell us, Leo," said clipboard man, who struggled to keep Leo's pace. "I swear she didn't tell us. You know we treat your pets good. Blanket usually calms 'em down, doesn't it?"

"You can read, yes?" Leo snapped. "It says right on the invoice that she is claustrophobic. Edward told me take precautions."

"Begging your pardon, but it says nuffink about 'er being claustrophobic. I wouldn'ta missed that, would I?"

In a room that reminded Rita of the veterinarian's office where her mother used to take her prize Burmese cats, Leo sat her down on the examination table and grabbed away the clipboard. She feared he would shred the papers as he riffled through them. The growl he offered as he shoved the clipboard back at the man was truly befitting his name. "Who gave you this?"

"Lorelei. She said Vivienne had approved."

Suddenly, Rita felt nauseated. Was there no escaping the bitch?

Leo dismissed the clipboard man, and she didn't protest as he eased her onto her side and carefully examined the welt on her bottom, which was still tender enough to make her wince. "My poor darling." He smoothed damp hair away from her face. "I'm so sorry that this happened. Why didn't you tell those men that you were claustrophobic?"

"Pets don't talk." Her voice felt scratchy against the back of her throat.

"Pets don't talk? What the…" His eyes widened, his face broke into a broad smile, and he kissed her forehead with such enthusiasm that she thought he might leave a bruise. "Of course. Pets don't talk, and you are already obedient pet. Edward is right, you are real treasure." Then the smile slipped. "But surely you must understand that

I would never do anything to harm any of my pets. I am contributor to RSPCA. I am volunteer in the shelters. I think anyone who would harm helpless animal should have their," he lapsed back into Slavic, and though she couldn't understand him, she was certain what he said was not nice. Then the smile returned as quickly as it left. "You will see." He kissed her forehead again, this time more gently. "You will love being pet, and you won't want to leave when time comes."

He snapped his fingers, and a woman dressed in a zoo uniform brought water—not in a cup, but in a silver bowl. Leo carefully helped her to sit, but when she reached for the bowl, he pushed her hands aside. "Pets use their hands for other things, darling. Feeding you, grooming you, and giving you to drink, those are responsibilities of your master." The woman held the bowl to her lips. She was aware of Leo gently stroking her back while she drank.

"There. Is better now, my little dovitsa?" Again he snapped his fingers and a man dressed in scrubs came into the room, looking more like a porn star than a veterinarian. "Dr. Marco will examine you now. Make sure you are OK to join other pets." He lifted her chin. "Some pets must stay in quarantine for little while, but I think claustrophobia is not contagious." He nodded to the vet, who moved forward.

"Oh she's lovely, Leo. What's her name?" The vet took her face in his hands and carefully examined the lymph glands along a sensitive path down her neck.

"Her name is Rita." Leo's hand moved possessively to stroke her belly, and suddenly she forgot about the ordeal of getting there. "She has had quite a trauma, Doctor. I need to know she is OK, and that she will be comfortable to get good night's sleep. You know how sensitive pets can be in new place."

The doctor placed a stethoscope, warmed to body temperature, between her breasts, listened, then gave a little nod. His breath was warm across her stippling areolae as he gently probed and palpated and cupped until she found it difficult not to move against his touch.

At her side, Leo reassuringly stroked and caressed first her hips, then her thighs, then the soft nape of her neck. In her peripheral vision she could see that the front of his safari trousers was well tented.

"She's exquisite, Leo, and in excellent condition," the doctor said as his hands moved over her belly, pressing and palpating. "You're lucky to have found such a specimen."

"Sadly, she is not mine. I am only borrowing her, but I shall enjoy her very much while I have her."

"Indeed." The doctor guided her on to her hands and knees and positioned her so that her bottom was only inches from his face. He traced the welt with a feather touch, tsk-tsking as he did so. "The brutes." Leo stroked her flank as though he were calming a prize mare. Then the doctor eased her legs apart and shifted her hips until her cunt was fully exposed. "There we go, that's a good girl," the doctor half whispered. "Hmm." He ran a finger down her perineum from just below her anus to separate her labia where the lips folded protectively around her pussy hole, an act that caused her to catch her breath in a soft moan. "She's very wet." He slipped a finger up into her, and she grasped down on it involuntarily. There was no hiding it. Phone sex with Edward and what was happening to her now had left her horny as hell and wet enough to mop the examination room floor.

The doctor slid another finger into her and pressed down low on her belly with the other hand. She whimpered, shifted her hips, and pressed back.

"She needs to be serviced, Leo," the doctor said. "You can't kennel her like this. The poor thing will never be able to sleep without some relief." The probing fingers had gone from examining to thrusting, and Leo was practically humping the side of the table, one hand migrating to stroke Rita's bottom.

Leo replied with a grunt. "All the males are sleeping and she hasn't been properly introduced. It would be big disruption."

"Shall I take care of her then?" When the doctor brought his thumb to circle her clit, Rita practically went through the roof.

"Leave her. If you need pleasure, you take with Fila or Rajka. They will take care of your cock, not my pet. It is the rules."

The doctor sighed and withdrew his fingers, and Rita groaned her frustration, but Leo pushed her hand away as it slid toward her cunt. "Leo knows his Ritichka needs to come, but pets don't touch their pussies. Trust me, I have something much nicer planned for little pussy." He produced a blue leather collar studded with rhinestones and clasped it around her neck. Then he attached a lead. "Come, my darling."

The doctor looked disappointed as Leo helped her from the examination table. "What will you do?"

"She will sleep with Blossom tonight. Blossom will take care of her until she can be properly serviced. Now do something about that before you burst." He nodded to the bulge in the doctor's trousers.

Leo led Rita into a moonlit courtyard, around a pool surrounded by a lush garden and up the path to the main house. "Wipe your feet, darling." He nodded to the braided rug just inside the door. "Millicent is very upset when there are paw prints all over the foyer."

He led her down a long hallway past rooms which were visibly opulent even in the muted tones of night. At last he opened double doors into a study, lit by the soft glow from a fireplace. Bookshelves with glass doors reached from floor to high ceiling, no doubt protecting rare volumes and leather bindings. A ladder of aging wood and wrought iron rested on rollers against one section of shelves. The furniture was comfortably worn cordovan leather, and the oriental carpets were, no doubt, expensive and hand-made. The room smelled of wood and leather and aging volumes and Rita felt instantly at home.

Leo slipped out of his shoes and poured himself a glass of something strong and amber from a crystal decanter on an antique table near the door. Then he sat down in a large wing-backed chair in front of the fireplace. He guided her to kneel next to him and rest her head on his thigh, his bulge scant centimeters from her cheek. As he stroked her nape and smoothed her hair, she reached for his fly, but he pushed her hands away with a light slap.

"That is no-no, Rita. Pets may certainly sniff, and nuzzle, but at the Zoo pets don't have sex with their minders. I brought you here so that Blossom could help you feel better."

For the first time, Rita noticed the dark form of a woman lying curled on the carpet in front of the fireplace.

Leo unclipped the leash from Rita's collar and stroked her tummy. "Go on now. Go introduce yourself." He shooed her toward the woman on the carpet whose dark eyes seemed enormous in the dancing firelight. She uncurled herself and stretched into a sitting position. It was hard to tell the exact shade of her skin, but even in the muted light of the fire it was dark. Her body was long and slender. Her small, high breasts were topped with enormous melt-in-your-mouth nipples.

"Blossom is the only one of my pets that stays in house all the time. Blossom, darling, this is Rita. She has had very rough journey to be here with us, and her pussy is very uncomfortable. Make her feel at home." Again he made a shooing motion, and Rita moved to join Blossom on the carpet.

She had barely dropped to her knees before the other pet buried her face, nose first, in Rita's bottom, sniffing and licking, making Rita's cunt gape and surge. Then, she presented her lovely arse to Rita, dark hole gripping and relaxing as Rita reciprocated, at first tentatively, awkwardly, until she got the hang of it, then more enthusiastically with her growing arousal. Once she and Rita were properly acquainted, Blossom slid her tongue in slow, even laps over Rita's body, beginning behind her right ear and working her way down the nape of her neck on to her breasts. She pressed with the pad of her tongue, then drew her lips closed between each lick in a nip of a kiss that made Rita's skin goose-flesh like a million tiny clits engorged with sensation. Each slide of the tongue and purse of the lips built on the last until Rita writhed helplessly beneath each caress, whimpering at the pleasure of it. Blossom licked her way over Rita's belly and on to her hip, easing her down onto the carpet, nudging her legs apart until Rita could feel the dark pet's warm breath against her pussy. Then she laid her head on Rita's thigh and snaked her incredible tongue over Rita's cunt, making her catch her breath in tight little grunts and bear down against the insinuations of mouth and lips and the occasional nip of teeth against her heavy clit.

Leo chuckled softly. "Our Rita does have a lovely pussy, doesn't she, Blossom? Make her come, darling. Make her feel better."

Rita pushed and scooted on the carpet until she could return the favor, laying her head on Blossom's thigh and burying her face in the musky femaleness of the pet, whose clit mirrored her nipples in sheer swollen deliciousness.

"Oh yes, that's Leo's good girls, that's my horny little darlings," Leo breathed.

Above their own grunts and moans, Rita heard the sound of a zipper and looked up to see Leo fondling his balls free from his trousers and caressing a heavy erection. The cordovan leather squeaked in protest as his stroking grew more urgent. The wet sounds of sex mingled with the smell of animal heat, and Rita found herself wanting to growl and bite and display her swollen cunt for Leo, like a red flag before a bull. She wished he'd join them. His cock looked positively equine. She could imagine the nice tight fit, with him taking turns in her pussy, then in Blossom's. Just then Blossom tongued her clit and nipped her with a throaty growl that sent her over the edge grunting and trembling. Blossom wasn't far behind. Leo watched them come, his cock thrusting in his tight fist like a wild thing he struggled to tame, until at last his body stiffened and bowed back against the chair, and he ejaculated in heavy spurts onto the polished wood floor.

They must have dozed. Leo woke them some time later. The fire had burned low. He was tucked back into his khakis, and the floor was clean. "Come on, girls. It's bedtime."

Blossom followed Leo and Rita followed Blossom up to the big master bedroom. The bed was nearly as big as Edward's. It was covered in rich Asian prints. Both pets sat on the floor near a large wardrobe and watched. Leo undressed slowly, placing all his clothing neatly over a straight-back chair, lingering to examine the hard planes of his large, well-muscled body in front of a full-length mirror, cupping the weight of his balls and penis, looking over his shoulder at the mounds of his buttocks. Rita was sure he was doing it for their benefit, and she was happy to watch. He had a wonderful body, one she would have gladly pleasured. She wondered at his refusal to fuck his pets.

At last he pulled back the duvet and sat for a minute on the edge of the bed, penis lying heavy, but relaxed against his thigh, then he cupped each pet's cheek, gave their breasts a stroke, and patted the mattress. "Come, girls. To bed with you."

He slid down between the sheets. Blossom crawled onto the foot of the bed, on top of the duvet, and curled up with a satisfied sigh. Rita followed suit. There, blanketed in moonlight, Blossom's fingers found their way to Rita's pussy, relieving the tension that had returned as she had watched Leo undress. Then both pets curled around each other and slept.

Chapter Ten

IN THE MORNING THE two pets followed Leo to a heavily laden breakfast table and sat on the floor near his chair. No kibbles for these pets. From his plate, he hand-fed them *prosciutto*, strawberries and melon, and fresh *pain au chocolat*, caressing them and praising them as he did so. The hand-feeding Rita liked, but learning to lap water from the silver bowl with her tongue was a challenge. When Leo saw her struggles, he lifted the bowl to her lips with a smile. "Never mind, darling, you will get the hang of it. In the meantime we don't want you dehydrated since you have busy day ahead of you."

Blossom looked as dark and exotic in the morning sunshine as she had in the firelight. She had closely cropped dark curls that showcased the strong bone structure of a very African face. She was more interested in Rita than she was in her breakfast, licking and sniffing until Rita found it hard to concentrate on the lovely food.

Not that she was complaining. She found it difficult to keep her mouth off Blossom's luscious nipples. Smeared with chocolate from the *pain au chocolat*, they reminded her of the delicious truffles Edward had fed her on the Eurostar.

At last, Leo pulled them apart, chuckling. "Stop it, you two. You're getting food all over. Such a mess you are making. This will not make Millicent happy." When breakfast was over, Leo delivered Rita, via a more private route, to the pet groomer back at the annex. He explained that the other pets would be up and about by now and one sight of her would set the more high-strung males off. "There will be no keeping their hands off their penises if they see you. It will be practically orgy. Of course I don't mind orgies. My pets need lots of sex. Is good for them, but all in good time, my dear Ritichka, all in good time."

Blossom had been allowed to accompany them, and, at the sight of the groomer—another man who looked as if he could be in porn films, she ran to meet him, dropped to her knees and buried her face in his crotch, sniffing and nuzzling wildly. He didn't try to stop her. Instead he stroked her neck and the top of her head, not bothered that he was bulging by the time Rita and Leo approached him more sedately.

"Pets live through their noses," Leo explained. "Most of the mammals do. There is reason why dogs and cats like to sniff crotches and bottoms. Our identity is all tied up in our scent. No two of us smell the same. Only we humans have forgotten how to use gift of smell. But," he nodded at Blossom, "it all comes back quickly when we are given opportunity. Most pets find the world is more interesting place when they experience through their noses."

On the Eurostar, hadn't Edward talked about all the wonderful senses humans take for granted? The thought made her ache slightly. Why did everything make her think of Edward? It would be so much easier if she didn't. She forced her attention back to Leo. "Go on," he was saying. "Give it a try." He gave her bottom a little smack and nodded toward the groomer, who was smiling at her expectantly.

This was just too strange, Rita thought, but she shrugged and dropped to her knees in front of the groomer, who chuckled softly and stroked her neck. "Hello there. Aren't you a beautiful thing?"

Mostly she could smell Blossom against the man's crotch. Of course, Blossom smelled like her, after spending so much time with her face between Rita's legs, but as the groomer's cock surged beneath khaki shorts, she caught the scent of a man who enjoyed his work. "Mmm," the groomer sniffed. "Don't you two smell like pussy this morning?"

Rita wondered if she'd ever get past blushing over the strange things that kept happening to her since her initiation began. Blossom was dismissed to play with the other pets until it was time for her own bath. Then the groomer took Rita's collar off and guided her into a tub full of warm bubbles. "That's a girl," he crooned. "Let's get you all nice and clean." He knelt next to the tub. "Oh, such nice titties. All the males will want to play with those, and the females too, I'll bet." As he ran the sponge over her, he inspected her with a running commentary. "Mmm, nice tight tummy muscles, pert little arse, and legs, goodness those legs go on forever. Aren't you a beauty?" He turned his attention to Leo, who watched attentively. "Who'll service her?" He began to soap her breasts, paying special attention to her rising nipples. "Dr. Marko said she needs it pretty badly."

"Is true. She needs male. Perhaps Brutus or Aralias could satisfy her. Would be lovely to see either of them mount her. Perhaps both. Aralias's dark body would be stunning contrast to Rita's pale skin. On the other hand, Brutus has nice buttocks, lovely to watch when he is thrusting."

The groomer nodded his agreement. "Whichever you choose, it'll be excellent, I'm sure." He turned his attention back to Rita. "Bend over, my lovely. Let's get your pretty little cunny cleaned and ready for receiving guests."

She obeyed, feeling embarrassed and insulted and incredibly horny. More so as the groomer opened her labia and dribbled warm water over her vulva. She couldn't hold back a little sigh. "Oh Leo," the groomer gasped. "This is a luscious pussy and so ready she might just come on my fingers."

"Just bathe her, Larry. Is not your job to make her come. You know the rules."

Fuck the rules, Rita thought. She didn't care who serviced her, but she wished to hell somebody would. The more they talked about her as if she were a bitch in heat, the hotter she got, until she buried her wet face against the groomer's crotch and began to lick and nip at his penis through his shorts.

Maneuvering himself until his body obscured Leo's view of what was going on, the groomer curled his hands in Rita's wet hair and held her to him, his breath coming fast and furious against her back.

Thwack! came Leo's hand across Rita's wet bottom. The surprise of it as much as the sting caused her to yelp and pull back. "Bad Rita! I told you last night, minders are off limits. Bad girl! We don't suck our minder's cock." He glared at the groomer. "You know better than to let her do this. If the Zoo will function smoothly, there must be rules, you know this. And those rules apply to you too, Larry. Now get her bathed."

If anything, the reprimand and the sharp smack on the bottom made Rita even more horny. She wasn't exactly convinced that being a naughty pet was a bad thing.

By the time the groomer had her bathed and shampooed and was caressing her dry with a thick terry towel, her whole body thrummed with arousal. It wouldn't have taken much squeezing of her girlie muscles to make her come, but the situation in which she found herself was so deliciously hot that every second of holding back, every second of waiting for Brutus or Aralias, or whoever would service her hot bitch pussy, was exquisite torture.

Leo carefully inspected her, then placed the rhinestone collar back around her neck. As he attached the lead, she felt every bit the animal she was pretending to be, rubbing her arse against his thigh and making soft little purring sounds at the back of her throat.

Leo sighed his approval. "Come on my beauty. Now we will introduce you to the other pets. Brutus will make your uncomfortable little pussy feel so much better."

As they headed for the courtyard, one of the safari women came to Leo. Rita couldn't hear what she whispered in his ear, but he nodded and handed her leash to the woman. "Wait here with Fila,

darling." He stroked her neck. "Leo may have a surprise for you."
Then he disappeared.

While they waited, Fila found a soft bristled brush, sat down
on a metal folding chair and guided Rita to sit on the floor between
her legs. Then she brushed Rita's hair, singing to her softly in what
sounded like Polish.

Rita rested her forehead on the woman's thigh, exposed below
khaki shorts. Leo was right about the sense of smell. She could just
make out the salt marsh scent of the woman's pussy beneath the
perfume of lavender soap. She could feel the heat radiating from
between Fila's legs as she brushed and caressed Rita's hair. Almost
without thinking, Rita slipped her fingers between her own legs and
wriggled them into the warm slippery folds of her pussy.

"Bad girl! You mustn't do that." Fila smacked the side of Rita's
bare breast with the back of the hairbrush just enough to almost
sting. Definitely enough to stimulate. She leaned in close to Rita's
ear, pushed the hair away and whispered. "Hold on just a little longer
and Brutus will take very good care of your pussy."

When Leo returned, he took up her leash. But instead of leading
her into the courtyard, where the other pets were, he led her back
toward the private entrance. Before they exited, he turned to Fila. "If
Brutus cannot wait to come, then put him with Mimi. But encourage him that it will be better if he can wait."

He led her swiftly back into the house, through a maze of hall-
ways and corridors offering none of the running commentary she
had grown used to. At last he led her into small secluded garden
and tugged her leash to pull her close to him. "This will be our
little secret," he whispered. He led her along a path behind a gur-
gling fountain full of frolicking marble nymphs to where the foli-
age opened up to reveal a secluded stone bench. On the bench sat
Edward, resplendent in his golden mask.

"Rita!" He gasped, coming up from the bench, but stifling

his urge to run to her. "Leo told me what happened. Darling, I'm so sorry."

A startled cry escaped before she could stop it. She nearly called his name, but quickly slapped her hand over her mouth as her pulse went into overdrive.

He took a step forward, as though he didn't trust his own legs. "Are you all right?" She stood next to Leo, frozen like the nymphs in the fountain.

"She is fine, Edward. I promise you. I have taken good care of her." Leo stroked her hair. "Go to Edward, darling Ritichka. Greet him like a proper pet. Go on. It's OK." His gaze held Edward's. "No one need know."

He turned his attention back to Rita. "Go on, darling, greet the nice man."

She recalled what Blossom had done with the groomer, and bounded toward Edward, dropping to her knees in front of him and burying her face against his crotch. He let out a surprised gasp and tumbled backward onto the bench.

He was hard, so deliciously hard, and the scent of him was like the woods, like a summer storm. God, he smelled like everything she wanted, and he was trying to push her away.

"Rita stop, we can't do this. I can't control myself. You have to—"

"Bad Rita! Bad girl." Leo's hand came down with a stinging smack against her bare bottom, and she howled her frustration as he yanked the leash and sat down next to the panting Edward.

"Edward. I am so sorry. She is pet, and not well trained yet. She can be unruly and overenthusiastic. And, like most pets, she is always so horny."

When Leo began to undo Edward's fly, Rita wasn't sure who was more in shock, her or Edward.

Edward shoved his hands away. "Leo, you know I'd happily let you do me, but not now." His voice cracked. "Not like this."

"Is not my intention to do you." He held Edward's gaze. "Now be still, and allow me to discipline my pet."

"You voted against her. What are you doing? Is this a trick?"

"Is no trick." Leo slapped Edward's hands as though Edward were the naughty pet, and continued undoing his fly. "I have no agenda, Edward. You know is true. My reasons for voting against this initiation, they had nothing to do with anyone else's wishes. But for me, admitting that I am wrong is not problem."

"Why the sudden change of heart?" Edward was still trying to push Leo away. And Rita was surprised to find herself whimpering much like the needy animal she was pretending to be.

"Pets don't talk, Edward. You know this rule, yes? I have seen what she suffered to keep the rules. She is worthy." Both of their hands were now suspended above Edward's crotch. "I know her rules too." He nodded to Rita. "I helped draft them. You may not have intercourse with the initiate. But those rules say nothing about an unruly pet who finds smell and flavor of your cock interesting."

Edward stopped fighting and let Leo tug his trousers down until his buttocks were bare against the bench and his thick penis stood out from his body like a sleek, pussy-sized battering ram.

"There now, is better." Leo inspected his work with satisfaction. "Now come here, darling, get Edward's scent, that's a girl. Leo knows that's what you want, oh that's my girl."

Trembling all over exactly as she had seen excited dogs do, Rita lowered her head and took the full length of Edward's cock into her mouth. She felt his body tense, felt his groan rumble even down through his cock. In her peripheral vision, she caught just a glimpse of him, head thrown back, mouth open, his fingers curled in her hair as he held her to him. She could feel Leo's hand stroking her back, and his heavy breathing made her suspect his other hand might be occupied.

"Oh God, Rita, that's so good, so good," Edward grunted

between barely parted lips, voice tight and breathless. "But it's not fair," he gasped. "It's not right. She deserves comfort too, Leo. Please, take care of her for me."

"You know the rules, Edward. I don't fuck my pets." Leo's voice came in tight little puffs against the back of her neck, and she could feel the heat radiating off his body, so close to her she could almost sense the shape of him beneath the khakis.

"Please, Leo," Edward pleaded, barely able to breathe. "Please, if you won't do it for me, do it for her. You owe her."

She heard Leo curse softly, and for a second, he pulled away from her. Then with a start, she felt his thick fingers slide between her parted labia to caress her clit.

"Is all right, darling. Lift your bottom for Leo, that's a good girl." She did as she was told without losing her rhythm against Edward's thrusting. At first there was a gentle, but insistent probing just inside her pussy lips, then she heard Leo grunt and her pussy yielded grudgingly, almost painfully, to his penetration, the very act of which made her throw back her head and howl as the orgasm she'd been holding off exploded through her.

As she lowered her mouth back onto Edward's cock, she wasn't sure one orgasm completely stopped before the next one blasted its way through her. She slipped both hands beneath Edward's arse and pulled him to her in a desperate effort to get as much of him in her mouth as she could. Behind her, Leo grunted and shoved, muttering in Slavic between gasps. One hand pinched and stroked the swell of her clit while the other rested on her thrusting bottom.

Edward's tight fist in her hair was nearly painful. "I can't hold back," he gasped. "I have to come, oh God, Rita, I want to make it last, but I can't wait." It seemed like he came for ages, and she swallowed hungrily, taking into herself his essence, even better without chocolate truffles. Her pussy had just erupted in another wave of orgasm when she heard Leo grunt. He pulled out so quickly that she nearly fell backward. She watched in amazement as he shot his load onto the grass, nearly doubled over himself.

Then Edward pulled her to him, kissing her long and deep. His embrace was bone-wrenching and demanding and enough to make her come again in great gasping sobs. When the tremors had stopped, and she clung to him spent, he whispered against her mouth. "I have to go, my darling." He turned his attention to Leo, who was still kneeling on the grass looking stunned. "I can't thank you enough for this."

Leo nodded and forced a smile. "Your feelings for each other is why I voted against initiation. This, you know will make things more difficult, cause pain."

"But you've changed your mind?" Edward said. Leo nodded, holding his gaze.

"Is motives I question. Her worthiness, I do not." Edward helped Rita to her feet. "I'm so proud of you, darling. Leo will take good care of you, and I'll see you soon." He kissed her, then disappeared into the thicket behind the bench, still tucking and zipping as he went. She looked after him until her eyes could no longer focus, then she turned to find Leo dressed and standing next to her. He took up her leash, which was still attached to her collar, and led her back into the house and up to his room without speaking. There, he led her into the bathroom, where he stripped and guided her into the shower.

As the warm water coursed over them, she waited for him to bathe her, but he didn't. As last, she knelt on the tiles and rested her head against his thigh. He released a long sigh and ran a hand down to caress her neck. "In all these years I have fed my pets, I have groomed my pets, I have enjoyed watching my pets' pleasure, but I've never once fucked one of my pets. Is the cardinal rule, and I have made sure that rule is kept. Until now."

Not knowing what else to do, she stood and slipped her arms

around him. For a long moment, he didn't respond, then he embraced her, pulling her close, kissing the nape of her neck. "Being inside you was exquisite. Is the best thing I have felt in a long time." He sighed. "But no one must ever know, and it must never happen again." He pulled away and looked into her eyes. "You understand this, my love?" She nodded, suddenly aware that the moisture on her face wasn't from the shower.

Chapter Eleven

IT WAS EVENING BEFORE Leo brought Brutus to Rita. The night promised to be warm and the moon was full. Leo had led her to another secluded garden and settled her on a thick rug spread on the grass. Next to it was a chaise longue and a small wooden table complete with crystal decanter and a glass. There she had waited for an undeterminable amount of time. She was amazed at how difficult it had already become to keep track of time, and at how quickly she was learning to relax into herself and simply be. Perhaps it was just her response to the environment Leo had created for his pets.

At last Leo returned with a tall, broad-shouldered male. His skin was lightly tanned and his hair was shaved close to his head, laying bare strong angular features and full expressive lips that Rita wanted pressed against her pussy. Beyond that the only thing that concerned her was his penis, which was already substantial at half-mast and rising. The moment he saw her, he strained at the leash and grunted. She took that to mean there was mutual interest.

"Rita, darling, this is Brutus. I've brought him to take care of you."

She lifted her hips and rearranged herself on the rug, making sure he got a good view of her pussy.

Leo didn't immediately unleash Brutus, who struggled and growled, every muscle tensed to get near her. Instead he let the pet get just close enough for a good sniff. Rita raised her bottom, feeling his humid breath tickle against her pout, feeling just the tip of his tongue in his strangled efforts to taste her, test her for readiness.

"Don't be too pushy, Brutus. Is the poor girl's first day, be easy with her," Leo cajoled. Rita didn't necessarily want easy, but she loved the fact that Brutus had to work to get to her. She moved just close enough for him to get a good deep taste of her, then she yelped and pulled back, torturing herself as well as him. He growled and lunged toward her, his penis now fully erect and bobbing against his belly where he knelt on hands and knees. She gave him another taste and he was practically humping air when she pulled away. While Leo struggled to hold the big male, she moved behind him to admire the buttocks Leo had praised, to sniff and taste, to flick her tongue over the exposed underside of his balls, sending him into a frenzy. Oh, she liked being in control.

Leo must have intuited exactly that because he yanked Brutus back onto his haunches, then flat onto his arse, securing the pet by placing a thick arm around his broad shoulders and stroking him as though he were calming a high-strung horse, exposing him for Rita's appraisal. "Is all right, Brutus. Relax," Leo coaxed. "You'll be mounting her soon enough."

At her leisure, she sniffed and nuzzled and took in the earthy pungent scent of maleness ready for the rut, a scent that made her mouth water, and her pussy clench. Brutus's penis surged and bobbed against her cheek and his hips ground against the grass until she feared he'd have grass stains on his much-praised buttocks.

"Shshsh," Leo crooned next to the big pet's ear. "Let her get used to you. Don't frighten her. You can wait just a little longer."

Rita wasn't sure she could wait, but oh it was nice to try. She ran her tongue up the shaft of his erection, tasting the salty pre-cum on the silky tip. Brutus's whole body tensed, every muscle quivered, and his cock surged against her mouth. She rose on her haunches to straddle him, but when he tried to thrust into her, she grabbed his cock with her hand and rubbed the substantial length of it between her sopping lips like a sausage on hot bread. His growl was not unlike a wild animal, she thought, as she leaned in and bit him hard just above the right nipple. He yelped, his penis strained in her hand, and Leo chuckled.

"Rita, dear, you shouldn't tease the poor thing so. He has been waiting all day for you. His balls must be nearly bursting by now. Come on, darling. You need it too."

Of course he was right. She moved back just out of reach, not quite sure what would happen next. Her heart raced with anticipation and even a little bit of fear. On her hands and knees, she turned her bottom to Brutus, making sure her legs were open enough for him to see how ready she was, how badly she wanted him, making sure he got the invitation.

He did.

Leo unhooked the leash from Brutus's collar, and she was instantly engulfed in warm, hard maleness. In her peripheral vision, she saw Leo settle into the chaise longue and undo his trousers. Then her attention was fully on the other pet.

She was surprised that Brutus didn't instantly enter her. Instead he folded himself over her, penis pressing against the crevice between her buttocks, hands moving first to cup her breasts, then to explore her pussy, lips and tongue on her nape and her ear, nipping her shoulders, then the back of her neck as she had seen male cats do when they mounted ready females. Finally he slipped inside her with a sigh, quivering all over with amazing control.

She could only imagine how badly he needed to ejaculate, and the thought was such a turn-on that she decided neither of them needed to wait longer. She thrust back hard and bore down on his penis. He got the blessed message and jack hammered as though she were concrete and he planned to break her. It didn't take long. As her pussy shuddered and she screamed her release, he grabbed her hips and thrust as though he would penetrate clear through her, and she thought he would never stop coming. The next three times were much more leisurely, and Leo stayed for all of them.

———

Life at the Zoo was pretty damn good for a pet once you got the hang of it. Rita never realized just how freeing it was not to have to speak, nor had she realized how much could be communicated without a word. In her fantasies, she imagined sharing all she had learned with Edward, but she knew reality wouldn't be so sweet once she wrote her exposé. She tried not to think about the story, but instead she tried to concentrate on the experience of initiation. Most of the time that was enough to keep her mind off what the consequences of the exposé would surely be.

But when she couldn't manage to keep her thoughts from straying to what seemed every day more like a betrayal of trust, she did her best to convince herself that all this was a game to Leo, to Alex, to Edward, and she was really nothing more than a pawn to them. Entertainment for the bored rich. When all the usual expensive toys no longer worked, they'd always find some way of entertaining themselves, and at the moment, she was it.

Vivienne wasn't even the cruelest among them, she told herself. Edward was much crueler. It was Edward who stood by and let the bitch torture her, sabotage her, repeatedly humiliate her. And yet still he deferred to her. Maybe they really were married just like Kate suspected. Why else would he let Vivienne come between them?

One of the best things about life at Leo's zoo, though, was that there were plenty of distractions, and she had very little time to think about the future. She lay on the grass near the fountain in a literal pile of pets, who were all relaxing in the afternoon sun. Aralias had just fucked her twice, effectively keeping the other males away from her. He lay with his head between her breasts and his arms around her possessively. It had been a constant competition between Brutus and Aralias for her attention, though occasionally one of the other, less alpha, males managed to at least feel her up. It wasn't her choice.

As long as she was Leo's pet, Leo chose who mounted her, and he usually chose Brutus or Aralias. She had to admit they both knew their way around female anatomy, and Brutus's attentions had gone a long way toward making her feel better after Edward's visit.

As for the females, they were all generous with their affection, knowing, as most women did, that having a cock in one's pussy isn't the only path to orgasm. In fact, she had two fingers buried to the hilt in Mimi's tight cunny at the moment, and, the way the little blond was squirming, Rita knew she was getting close.

The other thing most women know is that they can keep coming long after the men have shot their wads, so while Aralias's cock was recovering from the last fuck, Blossom, who loved the taste of sex, was licking and slurping at Rita's pussy. Leo sat in his usual chaise longue looking out over his pets with his cock in his hand.

True to his word, after Edward's visit, Leo had not offered Rita any more affection than he offered the other pets, though her place in the house with Blossom had remained secure. Millicent, the maid, complained about the extra work of having two pets in the house. But that same afternoon Rita and Blossom caught Leo in the big wing-backed chair straining under Millicent's squirming bottom with his face buried in the woman's ample cleavage. After that, Millicent didn't complain about pets in the house.

Rita was just coming again when Rajka came to Leo and whispered something in his ear. With more than a little effort, he tucked his cock back into his khakis and called for Rita. She disentangled herself from her fellow pets, who responded with a few grunts and groans of protest.

The glow of arousal was already gone from Leo's face when Rita approached him, and he sucked his bottom lip thoughtfully. "Rita, darling, go with Rajka up to my suite, and I will join you in a little while."

In Leo's suite, Rajka undressed herself, led Rita into the shower and began to bathe her. Rita bathed with the other pets now, a veritable pool party, morning and night, with several groomers on hand to help with the hard-to-reach places and to towel and massage the pets before bedtime. There had been no bathing in Leo's private suite since Edward's visit.

By the time Rajka had toweled her dry, Leo arrived. On a hanger in one hand he held a strapless blue sundress, in the other hand he carried a pair of sandals with kitten heels.

He forced a smile. "You have completed this part of initiation, darling, brilliantly, I might add. Sadly, Vivienne has decided that you have been my pet long enough."

"She makes decisions for everyone, does she?" The words came out after a week of silence and with far more venom than she could have imagined.

"She is head of High Council." Leo dismissed Rajka, then knelt to help Rita into a black lace thong, lingering to caress her curves in ways he would have never done when she was his pet. "I will miss you, my love."

When he stood to help her into the dress, she lifted her lips to his and lingered there exploring his mouth. He made no attempt to push her away. At last she spoke. "Being your pet has been an experience I'll treasure, Leo. But I'm not your pet any longer." She ran her hand down to caress the growing bulge in his khakis. "Remember that the next time you want to do more than just watch."

"I shall, my love," he breathed. "I promise I shall." Millicent knocked at the door and stuck her head in. "The limo's here." She caught Leo's gaze. "Mistress Vivienne has come for her."

Chapter Twelve

"RITA, DARLING. I HARDLY recognized you without your hoodie." Vivienne motioned Rita into the limo to sit across from her, then the driver pulled away.

The head of the High Council was as exquisite in a miniskirt and a lilac bustier as she was in the dressed-to-kill gowns she wore at The Mount. Rita hated to admit it, but in spite of all the bitch had done to her, the sight of the woman was still exciting, even arousing.

Vivienne raised a perfectly arched eyebrow. "Come on, girl. You're not one of Leo's little pets any more. You can speak. After all, we're practically family, aren't we?"

"I sort of enjoyed the quiet," Rita said, mentally high-fiving herself for being so glib.

"Well, I certainly wouldn't miss your horrible midwestern accent."

"I'm from Seattle," Rita said.

Vivienne waved her hand as though swatting away an annoying insect. "Never mind. I figured the ride back to London would give us some girl time. I'm sure you must have all kinds of questions about Edward, and no one knows Edward better than I do."

When Rita made no response, Vivienne offered a little pout. "Surely Edward hasn't already told you everything. Of course not." She raised a dumb blond finger to her mouth and pursed her lips. "If he had, you wouldn't still be here." She shrugged playfully. "Never mind, it'll be so much fun when all is revealed."

Before Rita could respond, Vivien leaned forward and stroked the fabric of the sundress. "Lovely outfit. Leo always did have exquisite taste. I let him dress me occasionally. Only when I'm not in a hurry, though. Leo likes to take his time." She ran a hand down her breasts to linger on the ribbon that laced the bustier. "Lorelei dressed me today. She knows how to showcase my best assets." She chuckled softly. "I can tell you agree.

"Oh don't look so surprised. I could feel you gawping at me from the moment you got in the limo." She gave the ribbon a tug and it loosened. Then she slowly began to unlace. "You want to see what's underneath, don't you? You want to see my tits, I know you do." She gave her breasts a knead. "Edward likes to pinch my nipples. Nobody can make them as tight and hard as Edward can. He makes it hurt. He knows I like it. Then he bites them. He has me bouncing all over the bed when he does that. Well, whenever we're actually in a bed."

Vivienne pulled the bustier open as she spoke, all the while her eyes were locked on Rita. "Does it bother you when I talk about what Edward does to me? Do you want me to stop?" She let out her breath slowly and shifted until her breasts were free. "I didn't think so. You want to know what he does to me. You want to know because it makes you feel like you know him a little better." She caressed her nipples between thumbs and forefingers, then slid her right hand down between her thighs.

Rita felt as though her chest would explode with some hybrid of anger and hurt. She couldn't listen. She daren't. It was too much to know, too personal. And yet she held her breath, desperate for Vivienne to continue.

"The way he touches me down there, it's like just by fingering my cunt, he can somehow get to rest of me. All of me." Vivienne moaned and kicked off her strappy stilettos. With the agility of a gymnast, she slid her foot up over Rita's belly, wriggling down in the seat until Rita caught a glimpse of the pink folds of her cunt, clean-shaven, open like a hungry mouth peeking from under the miniskirt. "He nibbles my clit like he does my nipples, until it hurts, and just when I'm about to cry, I come. I come so hard. Then he goes down on me, deep down, so deep that I feel like he's worked his way completely inside of me. You know, clear up here." She laid a hand between her breasts. "Then when he comes up his face is wet from me, like he's been in the ocean. And I taste me on him when he kisses me just before he pushes into me."

She slid her foot up on to the bodice of Rita's sundress, pausing to knead each of her breasts in turn with long, slender toes. Then she curled them over the top of the bodice and pulled it away from Rita's breasts, making a little purr of a giggle at the back of her throat as Rita caught her breath. "Shall I tell you more?" Then she gripped Rita's left nipple between her toes and pinched until Rita yelped. But before she could separate the pain from the pleasure, Vivienne withdrew and pushed Rita's knees apart with her foot. She maneuvered cherry-lacquered toes between Rita's thighs, and in spite of herself, Rita couldn't hold back a little whimper as Vivienne's agile toes curled around the crotch of her thong, pushed it aside, then wriggled in between her labia.

She felt like she would burst into flames. She wished she had the willpower to push Vivienne away, but instead, she slid down in the seat, opened her legs, and pressed onto Vivienne's probing foot, thrusting back breathlessly.

Vivienne pulled and tugged at her own nipples, shoving the clinging bustier out of the way with a soft curse. Her other hand caressed her pout in long flat strokes. Somewhere in the back of her sex-addled mind, Rita observed that Vivienne wore no panties. Her cunt lips were swollen and splayed wide as her fingers darted in and out of her hole, and the scent of their pussies blended in the air like some exotic perfume. Rita watched in fascination as the woman tweaked her clit until it burst from beneath its hood, pearlescent with the sheen of her juices.

Vivienne continued. "He can hold his load for ages, Edward can. He likes to make me wait for it, beg for it." She bit her lip. "He can be so cruel sometimes. But when he's inside me, I'm so full, so absolutely full, and I feel like if he pushes just a little harder, just the tiniest bit, I'll explode with such force that when it's all over, there'll be nothing left of me."

Then Vivienne became nonverbal, struggling to breathe, while Rita watched and ached, pressed against her thrusting toes. The woman ground her arse into expensive leather upholstery and humped the four fingers buried in her grasping cunt. Little mewling sounds escaped her throat. Her other hand assaulted her breasts in great kneading fistfuls of soft round flesh.

When Vivienne's orgasm convulsed over her and jerked her against the seat, she gave the crotch of Rita's thong a hard yank with her toes, tugging it tight between the folds of Rita's pussy, holding her splayed open and unsatisfied against the fabric, forcing her to watch while she came. She held Rita there while she caught her breath, then she released her, wiped her foot on the inside of Rita's thigh, and slipped it back into her shoe. "You're a voyeur at the gate, Rita, ogling what you can't comprehend, but think you want." Her eyes were ice, her lips were drawn tight against her teeth. "As for my relationship with Edward, well, you couldn't begin to understand what Edward and I share, so stop trying."

Rita felt as though she had been gut-punched. She could do nothing but gape in a cocktail of shame and anger as Vivienne fumbled in her bag for a silk handkerchief, leisurely wiping and caressing her folds before she laced her breasts back into the bustier and straightened her skirt.

Luckily, Vivienne's mobile rang, and she chatted happily to Lorelei about some planned trip to the south of France. It was as though Rita were not even there. She tidied herself, burning with anger and frustration, unable to believe she had let the bitch get to her, and on such a basic level. How could she have let anyone reduce her to this, to begging for glimpses into Edward's sex life, private glimpses that were not hers to have. But then none of it was hers to have. That was the problem. She didn't belong in this world.

All the more reason to finish the initiation, minimize contact with Edward, and just do her work. Once the exposé was out, she could take her pick of jobs and never look back. This was the break she needed, she reminded herself for the hundredth time. She should be thanking Vivienne for the stiff kick-in-the-ass reminder.

When the limo arrived at Rita's flat an hour later, Vivienne was still on the mobile and offered no good-bye, no sign that she had even noticed Rita leaving.

Inside her flat, Rita started the kettle, then listened to the messages on her mobile that had accumulated while she was away. Most of them were from Owen, wondering how their big project was coming along and asking if she could email him Rory's address, if she had it. It took her a few minutes to realize he was talking about Aurora.

She had barely got the coffee made and the computer booted, when her mobile signaled an incoming text.

R U alrite? Sorry abt V bringing U home. U wr amazng at L's. U
r always & endlessly amazing, my love. Thank U! EXX

It took a tremendous amount of restraint, but she didn't respond to the text. Vivienne was right. She didn't know anything about Edward. She wouldn't even know him if she met him on the street. How could she so easily and completely allow herself to forget something so disturbing?

The flat felt stuffy from being shut up all week. She opened the window next to the computer and breathed in the fresh air. As she pushed back the curtains, she noticed a lone car setting beneath the street light. The man inside seemed to be peering up at her flat. She squinted. Surely he wasn't looking through binoculars?

She quickly stepped back and pulled the curtains. Vivienne was making her paranoid. It was probably just someone who had pulled over to make a phone call. Maybe the wife had phoned him to pick up a curry on the way home. She turned back to the business at hand.

The best way to deal with The Mount and all its bullshit was research. She started back at the beginning. Every journalist knows how easy it is to miss the obvious when she's looking for something bigger.

After being trapped in a limo for two hours with the bitch, Vivienne seemed like a good place to start. Rita googled her, as she had before, and found exactly what she had found before. Vivienne Arlington Page managed The Mount. Part of The Mount's appeal was Vivienne's Garbo mystique. She was a master of showing herself at the right time in the right place, to the right people, but only very sparingly.

If information on Vivienne was scant, it was nonexistent on Edward. He wasn't mentioned in any of the write-ups she could find about The Mount. There was no last name, no first name, no photos, no Edward at all mentioned in connection with The Mount. There was a brief mention of Lorelei Grimes Slater, Leo Peregrine Banacek, Alexander Felix Benton, Morgan Tennyson Hanes, even Aurora Lytton Barnet. And though information on any of them was sketchy at best, there was absolutely nothing on Edward. It was as though he didn't exist. And certainly without a last name, there was no pursuing him further.

The thought of Edward's apparent nonexistence gave her a chill. How had she missed this before? Had she just not wanted to see? Vivienne said he was a monster. Vivienne said if Rita knew his secrets, she'd have nothing to do with him. She chafed her goose-fleshed arms, then remembered the window was open. As she stood to close it, she noticed the car had not moved, and the driver was definitely looking up at her flat with binoculars.

Damn The Mount! Damn the day she had ever set foot in the place. It wasn't bad enough that they had invaded her life, now they had to watch her 24/7 as well. That was it. She'd had enough of Vivienne's shit. She had no one's number but Edward's mobile, which she really didn't want to use tonight. But, damn it, she wasn't going to be spied on. She texted.

Y is V hvng my flat watched!?

Only seconds later she got a response.

No 1 frm TM watching your flat. Stay put. Sending someone 2 chk out situ. EXX

Sending someone! Goddamn it, he was always sending someone, never coming himself. Just as she was about to have a good rage, she noticed the message light blinking on the land line. She picked it up and listened to the message.

"Rita, darling. I'm so sorry for my part in all that's happened. You're my daughter and I love you. Please can't we make this right? Please call me."

There were four more messages just like it. As she deleted them, she suddenly realized what was actually happening, and she dropped onto the sofa still clutching the phone in her hand. Of course it wasn't Vivienne spying on her. She grabbed her mobile and texted Edward.

My mistake. Bloke stopped to use mobile.

She lied. She wasn't about to tell Edward that her own mother was spying on her. Jesus, the woman couldn't have picked a worse time. To her surprise, and disappointment, there was no text back.

Chapter Thirteen

"You Ms. Holly?" the delivery man asked.

She found herself fighting the urge to lie, not sure what Vivienne and The Mount would throw at her next.

"This is for you." He handed her a large oblong box in brown-paper wrapping and eyed her curiously as she signed his electronic pad. No doubt he was wondering what sex toys the pervy chick had ordered that arrived in brown paper. He'd be shocked if he knew what the pervy chick actually got up to. She offered him a sweet smile, and he blushed before turning quickly and disappearing down the hall.

In the privacy of her lounge, she opened the box to discover a black leather catsuit heavily weighted with zippers, snaps, chains, and other pieces of metal which made Rita shiver to even contemplate. She was pretty sure the suit weighed as much as she did. The costume was complete with thigh high boots, a bomber jacket, and a hand-written note that read:

> *Don't touch, don't fondle, and don't experiment. Just put on the suit and nothing else, then wait for me.*
>
> *—Morgan*

Visions of the high councilman with the leopard tattoo flashed through her head—and her cunt.

Morgan needn't have worried that she would experiment or play with the suit, and certainly not that she might put something on under it. There was barely room for skin under it. With the efforts of a contortionist and a fair amount of cursing out loud, she finally got it up over her hips and shoulders, but thoughts of zipping it above her navel made her break out in a cold sweat.

She didn't have to wait long before there was a soft knock on the door. A glance through the peep hole assured her that it was Morgan. The intriguing tattoo was completely covered in black leather, all topped off with a heavy bomber jacket. She opened the door just enough to let him in.

Immediately his brown sugar gaze took in the unzipped front of the suit and the way her arms were folded protectively over her breasts.

She blushed hard. "I'm sorry, but I'm—"

"Claustrophobic. Yes I know, kitten." She noticed the tiniest bit of Western twang. "Edward threatened me about it ad nauseam downstairs just now. That's what took me so long."

Her heart suddenly leaped into her throat. "Edward's downstairs?"

"Well, he was. I sent him home. I'm here now, luv, and I promised I'd take good care of you."

She tried to sound matter-of-fact. "How long had he been down there?"

"Ever since he got your text about someone spying on you."

"Why didn't he come up?"

He held her gaze. "Sweet cheeks, you know why he didn't come up." He changed the subject. "Now about this lovely suit. Just let me help you with it, and you'll see why it's so perfect for someone who suffers from your affliction."

She struggled to drag her thoughts back from Edward as Morgan coaxed her arms away from her chest and released a long sigh at the sight of her breasts barely covered by the unzipped front of the cat suit. "Oh we're gonna have so much fun." He covered her lips in an open mouth kiss that tasted of caramel and coffee. His tongue flicked across her hard palate and wrestled lightly with hers. He slipped his right hand inside the cat suit to cup her breast and raked a thumb over her heavy nipple. Then he rolled it against his index finger until the pinch of it was so close to pain that she held her breath waiting for it. Or was it pleasure she waited for?

Morgan's chuckle was hot against her mouth. "You're so full of anticipation, kitten, so full of needs you don't even know about yet. I smell it on you, all of it and more." He lowered his mouth to her nape and bit. And she definitely felt pain, but her pussy felt something a whole lot nicer.

Then as though he were about his everyday business, he began to fiddle with the chains on the front of the suit. She could see little of what he was doing, but she could hear a snap here and a chink there and occasionally feel the cool metal against her sternum. At last he pulled away and inspected his work.

Where the zipper would have confined her tits into a breathless hug, there was a loose lacing of chain-linked and crisscrossed bustier-fashion revealing the mounds of her breasts while concealing nipple and areola. "There," he breathed. "That's better, isn't it?"

He walked around behind her to take in the overall effect. "Ever ridden a Harley?"

"Motorcycle? No."

"Don't look so frightened, sweetness. I've been riding since I was a pup." His lips curled into an edible smile. "I promise I'll make it good for you."

He knelt and helped her into the boots, lingering to suckle her toes and kiss her insteps before guiding her feet into the soft insides, then slowly zipping them up and up and up. At last he stood and held the bomber jacket for her. "Our steed awaits."

Outside a few neighborhood teenagers had gathered around to admire the biggest, sleekest vintage Hog Rita had ever seen, complete with silver wings painted stylistically across the petrol tank along with the words *Pegasus III*. It took her a few seconds to realize that the boys' attention had shifted away from the Harley. "Could we please go," she whispered, feeling like she did in her dreams when she found herself suddenly naked at the office or in the queue at the grocery store.

But Morgan took his time buckling her into the helmet, making sure it wasn't too tight, making certain she wasn't claustrophobic. When she started to get on behind him, he shook his head, scooted back slightly, and patted the leather seat in front of him.

She balked. "Isn't that illegal?"

"Not if we don't get caught." He patted the spot in front of him again and chuckled. "Trust me. It's the best seat in the house."

Trying to ignore the mutterings and the stares of the teenagers, she climbed on the Harley in front of him, a little less gracefully than she had planned. Fortunately the resulting blush was contained within the helmet.

Morgan knew only one speed and that was suicidal. The g-force of acceleration strong-armed her back against his chest with a yelp that was fortunately drowned by the roar of the Hog. It seemed to her that Morgan was taking the fastest way out of town, weaving in and out of traffic with such terrifying maneuvers that she feared heart failure was imminent. They had only gone a few blocks when she gave up shouting at him to stop. He either couldn't hear, or was ignoring her.

As the traffic lessened, and he headed out on the A3, she realized he was controlling the Hog with one hand. The other arm was wrapped low around her waist. There was an electronic crackle next to her ear, and his voice filled the inside of her helmet. They had contact. "Just relax, sweetness. This is gonna be so good."

His hand slid lower on her belly until it rested against her pubic bone, where it began to fumble until she felt a tug and a zip, and suddenly cool air bathed a horizontal swath of flesh exposed to the night. "I love zippers. Don't you?" His voice was like a kiss against her earlobe.

There was more tugging and zipping until she felt the pressure of the cat suit lessen against her crotch, as though she had just split her trousers. She caught her breath.

"Mmm, there. Oh that's nice." His voice was inside her helmet again just before his fingers slid down between her folds and pressed up into her in such a way that the vibration of the big bike beneath them seemed amplified as though it were a giant vibrator. She was suddenly in danger of forgetting that she was in danger of losing life and limb. My God, the bloke's fingers were expressive as he slipped the middle one deep into her cunt while his thumb raked her pebble-hard clit.

He swerved to pass a lorry. "We're gonna die!" she yelped inside her helmet. Then she bore down against his hand and the vibration of the Hog, hoping he could keep from crashing until *after* she came.

She didn't know if he had heard her yelp, but she wondered if he'd heard her thoughts. "Lift your bottom," his velvety voice filled her helmet again.

"Are you crazy?" She gasped.

"Trust me. Lift your bottom. Don't worry. I'll keep you safe. I promised Edward, didn't I?"

She held her breath, cursing between her teeth, and struggled to do as he said. She grabbed on to the petrol tank until she was sure her fingernails would dig holes in the paint. Then she squealed as another zipping loosened the hug of the cat suit even further until she was certain the whole crotch of the garment had been zipped away. As if to confirm her suspicions, Morgan's large hand now stroked her from behind, spreading her lips.

"Sweet Jesus, you're slippery, kitten. I believe you really like riding a Hog." Then she felt him inch forward on the seat.

He wouldn't…Surely he couldn't…"Oh my God," she gasped.

What was crowding against her bottom and nestling up to her pout was too thick and too stiff to be his finger.

"That's my girl," came the voice in her helmet. "Lift your bottom for me. Just a tiny bit more now. Almost there. I've got you. I won't let you fall." He tightened his arm around her and maneuvered his hips. "That's it, oh yes that's the place I want to be. Jesus, Rita Holly, that's some hot pussy you got there." Then all she could hear was accelerated breathing followed by a hard thrust that nearly sent her over the handlebars but for the strong arm wrapped around her. And he was in. Her pussy felt like it would split in two from the sudden, unexpected fullness.

"That's my girl. Now lean forward. All the way forward and let the Hog do the work. She felt him downshift, and the beast rumbled beneath them. With the substantial length of him so far up inside her, she felt physically compelled to lean forward over the petrol tank until she could feel the cool chains of the cat suit pressing into her bare flesh, until her erect nipples felt like they'd drill clear through the tank.

Then with a hard thrust, Morgan scooted forward again, and she heard him sigh. After that the thrusting and maneuvering became much more subtle, using the power of the Harley roaring beneath them as the driving force. He had positioned himself perfectly so that each undulation of his hips drove her distended clit against the vibrating leather of the seat. My God, she thought, it was a brilliant way to die.

His breath was soft little grunts inside her helmet coming faster and faster until she thought he must have stopped breathing altogether. The movement of his groin against her became less and less, all the while building in intensity until each minuscule shifting penetrated up her spine clear into the crown of her head, until she was certain the imminent orgasm would surely explode her brain.

When his ejaculation erupted inside her, she felt as though his cock had suddenly expanded to fill the entire space within her pelvic girdle, and her own orgasm tightened and gripped on him until he cried out.

She would have surely catapulted off the Hog with the double explosion in her pussy had Morgan not held her tightly with his free arm, as they sped down the A3 toward the Guildford exit.

She wasn't sure she hadn't passed out completely with the intensity of their dual orgasm atop all that horsepower. They were now hurtling down some back road in rural Surrey. Morgan was still controlling the bike with one hand. The other found its way inside her bomber jacket and between the chains to knead and caress her breasts until she was once again bearing down to take advantage of the vibrations of the Hog.

At last he pulled on to a farm road and drove the Harley inside an open barn. There he turned off the engine, dismounted, and took off both their helmets. As he moved to shut the door, she couldn't help feeling a frisson of fear cold and low against her spine.

Near the door he flipped on a light switch that cast the cavernous space into a wild array of dancing shadows, but at least it wasn't pitch dark. Then he turned to face her, eyes black in the gloom. "Now, kitten, I'll educate you in the pleasures of a Hog, and more specifically the pleasures of a Hog in that suit you're wearing. Lose the jacket."

She hurriedly obeyed.

He shifted her until she straddled the seat with her back now facing the petrol tank and handlebars. Then he climbed aboard the big bike as he would if he were getting ready to take a Sunday drive, pushed forward toward her, and reached for her breasts. A loud zipping noise echoed into the room causing her to jump.

Zippers that she thought were to breast pockets were actually pockets to her breasts. Morgan manipulated her tits from openings similar to those she had seen on night dresses for nursing mothers.

And nurse he did, noisily, greedily until she found herself practically humping the big bike just from the feelings being generated in her breasts by his mouth.

While she squirmed he lowered both hands to her thighs, but instead of lifting her onto his lap as she expected, there was more zipping and both legs of her cat suit detached. With a little more tugging and zipping, he pulled the detached leggings free from the high boots and tossed them on the straw-covered floor. She lifted her arse off the seat and whimpered, sighing with hopeful relief as he chucked off his bomber jacket and practically crawled on top of her, pressing her back until her spine arched against the petrol tank.

He raked splayed hands along her ribs, breasts, and shoulders, then coaxed her arms up over her head until she curled her fingers around the handlebars to brace herself. Metal clinked and jangled, and with a little maneuvering on Morgan's part, the chains she thought had been decoration on her sleeves became handcuffs securing her to the handlebars.

She cried out in alarm and struggled, but he pressed his middle finger into her snatch and soothed her fears with pleasure. "There, there, sweetness. Trust me. It'll be so good. So very good."

Once she stopped struggling, he began to unzip what was left of the suit. She watched in fascinated arousal as Morgan uncovered her bit by bit, a zipper here, a snap there. As the leather fell away, Rita could hear the detaching and reattaching of the chains that had adorned the suit. The heaviest link he had augmented with chains from the panniers of the bike, chains that bound her to the petrol tank, encircling her just above and below her breasts in tight bindings that crossed and twisted between her tits and forced them upward and outward until they bulged like overinflated balloons atop her chest. The pressure made her nipples and areolae swell and ache.

The leather cuffs of the sleeves remained to soften the rubbing of the chains that bound her wrists. The high leather neck, now fastened by metal buckles, formed a collar not unlike the blue pet collar she had worn for Leo, but thicker and much more sinister with its heavy metal rivets. It was attached to a strip of leather running down her spine and ending in a buckle just above her coccyx. It was all that was left of the cat suit.

Attached to the front of the collar by a spring clip was another chain, which Morgan had also taken from the panniers. It clipped into the chains that crossed between her breasts, then ran down over her belly where it ended in a buckle that lay loosely just above her pussy.

At last, Morgan stepped back and inspected his work. "Almost finished sweetness. Just have to add the finishing touches." Once again he dug in the panniers and pulled out a leather strap about as wide as the crotch of her knickers. It contained two holes.

She squirmed as Morgan attached it to the chain resting low on her belly. He offered her a wicked, but somehow reassuring smile. "Don't worry, darlin', a chastity belt this ain't."

Then he rummaged in the panniers again, bringing out a thick black dildo, which he secured into the belt before he inserted it into her grudging cunt, making her gasp. "There, now wasn't that easy, just slipped right in, didn't it?"

The butt plug came next, but not before he lubricated it well with his own saliva. She was surprised that the invasion of her back hole served only to make her cunt more slippery.

As he secured the attachments, he spoke softly to her. "You're scared, kitten. I can see it in your eyes. I won't tell you there's no need to be because the one thing I'm not is a liar. What I will say is that you'd be amazed at what other feelings can erupt out of a little bit of fear and a little bit of pain." He leaned over to suckle each of her breasts in turn as he cinched the butt plug and the dildo into place and tightened the straps until Rita cried out.

"There," he said, rubbing his hands together and approving the overall effect. "That's perfect."

Then he left.

Rita waited.

The light was on. It wasn't so bad, she told herself.

And she waited some more.

Outside somewhere in the trees an owl trilled.

Morgan couldn't have gone far, she reassured herself. After all, she had the Harley.

But what if there was a car nearby? What if someone had been waiting to take him away? What if this was that dreadful end she had imagined back the first time Aurora had locked her in the office and spanked her.

Oh that spanking. That delicious spanking. She felt her pussy clench against the dildo and her anus tightened on the butt plug in sympathy.

She pulled her thoughts back to the rather disturbing situation in which she found herself. They wouldn't do that to her. They wouldn't leave her here. Everyone but Vivienne had been straight-forward and above board. Of course it was all a part of the initiation, but surely they wouldn't hurt her. Not really.

Would they?

She waited a little longer and began to wonder if she should try to get loose. She lay chained over the petrol tank, her breasts saluting the ceiling, and her knees bent with her feet on the seat. The position created a delicious fullness low in her belly, and the shifting of her hips caused the front of the leather gusset to rake against her distended clit, which caused her pussy to clench, which caused her arse to clench, and when it all happened together, the sensation was much too powerful to ignore. The thought that she could be left to die crossed her mind, but there was nothing for it. Die or not. She had to come.

She concentrated on gripping and releasing the attachments that filled her. She couldn't play with her tits, but the way they were trussed up was the next best thing. Once she got the grip and release just right, she began shifting her bottom, grinding her hips against the big leather seat.

With each shifting and gripping, the scent of her pussy grew stronger and all the training as a pet helped her to pick up Morgan's scent as well, which had more horsepower than the Harley and was all over her body. When the first orgasm broke, she cried out, shuddered hard and had to brace herself to keep from falling off the Hog. It was a big machine, and if in her heat, she pulled it over on top of her, that probably wouldn't end well.

Once she was stabilized and able to breathe again, she found that nothing had diminished. She still had both holes stuffed. She was still wet and her clit was still thrumming. By the third orgasm she had perfected her technique. As she lifted her hips and tightened her thighs, she wondered if she could OD on orgasms. With only her own pleasure to concentrate on and with movement restricted, each orgasm built on itself, and instead of leaving her more tired, each time she came she felt more energized. Her head buzzed with endorphins, and she was certain that if Morgan returned this second, she could easily race the Harley back to London and win.

For a second fear gripped her belly. Had Morgan given her some sort of drug, maybe introduced through her skin? Maybe she really would die of orgasm overdose. But then she came again, and the orgasm was so fantastic, it really didn't matter. Everybody had to die of something. The smell of leather and metal and pussy and sweaty male mixed with the undertones of clean stable straw and motor oil washed over her in a pheromonal cocktail that pushed her into an altered state, and it was from that altered state, just after a particularly earth-shaking orgasm, her eyelids fluttered open to find Morgan standing next to her with his cock in his hand.

She smiled up at him and opened her legs. "Wanna play?"

"Could do."

She nodded down to her attachments. "You'll have to make room."

He straddled the bike and scooted into position, his big cock anxiously stretched between them with just enough of his groin exposed to give her a glimpse of the leopard skin tattoo. He unhooked the front of the gusset and removed only the dildo.

For a brief second she felt the void, but only for a second, then his warm, dark cock slipped into place, she half perched on his lap, half reclined over the petrol tank straining against the chains. His rough fingers pinched her nipples to cherry licorice peaks, then pinched and stroked her clit until she flinched and thrust alternately, right at the threshold of pain until she reached the tipping point. Then she screamed and grunted the orgasm that tore through her until her throat was raw, tightening her hold on Morgan until he grabbed her buttocks in a bruising grip and pistoned out his load, his own growls echoing off the rafters.

Some time after that a limo came. Two women dressed in black suits and ties, not unlike the bouncers, or Aurora, carefully cleaned her, dressed her in a soft velour track suit, and returned her home just before dawn. As she got out of the limo, she looked around for signs of Edward, but there were none. She felt disappointed.

Chapter Fourteen

EDWARD SWITCHED OFF THE DVD player and cursed out loud into the darkened room. He sat on the leather sofa in a pair of faded jeans and nothing else. The fly was open and he gripped his cock in a strangle hold. Fuck it! He could easily come in his hand watching the DVD of Rita. He could pretend he was Morgan pushing his way into her exquisite snatch, but that's all it would be, just pretending. Hell, if he just wanted pussy, it wasn't hard to get at The Mount, but it wasn't pussy he wanted. It was Rita he wanted. And he wanted all of her, every inch of her, nonstop until they were both completely sated. He figured that would take a very long time.

Then he wanted to start all over again.

She was doing great with the initiation. Morgan couldn't stop talking about how she had ridden him on the Hog. Christ! *She* was doing magnificent; he was the one not handling it very well. Damn it, everyone got to experience Rita but him. He would never forgive Vivienne for that.

There was a soft knock on the door. He wrestled his cock back into the jeans and answered it.

Alex stood before him still dressed in his dance costume. "Leo has a couple of his men keeping an eye on Rita tonight. She'll never know he's there. But if anyone else shows up snooping around, we'll know about it."

"I should be there myself," Edward growled.

"You can't risk any further contact, and you know it. Whatever else, if anything else, is going on with Rita, it has nothing to do with you. Personally, I wouldn't put it past that sleazy boss of hers." Suddenly the dancer was shifting from foot to foot and avoiding Edward's gaze.

"What? What is it, Alex?"

He cleared his throat. "She wants you."

"Bloody hell! I don't want her."

"Not like you have much choice, is it?" Alex took in Edward's state of undress and the unsettled bulge in his jeans. "Morgan gave you the DVD?"

Edward nodded. "You'll be back in the cock stock if she finds out about it."

Edward winced at the thought of the chastity belt and his hand came to rest protectively against his overworked fly.

"I heard about the bet," Alex said. "Do you really think she'll honor it?"

"She has to. She had Lorelei write it up, and now everyone knows."

Alex let out a low whistle. "Jesus, I can't believe she'd even make such a bet. I wouldn't trust her, Edward. She has everything to lose."

"And I have everything to gain. I'll have my life back. Don't you think that's worth the risk?"

"Of course it's worth the risk. All I'm saying is be careful." Alex kicked off his shoes and padded to the refrigerator. "Mind if I watch a little telly? Mine's on the blink again." He helped himself to a beer.

"Just let yourself out when you're done." Edward reached for the door.

"You going like that?" Alex nodded to Edward's bare torso and feet.

"She's come to me in less. What does it matter?"

Alex shrugged. "Suit yourself." He plopped down on the sofa and began to channel surf.

Edward took a deep breath and pulled the door shut behind him. Best get it over with. Putting it off only made matters worse.

He was surprised when Vivienne answered the door herself dressed in an ice-blue kimono he'd given her as a birthday present. Judging from the exaggerated hourglass shape of her, she was wearing a corset beneath. She loved corsets, and she wore them well. She wore everything well. The flat was quiet, other than soft jazz playing in the background. She knew he liked jazz.

"Where's Lorelei?" he asked.

"Business. Diego from the Argentine House." She handed him a glass of fizz, Moët et Chandon, he noticed. "Lorelei has a good rapport with Diego, and they enjoy each other's company." She sipped delicately and released a deep sigh. "You've seen Morgan?"

He nodded.

"I wasn't told about his little task for your girl."

"You know Morgan, always the spontaneous free spirit," Edward lied. The truth was no one wanted to risk another sabotage attempt by Vivienne.

She forced a laugh. "His enthusiasm is practically contagious. Whatever your little darling did, I think we can safely say Morgan was impressed. I thought he was going to shoot his wad just telling me about her."

"Can we talk about something else?"

"He said she wore the suit well."

"Please." He tossed back the champagne as though it were cheap ale. She moved close to him and ran fingernails the color of the inside of a seashell down over his chest, bringing them to rest just below his navel. "You wish it had been you, don't you?"

He set the champagne flute down on the end table. "Please, Vivienne, do we have to do this again?"

She leaned in and kissed the hard muscles of his pecs, her hair falling against the rise of his nipples. He caught his breath as she slipped her fingers down beneath the waistband of his jeans, a tight squeeze, since his penis was still at half-mast. "I thought you might be needing a little help with this tonight," she breathed.

Hers was not the help he wanted. But, damn it, he was horny and frustrated and Vivienne was willing, and she was a good lover when she didn't have an agenda. It was the agenda part that worried him.

Slowly, with endless fascination, she undid his fly, then chuckled softly. "What's this? No underpants? Aren't you the cheeky boy?" She teased the head of his penis until it jutted up against his belly, then she bent and kissed just the tip, flicking her tongue over it as though she were tasting a new flavor of ice cream.

The muscles low in his stomach contracted like he'd been punched. Interesting that the response was the same, pleasure or trauma. He just had time to caress her hair before she pulled away. Holding his gaze, she slowly, deliberately untied the sash of the robe, unwrapping herself as though she were a work of art, and so she was. In the beginning he had wanted her like he had never wanted anything. She had been his wildest obsession, and his most costly. Even after what she had done to him, it was a long time before he was out from under her spell. And now that he was, well, sometimes that was almost worse.

She looked virginal in the white corset, like an innocent laced tightly in silk and ribbon for her own protection, but she was never the one who needed protecting. Her breasts mounded above the tight lacings like apples overflowing a basket, and they evoked a similar desire to taste.

She turned her back to him, offering the view of her perfect bottom, peeking from beneath ribbons and lace, her legs parted just enough to intimate what was to come. "Unlace me, Edward. Be a dear."

He moved behind her, so close that in its present state, his cock could almost reach out and touch her. As his hands came to rest on her back just above the swell of her bottom, she sighed a little whimper of a sigh and shifted her hips back toward him. He undid the knot and, with well-practiced hands, undid the lacings until at last the corset parted, yielding grudgingly to expose the exquisite narrowing of her waist. Everything about her was exquisite, he thought, as he let his finger trace a path down her spine until his hand came to rest just above the crevice of her pillowed bottom. How could it have taken him so long to see the flaws beneath?

Unaware of his machinations, she turned and knelt in front of him, looking up from under long lashes, a gaze of adoring innocence perfected. Then she slid his jeans down just enough to take the length of him into her mouth.

He struggled to relax into the pleasure of it, to think only about how much he needed to come, to think only about how erotic their situation was. But he knew Vivienne too well. No gift was ever freely given.

Just when he had almost forgotten the niggle, just when he was almost able to give in, she stood and took his hand. "Come to bed with me, Edward. It's been a long time since I've made love to you."

"It's been a long time since you've wanted to." The minute he'd said it, he knew he shouldn't have.

Her grip on his hand tightened and the soft laugh at the back of her throat sounded slightly predatory. "Consider it a sympathy fuck, then, if you like."

By the time they had reached the bed, the patina of adoring innocence was gone. She pushed him back on to the satin duvet, tugged his jeans down and bit him just barely above his penis. "Ouch! Vivienne, that hurt." Another mistake, letting her know, especially since the surging of his cock clearly indicated the pain was anything but intolerable.

She grabbed him by the hair, pulling his face only inches from the bow of her mouth, now contorted into a snarl that would have made a lesser woman look ugly. "What? Doesn't she hurt you enough, Edward? What's the matter, are you getting soft on me?" With a quick shift of her hips, and a devastating downward thrust, she slipped onto his cock, then gave a little sigh. "Oooh, not soft at all." Her grip was tight and angry, and he couldn't help thinking of Rita in chains, her delicious girlie grip milking the dildo and the butt plug until she came. My God, to have her do that to him. Jesus, there must be nothing sweeter on earth.

And suddenly he scooped Vivienne in his arms and rolled on top of her, then he thrust so hard that she yelped, and there was just enough pain in the yelp to encourage him. He bent and bit each of her nipples in turn, and she squealed, wrapping her legs around him, digging her nails into his back, making him flinch, making his balls feel like they would surely burst. That must have been what Morgan felt like when he saw Rita coming and coming, endlessly coming.

Vivienne bucked and dug her heels into his back as her first orgasm hit, and her pulsing grip only made him pump harder, feeling the weight of his own need like a boulder around his waist. Morgan had emptied such a load into Rita. Such a load. Watching the DVD, Edward had thought the man would never stop coming.

"That's it, fuck me hard, you cunt-licking bastard." Vivienne's dirty talk barely registered in the back of his mind. There was no room for it next to the picture of Rita chained to the Hog, the picture that now filled his head, and his balls. Rita in chains, Rita in leather, Rita riding the Hog, her slippery pussy sliding over the hard leather saddle. The fullness in his balls was unbearable, his penis felt like it had a mind of its own, wanting nothing but relief, surrogate relief if necessary. But he knew any sort of relief would only be temporary until he could have what he wanted. "Oh God," he gasped.

"That's it, you fucking bastard, jizz my cunt." Vivienne tightened her grip and thrust harder, but he had forgotten himself, and the circumstances no longer mattered in his desperate state.

His mind was no longer capable of caution, and his body less so.

As her second orgasm broke over her, he came. "Oh God, Rita, I'm coming." Too late he realized his slip.

Vivienne growled like an angry lioness and shoved him so hard he fell off the bed, ejaculating long arching spurts of semen onto the white carpet. "Get out," she bellowed. "Now!" She kicked at him, but he was too fast for her, and amazingly agile considering the uncomfortable situation he found himself in.

He stood and stumbled before realizing his jeans were still around his ankles. Convenient for a quick escape, he thought. As he yanked them up and slipped hurriedly out the door, he reminded himself that there was no quick escape. He'd pay dearly for such a slip.

Inside his flat he found Alex stroking a boner in empathy with Morgan, who was doing the same on the DVD. When he saw Edward, he fumbled for the remote. "Sorry, mate. Didn't expect you back for a while."

"It's all right." Edward plopped down on the couch next to Alex, the sight of Rita writhing making him hard again. "She wouldn't mind. In fact, it would turn her on, the two of us having a wank watching her and Morgan have a wank." And suddenly his mood lightened. As he watched Morgan climb on the Harley and remove the dildo from Rita's pussy, he was reminded there might yet be an escape for him.

Alex glanced over at him. "You look worse for the wear. Things didn't go well with Vivienne?" He resumed the leisurely stroking of his cock.

"Do they ever?"

For a long moment, the two sat in silence, watching the sexy drama unfolding on the DVD. "God, she's amazing." Alex's voice was breathless as Rita invited Morgan for a ride.

A glance at the dancer's erection made Edward chuckle. "What?" Alex looked down at his cock. "What's so funny."

"It turns her on."

Alex smiled and gave his cock an affectionate stroke. "Glad to hear she likes it."

"No, I mean yes, she likes your cock, but the thought of the two of us fucking turns her on."

Alex chuckled softly, his attention back on the DVD. "You told her about that?"

"I did, and it made her really hot."

In an effort to release his balls from the restraint of his trousers, Alex shifted on the sofa, then he stopped mid-grope. "I have a brilliant idea. Course it would get you into more trouble with Vivienne, which I doubt you need right now." His face broke into a broad smile. "But only if she finds out." He nodded to the view of Morgan's straining backside as he pistoned Rita's snatch. "It's hardly fair you get to watch her, but she doesn't get to watch you. Don't you agree?"

Edward's pulse went into overdrive. His balls ached at the very thought. He'd had more than a few fantasies about Rita watching the two of them, then joining in the fun.

Alex had already flipped the remote control, and the light on the camera, positioned to take in any interesting activity on the sofa, blinked. "Quick, put this on." He practically threw Edward's mask at him from where he had tossed it on the coffee table after his return from Leo's. Once it was on, it was Alex's turn to chuckle. He nodded at the mask. "Can you suck cock in that?"

"You'd be amazed at what I can do in this." As if to demonstrate, Edward pulled Alex into his arms and took his mouth in a rapacious kiss. It was a relief to have sex with no agenda. He and Alex didn't have sex often. When they did it was always spontaneous and always free of ulterior motives. When Edward pulled away, Alex bit his lip playfully. "Do you kiss Rita like that? Come on, don't be shy. Show me how you'd kiss Rita, and when she watches, she'll know you were thinking about her mouth."

Alex was as good at acting as he was at dancing. This time when Edward kissed him, his mouth suddenly felt softer, more feminine. Edward had to open his eyes to make sure he was still kissing Alex.

But Alex didn't give him much time to dwell on his acting skills, he was already helping Edward out of his jeans, which was not too difficult since he'd returned from Vivienne's still too hard to manage the fly. Finding Alex having a wank hadn't lessened the load. The dancer tugged and maneuvered until Edward sat bare-arsed on the sofa, his hips thrust forward, his erection standing to attention. Alex sighed. "Bet I know what else you like to do to her mouth."

As he began to tease the end of Edward's cock with the tip of his tongue and the round O of his mouth, Edward thought of Rita naked except for Leo's leash. He thought of her sniffing and nuzzling and sucking his cock while Leo mounted her from behind. So much like a wild thing, he thought. He curled his fingers in Alex's hair and pulled his face down until he felt full contact of strong, determined lips and a deliciously deep throat, room for him to thrust unhindered. And he did, making no attempts to stifle his groans of pleasure.

Dancer coordination served him well as Alex kept the perfect rhythm to his thrusts while at the same time stripping off until he too was completely naked, his thick cock bouncing against his thigh each time Edward thrust into his mouth. Edward ran a hand along the dancer's flank until he could cup and knead his arse cheek. Then he slid his curled fingers into Alex's crevice and fondled the twitch of his anus.

But instead of lingering to enjoy Edward's caresses, Alex rose up and pushed Edward back on the sofa until he was lying down, then he reverse-straddled his face and lowered his bottom close to Edward's mouth. When he was satisfied the position worked for both of them, he leaned forward and continued deep throating Edward's heavy cock, occasionally running a muscular tongue over his balls.

The sight of Alex's tight bottom clenching and unclenching just above his face combined with the yeasty tang of male sweat made Edward's mouth water. He pulled him down close and raked his tongue over Alex's anus until it glistened with a fine sheen of his saliva. Then he thrust with his tongue, knowing by Alex's muffled moans that he was appreciating the efforts. Finally he pulled the dancer back so he could nibble and lick his smoothly shaved balls and reciprocate with a good deep throating while he scissored two fingers into Alex's wet pucker. By that time they were both in danger of propelling themselves off of the sofa in their thrustings. At last Alex pulled away and gasped. "Fuck me, Edward. I need you to fuck me now."

As they scrambled to reposition, Alex pushed onto the sofa and maneuvered his way beneath Edward. "I want to see your face," he spoke between labored breaths. Then he lifted his legs onto Edward's shoulders and wriggled his hands down to spread his buttocks, exposing his dark, deep hole. It was an invitation Edward did not resist. His penis was still slippery from Alex's mouth, and the tight pucker of the dancer's anus yielded as he thrust upward until he was fully impaled with his bottom high in the air. Edward rose onto his knees for better positioning, then braced one foot on the floor next to the sofa.

Sandwiched between them, intriguingly close to his own mouth, Alex's enormous erection bounced wildly with each thrust. With his arms raised over his head, he braced himself against the sofa and thrust back with a force that threatened to catapult Edward over the coffee table.

The camera recorded every move as the two men humped and shoved their way toward ejaculation. Edward thought of how Rita would play with herself when she received the DVD. He could imagine her pulling aside her panties and thrusting against a large dildo, harder and harder as the DVD progressed, hard enough to make her breasts bounce, hard enough to make the sofa creak with her humping and thrusting. And he came, grunting and hammering into Alex, feeling like his balls would explode with his release. He could tell by the way Alex tensed and held his breath that he was about to come as well. Quickly, he pulled out. "I owe you, Alex." He barely got Alex's cock into his mouth as the first eruption of semen hit the back of his throat and Alex thrashed out his own load.

It seemed ages before they collapsed back onto the sofa. Edward wiped his mouth, then wriggled and shoved his way closer to his friend, who pulled him into a tight embrace knocking the mask askew. It didn't matter. Edward's back was to the camera.

"You think Rita will like it?" Alex asked when at last they could both breathe again.

"I hope she does," came Edward's breathless reply. "She said it would turn her on, and since I can't…since we can't…"

"Don't sweat it, mate." Alex pulled Edward closer and stroked his back. "You'll be with her soon enough, and you can tell her how you feel." He fumbled with the remote control of the camera. "Though I can't imagine that she doesn't already know how much you—"

Chapter Fifteen

"GIVE ME THAT." RITA grabbed the remote away from Kate and fumbled to switch off the DVD.

Kate folded her arms across her chest and held Rita's gaze. "You should have told me we were going to watch a film. I'd have brought popcorn."

"Can't you ever just leave things alone? I told you I'd be right back." She held up the carrier bag with the bottle of malbec she had just slipped out to the corner store for. When she left, Kate had been on the phone with one of her students.

For a long moment the two glared at each other in the dim evening light of the lounge. Then Kate released a long sigh. "So are you gonna fill me in, because I'm getting tired of your rubbish."

Rita sat down cautiously on the couch next to her friend. "I'd rather not."

"Bloody hell, Rita, I'm your best friend, or at least I thought I was, then you go off to The Mount for a date with Mr. Shag-me-in-the-dark and suddenly you're like a stranger. Are you trying to push me away? Is that it?"

"No! Of course not." Rita buried her face in her hands and shook her head. "God, Kate, I'm sorry. It's just that nothing like this ever happens to me. My life's boring, and then all of a sudden I'm in the middle of it and it's getting deeper. I hardly know where to begin."

"At the beginning maybe?" Kate nodded to the television. "And it better include an explanation of that hot DVD custom made for you, unless I'm totally daft."

Rita suddenly felt desperate to tell someone about what was happening to her. And here was her opportunity in the form of exactly the person she wanted to talk to, the person she talked to about anything and everything before Edward and The Mount. She blinked hard, surprised to find she was fighting back tears. "If I tell you, you've gotta swear on your life that you won't tell anyone. Not anyone. I mean it."

Kate rolled her eyes. "I'm your best friend, Ree. Of course I'm not going to tell anyone, you stupid cow."

Rita wiped her sweaty hands against her jeans and released a shaky breath. "If anyone finds out I've told you, then it's all over."

Kate uttered a little gasp and pulled her friend into such a tight embrace that it forced the breath from Rita's lungs and made her gasp. "Oh God, it's true then? I was afraid of this. What is it, hon? Organized crime? Drugs? White slavery?" Her voice got higher and higher with each new speculation.

"No!" Rita extricated herself and rubbed her crunched ribs. "It's nothing like that. It's…"

Kate leaned closer. "It's what?"

"It's an initiation." There! She'd said it, and she'd said it out loud. For a horrifying few seconds, she held her breath, half expecting Vivienne and her gang of thugs to show up with a newly made chastity belt, one that covered her whole body, one that she would never get out of.

Kate blinked. "A what?"

―᭣᭣᭣―

By the time Rita finished the whole story, the bottle of wine was long gone along with two pots of tea, Chinese takeout, and serious amounts of Jaffa Cakes. OK, she didn't need to give every detail, but this was Kate she was talking to, and hadn't she been absolutely bursting to tell her everything from the beginning? Anyway, once a little of the truth was out, what was the difference if she told the whole thing? At last the two sat in silence, Kate dragging her teaspoon through the trail of sugar strung across the tea tray. "Bloody hell, Ree, if anyone else told me what you just did, I'd swear they were barking." She nodded to the blank television. "The guy in the mask, that was Edward?"

Rita nodded.

"How can you be certain if you've never seen his face?" She raised a hand. "Never mind, I guess that's a pretty stupid question under the circumstances. And Alex?" She scooted closer. "Does he have a girlfriend?"

"The subject never came up, but based on my experience, I don't think having a girlfriend is very popular at The Mount."

"Well, maybe you're in the process of changing that."

Rita couldn't quite muster her friend's optimism.

"I've always considered myself open-minded," Kate said. "Though I never did get the guy on guy thing. At least not until tonight." She nodded to the television. "Can I have a copy of that DVD?"

"I don't think that's a good idea."

Kate drummed her fingers on the coffee table and studied her friend with hard eyes.

"What?"

"You really don't expect me to believe you've put yourself through all this just for the story, do you?"

Rita sprang from the sofa and began to pace. "Of course it's for the story. Jesus, Katie, Vivienne's a sadistic bitch, and I expect to be well compensated when I burst her little bubble. I want the satisfaction of watching that slut squirm when it all gets exposed. Don't look at me like that. You don't know what I've been through."

"Let me see," Kate began to tick off a list on her fingers. "There's fucking, then there's sex with hot blokes, oh, and let's don't leave out sex with hot chicks, then there's more fucking." She shrugged. "I'm trying to be sympathetic, really I am, Ree. Then there's this." Kate switched the DVD back on just as Alex said, "Show me how you'd kiss Rita, and when she watches, she'll know you were thinking about her mouth."

"Stop it, Kate." Rita reached for the remote, but Kate jerked it away and fast forwarded. "Don't sweat it, mate," Alex was saying to the brooding Edward. "You'll be with her soon enough, and you can tell her how you feel. Though I can't imagine that she doesn't already know how much you—"

"Stop it!" Rita grabbed the remote and switched off the DVD, but not before she got a tender view of Edward's back and buttocks, curled against Alex, and the ache beneath her breast bone seemed suddenly bottomless. "I'm a journalist," she spoke over the hammering of her heart. "I didn't ask for any of this, but now that I'm in it, only a fool would not take advantage."

Kate grunted. "And all for that skank, Owen? You know he'll find a way to weasel credit for it. Jesus, Rita, what happened to your high American ideals? She nodded to the television. "I mean, Edward's fucking a bloke for you. The man loves you, for Christ sake. Any fool can see that."

"No." Rita stamped her foot. "Any fool can't see that." Thoughts of her conversation with Vivienne on the way home from Leo's flashed through her head and made her face burn. She drew her arms around herself in a tight hug as though she were suddenly cold. "You don't know. You weren't there. If he loved me, he wouldn't make me go through this." The words caught in her throat and pushed past the lump.

Kate shook her head slowly. "You can't really be that stupid can you?" She grabbed up the tea tray and padded into the kitchen as though she were off to a fire. "I won't argue with you. But don't come crying to me when it all goes tits-up." She came back from the kitchen and plopped down on the couch next to Rita. "Before I discovered your great new porn, I came here to tell you that I've had a visit from a private eye." She held Rita's gaze. "He was asking all kinds of questions about you. And you're not surprised, are you?"

Rita shook her head.

"I told him it was none of his damned business. If he wasn't the cops I had nothing to say to him."

"And?"

"He left. That was this morning. Is that a part of your initiation?"

"No." Rita rubbed the bridge of her nose to ease the beginnings of a headache just behind her eyes.

"Jesus, Ree! You mean there's more?"

"It's my mother." The words came out sounding too much like a whine.

"Are you having a laugh?" Kate let out a low whistle. "Doubt if she'll approve of her daughter the porn queen, even if a Pulitzer is imminent."

Rita shook her head. "The damage is already done. I'm sure my mother knows how many times I go to the loo by now."

"You think she knows about The Mount?"

The thought made Rita's stomach ache. She so didn't need her mother's interference right now. Please God let her stay away just until the initiation was over and she had the information she needed for the exposé.

Chapter Sixteen

THERE WAS CHILLED CHAMPAGNE and canapés on a table covered in white linen, and there was a single red rose in a crystal vase. Beyond that, standing at the window, taking in the view of the city, was Lorelei.

A business proposition, she had said when she called. But a clandestine meeting in a swank hotel room was definitely not the kind of business meeting Owen was used to. Mind you, he wasn't complaining. No red ties, no charcoal suits. Instead, the turquoise dress she wore looked like it was painted on. It was some fifties style, to the knees and slightly off the shoulder. The matching shoes were unbelievably high-heeled making the muscles of her calves look positively edible.

"Good afternoon, Mr. Frank." She turned to face him and offered a cock-stiffening smile. "Owen. I've been looking forward to our meeting." She nodded to the champagne. "Would you do the honors?"

Once champagne was served, she invited him to join her at the table near the window. She toasted new friends and endless possibilities. Then she sat her glass down and ran a French-manicured nail around the rim. "I'm sure you must be wondering why Vivienne sent me to meet with you today, so I won't keep you waiting."

He offered himself a mental pat on the back. It was as he'd hoped. Vivienne had sent her. *The* Vivienne. In his mind's eye he could already picture the cover of next month's *Talkabout*. He would be sitting next to Vivienne inside The Mount, in one of the more intimate dining rooms. She would be wearing some wispy little number, a one-off that some designer had made especially to showcase those luscious breasts and that tiny waist. They would be toasting each other with expensive bubbly, and she would be looking at him adoringly, with just a hint in her eyes that told him their time together would not end in the dining room. And he'd be the envy of—well everybody.

His fantasy left him breathless, and he forced his attention back to the present. He leaned across the table into Lorelei's stunning gaze, offering his best business face. "How may I be of assistance, Lorelei?"

"Both Vivienne and I, along with others at The Mount, are quite impressed with the work you've done at *Talkabout*. The magazine seems to have flourished since you've taken the reins." She sipped her champagne. "You might not think so, but The Mount is always concerned about publicity. Of course the publicity we don't get is probably the most important."

"Of course. Part of the mystique and all."

She nodded. "Exactly. But, the time has come when Vivienne feels we should be a little more forthcoming with information about ourselves."

"Oh?"

She held his gaze as though she were sizing him up. Clearly there was an astute businesswoman inside that slinky dress. "Of course all this must be done with the utmost discretion and taste in keeping with our reputation."

"Of course. Go on." He kept his voice neutral, which was no small task under the circumstances.

"Vivienne thinks you're the man to write a story on The Mount. It would be an exposé, of sorts, in that nothing like this has ever been done before."

My God! It was even better than he'd hoped. There would be

a Pulitzer, there would be his pick of positions. At last there would be the hard-earned recognition he so deserved. Of course he'd try to break the news to Rita gently. Surely she would understand that they wanted someone with more experience to do the exposé. If she didn't, well it really didn't matter, did it? He was the boss, after all.

"Owen? Mr. Frank? Are you all right?"

Owen remembered to breathe. He pressed his feet hard against the floor under the table to keep his knees from trembling. My God! This was a dream come true. "Fine. I'm fine. I must say, I'm a little surprised, that's all. Of course! Of course I'd be happy to do it. Whatever you want."

"Good." She offered a breasty sigh and relaxed back into her chair. "Wonderful." There was that smile again, the one he wanted to eat. But it was quickly subsumed into her business face. "There are a few finer points Vivienne has asked me to discuss with you." This time she leaned so far over the table that her well displayed tits were indeed well displayed and she didn't seem to mind if he looked. "Remember, The Mount has always benefited from gossip and rumor. When I tell you what will be expected of you, I'm sure you'll keep that in mind."

"Of course, naturally. Go on."

"First of all, Vivienne is to have complete editorial control."

He blinked and jerked back in his chair feeling almost as though he'd just been slapped. This was not a part of his fantasy. This wasn't at all what he had in mind. He took a deep breath, biting the inside of his cheek to stop the nervous twitch he felt threatening his upper lip. "My dear Lorelei, journalism doesn't work that way. I run a magazine, not a PR firm."

Once again, Lorelei offered that steamy smile. Definitely unfair negotiating advantage, he thought. "Vivienne was certain a fine journalist such as yourself would feel that way, so she asked me to offer you this as a part of her effort to convince you that you're the right man for the job." She stood and walked slowly to the dressing table, making sure he had plenty of time to admire her well-rounded bottom. From her bag she took a plain white envelope and handed it to him.

While she waited for him to open it, she nibbled a canapé, doing things to smoked salmon with her mouth that caused his cock to jerk in his trousers, making it hard to concentrate on the envelope. But at last he worried it open and pulled out a single slip of white paper that read, *five million*. "What's this?"

"If you agree to our little offer, that's the number of pounds you'll find deposited in your account by the time you get back to your office today."

For a second he could barely hear over his sudden struggle to breathe. "Are you serious? You can't be serious?" God, he sounded like a stupid amateur.

She leaned down and kissed his ear, nibbling the lobe like it was a delicate canapé. "Oh I'm very serious, Owen. Very serious indeed."

His pulse threatened to hammer its way through his throat. He stared at the words on the paper until they slid out of focus. Even the close proximity of Lorelei's luscious mouth paled in comparison to the visions of Ferraris and country cottages and supermodels on his arm that danced through his head.

"Owen?"

"What do I have to do?" His voice sounded breathless, like a gale had caught in his throat, and threatened to strangle him.

She knelt in front of him and rested her hand on his fly, her blue eyes shining beneath enormous lashes. "All you have to do is write the story that Vivienne tells you to write. Do exactly as she says, and the exposé is all yours, the money's all yours," she ran a lacquered nail over the buckle of his belt, "and other fringe benefits as well." She leaned in close and rubbed her cheek against the beginnings of a bulge. "All yours for the taking."

She stood so quickly that it took serious restraint to keep from grabbing her and pulling her face back down to his crotch. But then she reached behind her, unzipped the turquoise dress, and stepped out of it. Owen found himself looking at the most perfect body he had ever seen, displayed in burgundy silk lingerie that he had no doubt would have set him back a good three months' salary, but oh God, she was worth it. Her breasts practically spilled over the top of the deep lace plunge, and the thong made a matching lacy V just above her pussy.

Now her smile was almost shy. "Vivienne sent me to persuade you to work for us." She knelt in front of him again. "She said use any means at my disposal." With amazing agility, considering the length of her nails, she undid his belt and trousers and reached inside. She looked up at him with a pout that was almost innocent. "Please say yes, Owen." Her voice was thin and girlish. "For me."

Before he could even feign a protest, she pulled his cock into her mouth so deeply and with such delicious suction that he nearly fell off the chair. Just when he had almost forgotten everything else in the world but his cock in her mouth she pulled away and whimpered, slipping a hand into her panties, making no effort to hide her squirming. "Please say yes, Owen. Please do what Vivienne asks so we can fuck."

"This is highly…I normally don't…urgh."

She took him into her mouth again, snaking her tongue along the length of him, doing things that made him certain her tongue was prehensile. He groaned out loud and humped her mouth like it was a pussy. "Please," she said when she came up for air. "It'll be so good for all of us, I promise you. Your career will be made, and you'll be able to do whatever you want." She guided his hand to her breasts. "You'll have your own private table at The Mount with me, or even Vivienne, to share it with you."

She unhooked her bra, releasing her lovely tits, eager nipples first, and he was convinced. Oh God, how he was convinced! "Tell Vivienne I'll do it." He stood and pulled her to her feet, then he pushed and nudged her toward the bed with her frantically tugging and shoving at his clothes and whimpering like she was gagging for it.

"I'm so glad. I'm so glad," she gasped as they fell onto the bed. He pushed aside her thong and shoved into her smoothly shaven cunt. She was tight, so tight and slippery. He knew he couldn't last long. She wrapped her legs around him, shoes and all, shoving and humping like she couldn't wait either. He drilled harder and faster, figuring this was just a prelude, as badly as she wanted him. They both needed to come, just get rid of all that tension that had built up. Then they could take their time. He'd take the afternoon off. After all, they had the room.

"Oh God, oh God! Owen, I'm coming," she gasped. And he came too.

Chapter Seventeen

VIVIENNE'S FLAT WAS EMPTY. Lorelei shivered and chafed her arms. She couldn't remember Vivienne's flat ever being empty. This time of evening the place was always buzzing with activity. It was true Lorelei had returned later than she had expected, but Vivienne had ordered her to stay until the job was done. How was she to know that in spite of Owen Frank's sleazy reputation, the man was into marathon sex, and not half bad at it either. Fucking him might be an inconvenience, but it was certainly no hardship.

Edward was at work in the study, Alex was teaching a dance lesson, and Aurora was in the dungeon punishing the errant CEO of some bank. No one had seen Vivienne in the restaurant either. Lorelei wandered down the narrow hall toward the back entrance. Sometimes Vivienne sought out unlikely spots to take lovers. It was a kinky thing with her, having sex in unusual places. The only thing she liked better than sex in unusual places was being caught in the act. There were no grunts of pleasure coming from the linen closet, nor the pantry next to the lift.

Lorelei stepped out into the alley where two sleek limos stood ready for the private use of members. One driver was busy reading a novel, the other talked quietly on his mobile. Both offered her a polite nod.

She was about to go back inside when a muffled whimper further down the alley got her attention. Careful not to turn her ankle on the cobbles, she tiptoed behind the limos and around to where the dumpsters from the kitchen sat. As she moved closer, she heard it again, a muffled grunt followed by a whine.

She thought she recognized the faded blue gym suit with the hood pulled up, but it was those ugly pink flip-flops that gave her away. What the hell was Rita Holly doing behind the kitchen bins?

Then a masculine voice mumbled something Lorelei couldn't quite catch, and she froze in her tracks. Surely Rita wasn't stupid enough to meet Edward here like this? But hadn't she just seen Edward hard at work in the study? Vivienne always said the chick was a slut. Lorelei had masturbated more than once thinking about Rita pleasuring the two guards the night she was brought before the High Council.

Whoever she was with, his face was buried in Rita's cleavage and he was nursing hungrily.

"I believe in reciprocity," Rita said. She sounded strange, like maybe she had a cold. She dropped to her knees and took the man's insistent cock into her mouth, and suddenly Lorelei could see that the man was Gavin, the guard. Had Rita really liked him that much? Lorelei had always thought him a bit creepy. She watched in confusion as Gavin humped hard. "That's right you little bitch. You love sucking cock, don't you? And mine's fully loaded and ready for that dirty mouth of yours." He grabbed the back of Rita's hooded head to pull her further onto his penis, thrusting rough and fast.

Rita gagged and sputtered and shoved him back.

Gavin uttered a breathy curse. "It's a big one isn't it? A filthy mouth like yours needs a big one, doesn't it?" He slapped the back of her head. "Doesn't it?"

"Mph," came the reply.

"You hot little bitch. You need someone to teach you your place. And on your knees, well," he thrust hard, "that place works for me."

Rita gagged again and pulled back, gasping and sobbing, her hands kneading her breasts with a vengeance. "Please fuck me. I need to be fucked so bad."

"I'll fuck you all right, you little chav slut. I'll fuck your pussy till you can't walk straight, then I'll fuck your tight little arsehole." He jerked her to her feet and pushed her against the bin with her back to him. She let out an anxious sob. Then he slid his hand down the back of her yoga pants. "What? No knickers? You're such a slutty little whore."

"I am. I'm a slutty little whore," she whimpered, then thrust her arse back at him like an open invitation. But he didn't mount her right away. Instead he shoved a rough hand further into the trousers between her legs and began to thrust. She went into a frenzy humping his fingers. He chuckled. "Oh, you're gagging for it, aren't you? All slick and quivery and pouting, you dirty girl. No knickers, no bra, just that soft fabric rubbing up against your twat." With a violent tug he ripped open the crotch of her track suit, and Lorelei flinched at the sound of tearing cloth as he exposed Rita's arse completely, then he began to spank her, hard enough to make her squeal.

"Hurts, doesn't it? You like that, don't you?" Gavin smacked her again. "Tell me you like it."

"I do. I like it so much."

He spanked her until she was properly sobbing.

"Please, put it in me," she begged. "I can't stand it anymore. Please fuck me. Make me come, please."

Cautiously Lorelei stepped closer holding her breath and ignoring the urge to slip her fingers into her own pussy and have a little voyeuristic come along with them. She wasn't sure why, but something didn't seem quite right.

Gavin took hold of his cock like he was gripping a sword, and with one hard thrust, pushed into Rita, growling like an angry bear as he did so. Then he grabbed her hips and hammered into her with such force that Lorelei caught her breath at the violence of it. As for Rita, well it was really hard to tell if she was in ecstasy or agony. She whimpered and whined and made little mewling sounds with each angry thrust.

Gavin looked like he was about to burst. His face and neck were now an angry shade of red as he grunted out a stream of obscenities with each thrust. Then he yanked off her hood and grabbed her by the ponytail, twisting it into his fist. She gave a strangled yelp as he yanked her head back toward him.

And suddenly everything made sense. The ponytail was blond, not chestnut, and there was no mistaking Vivienne's profile. "I'm coming, I'm coming!" She shouted. Gavin kept shoving into her as though he had every intention of splitting her in two. Then he pulled out of her, shooting his wad up her back and onto her hoodie. While he gasped for breath, he still held her pinned against the dumpster, and when he was done coming, he wiped his cock on the leg of her pants. "Just what you deserve, bitch, a fuck in a back alley, now get out of here. Go home where you belong."

It took Lorelei a few seconds to realize that, as Vivienne dropped to her knees, onto the filthy cobbles next to the dumpster, she wasn't sobbing, but rather she was still convulsing with orgasm. Her eyes were closed, her head thrown back and the moans escaping her throat were nothing short of ecstatic. As intimate as Lorelei was with Vivienne, she had never seen her like this before.

And suddenly she realized she wasn't intended to see. The trance was broken. Heart pounding in her chest, Lorelei turned and ran back past the limos, back into The Mount, nearly twisting an ankle on the cobbles. Inside, she hurried upstairs to Vivienne's flat, not for the first time, wishing she had a place of her own.

<center>~~~</center>

"The money's been deposited, and he has the mobile I gave him," Lorelei said. Vivienne had called her to the office she kept on the ground floor behind the main restaurant. It was mostly there for appearances, but it was always a quiet and private place to meet. ·

She tried not to think about what she had seen in the alley not yet an hour ago. Vivienne could pick up on the tiniest signal when something was wrong, and that was often dangerous for people who got in her way. Poor Edward was proof of that. Lorelei forced her thoughts back to Owen Frank. "You pegged him right. The man'll do just about anything for money and tail."

"Is he any good?" Vivienne asked. "In bed, I mean?"

Lorelei shrugged. "He's all right. It's hardly fair to compare when I live at The Mount and get the best."

Vivienne pulled a compact from the top drawer of the desk and powdered her nose. There was now no sign of the faded sweat suit. Lorelei marveled at just how quickly she had transformed herself from slutty chav into the Goddess of The Mount. The change was so complete that she could almost wonder if she had imagined the whole sordid incident. "You were gone a long time," Vivienne said.

"The man has a lot of endurance."

"He's willing to write exactly what I tell him?"

"You could tell him you're Hera and The Mount is really Mount Olympus and he'd write it. Don't worry. He has no loyalty to Rita, only to himself. He's just the kind of bloke you're looking for."

"You hinted to him that Rita might have information we need to access?"

"I did. But if she's writing anything about The Mount and he knows it, he kept it quiet. I figure he'll try and access her files, then we'll know."

Vivienne bit her lower lip delicately. "It would be so much better if we could actually catch her in the act of betraying The Mount. That would end this travesty of initiation quickly and painlessly." She grunted. "Well for everyone but Edward, of course."

"Does that matter?"

"Not really. I want him to suffer. He deserves it. He knows he belongs to me, and he'll always belong to me. How can he possibly think she can help him?"

"But you made the bet."

Vivienne chuckled softly and examined her nails. "You know Edward can't resist a good bet. Besides, I was bored."

~~~

Later, as they lay curled around each other in Vivienne's big bed, Owen called. Lorelei stayed on the line long enough to be certain she had made his cock hard and long enough to reassure both her and Vivienne that he was theirs. When she hung up, Vivienne pulled her back into her arms. "Well?"

"I'll meet him tomorrow night at the hotel again for another fuck. Don't worry. He's hooked."

"Good. I don't want him brought here. Edward would get suspicious." She curled her fingers in Lorelei's hair and gave her a long, lazy kiss, her tongue moving in small darting motions over Lorelei's hard palate, intimating what she could do to Lorelei's cunt, if she wanted to. And just when Lorelei was beginning to squirm and grind her bottom against the mattress, Vivienne pulled away ever so slightly. "I'm sorry you have to fuck him, darling, but there's really no one else I can trust. You understand."

"Of course I understand, and I don't mind. Slumming can be a turn-on sometimes." The minute she had said it, she realized her mistake, but it was too late.

Vivienne kissed her again, this time harder, pulling away with a painful nip on her lip. "If you tell anyone what you saw this evening in the ally with Gavin," she curled her fingers tighter in Lorelei's hair until Lorelei flinched, "I promise you, darling, your punishment will be very long and very unpleasant." She lowered her mouth to Lorelei's nape and bit hard. "Are we clear?"

Chapter Eighteen

THE GOWN ARRIVED, AS had the cat suit, in an oblong box with brown-paper wrapping. It solicited the same tense butterfly dance in her stomach and the same dryness in her mouth. This was all becoming rather routine for the delivery man, who offered her a knowing smile as she signed for the package. No doubt her mother's bloodhound had seen it too, along with her leaving the house in the cat suit, on the Harley. She wondered how long it would be before the woman showed up and made a scene.

A peek out the window before she opened the box showed the coast was clear. Maybe she'd get another day's grace. Her whole life had turned into a bizarre lopsided tango, dodging her mother's calls, and wondering at every turn just what Vivienne would pull next. It had been unusually peaceful for several days now. She was enough of a pessimist to figure that wasn't a good sign.

In the lounge, she opened the box with trepidation, wondering if there was such a thing as a full body chastity belt. But when it was opened she gasped in delight. Folded neatly, in soft pink tissue paper, was a gown of blue-gray silk. The neck line was cut square and low in the back and in the front. It was designed to display her breasts at their luscious best. There were matching shoes, more romantic than sexy, and the accompanying necklace and earrings of opal were set in white gold. There was no note, no message, nothing, but everything fit perfectly, almost as though it were designed especially for her.

While she admired herself in front of the mirror, her mobile signaled an incoming text.

M sure gown is exquisite on U! Can't w8 2 C. Limo will pick U
up at 8. EXX

This time, instead of being sneaked in the back door, the limo delivered her to the front entrance. Leo met her dressed in a tux that made him look like he owned the whole world and enchanted all the women in it.

He offered her his arm, giving her an admiring once-over as though she were his favorite pet again. "My dear Rita, never have I seen such a stunning creature in all my life." He laid a warm kiss across the back of her hand, folded her arm over his, and guided her toward the entrance.

She felt like all eyes were now on her, as they had been on Vivienne that first night. Was it only a few weeks ago, her first visit to The Mount? It seemed years. She felt as though her feet weren't touching the ground. She felt as though she were suddenly a goddess surrounded by worshippers there to do homage. Was this what Vivienne felt when she made her grand entrances?

Thoughts of Vivienne brought the knot back to her stomach. Surely this was too good to be true, at least if Vivienne had anything to do with it.

Inside diners stopped eating and stared, discreetly of course. The wait staff gave respectful little nods, to Leo, no doubt. They would have known him. And yet, it felt as though they were looking at her with admiring eyes. Not for the first time since her whole adventure at The Mount had begun, the thought that she might have been drugged popped into her head.

When they came to the staircase that led down to the Presence Chamber, Leo stopped and turned to face her, lifting her chin so that their eyes met. "You know what today is, yes?"

She shook her head. "Is new beginning for you, my darling. Is the day your initiation ends and you become full-fledged member of The Mount. This is a position well deserved, no one would doubt."

She suddenly felt as though all the oxygen had gone out of the room, and along with it, all of the sound. Even her own breath seemed caught in the claustrophobic confines of her ribs, where it raged with her pulse. "But what about Lorelei? She hasn't given me a task yet?" The thought left a sour feeling at the back of her throat.

"In the first place, not everyone has to make task for you. Is not required. In the second place, Lorelei is Vivienne's girl. No one would trust her with such important responsibility. She is, as you say, butt kisser." He raised his hand as though he were shooing away a fly. "We will not speak of this now. This is a happy occasion. Is not the time to talk such unpleasantness." Leo dropped a reassuring kiss along her earlobe. "You have earned your place. Now come. We must not keep the High Council waiting." He opened the door and they descended the long flight of stairs.

When the doors swung open at the bottom, a sense of déjà vu welled up inside her as she was led into the center of the stone chamber. Her eyes locked immediately on Edward in his golden mask. Beside him sat Lorelei and Morgan. Even Aurora was dressed in a gown, black and gothic. One look at Alex brought to her mind a quick flash of him making love to Edward. Leo's chair would soon be filled. But Vivienne's chair was empty.

They stood for a moment in front of the approving gaze of the council. The moment grew and expanded to become uncomfortable. It was impossible not to notice the council members whispering among themselves, nor their surreptitious glances behind the curtain. Vivienne was nowhere to be found. The only one who seemed comfortable with the situation was Lorelei. She whispered something in Edward's ear, then excused herself. The silence stretched to the breaking point.

Leo said something in Slavic under his breath, then he motioned to one of the guards. "Bruce, bring a chair. This lovely lady has been kept standing long enough."

From somewhere the guard produced a cushioned, high-backed chair. In the shuffle, Rita hadn't noticed that Edward had left the dais and was now standing next to her. As she sat, he knelt before her and took both her hands in his. "You look like heaven itself, Rita Holly." Though she couldn't see his eyes, she could hear the thickness in his voice that seemed to grow with each word. "What's this magic you've worked on me, from the very moment I met you on the train in the dark?" He kissed her fingers folded over his. "I'm undone."

There was another shuffling about as Lorelei came back into the room with an envelope in her hand. When she saw Edward kneeling next to Rita, she hurried down the steps of the dais and handed him the envelope.

Edward opened it and took out a single, clearly expensive sheet of stationery. The whole room held its breath while he read it. Then he exploded. "That bitch! That ruthless bitch. She can't do this. She cannot do this. She has no right." He wadded the paper into an angry ball and tossed it across the room. Then he grabbed Rita's hand and pulled her from the chair. "Come on. We're leaving. It's done. It's over."

"You can't leave, Edward. You know you can't. And it isn't over." Lorelei's voice rang out above the confusion on the dais. "Vivienne has every right to demand this of the initiate. It's in the statutes."

Leo laid a restraining hand against Edward's arm, stopping him mid-stride. Then he picked up the paper from where it had landed at the feet of one of the guards and unwadded it. As he perused it, his face became redder and redder with each word. Whatever he said in Slavic was said with such venom that no one in the room could doubt the general nature of it. He looked up at everyone.

"Well?" Morgan asked. "What is it? What does it say?"

"If I may." Lorelei plucked the paper out of Leo's hands, smoothed it meticulously, and cleared her throat. "As you have all, no doubt, gathered by now, this is from Vivienne, who has refused to be present tonight because this initiation has not been completed."

A wave of protest broke among those still remaining on the dais, but she raised a hand to silence them. Then, as though she were the mayor of the city with an important proclamation, she began to read.

> *My dear fellow council members,*
>
> *I will not sanction the membership of Rita Ellison Holly into The Mount until her initiation is complete, and to the best of my knowledge there is still one task remaining for Ms. Holly. That is the task offered up by the head of the High Council.*

"But she's already had her task," Alex interrupted. "It's not our fault that she broke the rules of initiation and had her task nullified."

"As far as I'm concerned this initiation is over," added Morgan, stomping his booted foot on the floor for emphasis. Lorelei raised her hand. "If you would let me finish." When there was silence again, she read on.

> *Under the Laws of Initiation, chapter 14, subsection 121, an initiation is not complete until the task offered up by the head of the High Council is completed by the initiate, and completed to the satisfaction of the head of the council. Since the rest of the council saw fit to void my first task, Rita Ellison Holly has not completed the task set forth for her by the head of the High Council. When she has completed said task, then and only then will she be a full-fledged member of The Mount.*

The task set forth for Rita Ellison Holly is this: She shall immediately be conveyed to my quarters. There she shall be stripped of all rank and possessions and shall assume the position of personal slave to Vivienne Arlington Page, head of the High Council of The Mount, London Coven. When she has completed that task to the head of the High Council's satisfaction, then, and only then, shall she be considered worthy for membership into The Mount.

The council chamber erupted into chaos, but Rita hardly heard it. Edward was yelling something about broken rules. Lorelei was yelling something back about Vivienne's demand being perfectly legal under the codes. None of it mattered any more. It was over. This was more than even she could endure, and if no one was willing to stand up to Vivienne, then Rita had a snowball's chance in hell of ever completing the initiation. While the world around her was in chaos, she turned and fled up the stairs. She took the back door and caught a taxi at the end of the street.

As the cab sped away from the waterfront, she looked out the window, feeling cold and numb. She had enough, she reassured herself. She had everything necessary for a good story, so why did she feel so awful? They deserved it. They all deserved to be exposed for letting Vivienne get away with such blatant breaking of the rules, for letting Vivienne hurt and humiliate her.

And Edward...Suddenly the world outside the window refracted with the welling of tears. Edward deserved it most of all. She forced thoughts of him out of her head and tried to occupy herself by planning the story, the writing of which would now fill her time.

Rita Ellison Holly. Why had Vivienne referred to her as Rita Ellison Holly? Granted, she hadn't used her family name in a long time, but there were no Ellisons in her family that she knew of, and even if there had been, Vivienne couldn't know that.

She paid the taxi driver and got out of the cab before she noticed the waiting limo. Alex had her by the arm and was guiding her toward its open door before she knew what was happening. "No," she balked. "I'm not going to be that bitch's slave. Now leave me alone. I've had enough."

"I know you have, darling, and I'm so sorry." Suddenly she was engulfed in Edward's arms. "But please just hear us out. Just get in the limo and listen. Then if you still want to end it, I'll understand."

"You let her do it." Even as she spoke, she allowed the two men to guide her into the limo. "How could you let her do this to me?" She gave Edward a hard shove with the flat of her hand.

Alex intervened, pulling her away from Edward and holding her tight. "He had no choice, Rita. I know you don't understand now, but it's true. Please you have to trust him. You have to trust that Edward—"

"Shut up Alex. You'll only make matters worse."

"Make matters worse?" Rita half shouted. "How the hell could matters get worse? How?"

"Trust me," Alex said, holding Edward's gaze. "They can."

Inside the limo, the driver offered her a shot of whisky, which she downed without a second thought, then she sat glaring at the two men, pushing Edward away when he tried to take her hand.

"Listen to me, Rita. Leo, Morgan, and Aurora have gone to plead your case before Vivienne. That'll buy us some time."

Rita exploded. "Doesn't anyone ever just tell that bitch to fuck off? And what is someone like her doing in such a position of power in the first place? Has she got you all by the balls?"

In spite of her evident anger, Alex forced a half smile. "I guess that's one way of putting it."

"Why would I want to be a part of an organization where I have to kiss her arse whenever she demands it? Tell me why?"

"Because you're the tipping point, Rita, don't you see?" Edward grabbed her hands this time and held them so tightly she feared he'd crush her fingers. "You change everything. I can't explain it to you now. You'll have to trust me, but if you pass the initiation, you break Vivienne's hold."

"Oh, so I should do it for The Mount? Is that it?"

Edward took her face in his hands and kissed her. And in her mind's eye, she heard Alex saying on the DVD: "Kiss me like you'd kiss Rita, and she'll know you were thinking of her." My God, it was true. When Edward kissed her, it was like he was giving her life, breathing into her a fullness she could barely contain, and yet she hungered for more. When he kissed her, she wanted to devour him, to take him into herself, to fully possess him in ways she couldn't even possess herself. It made no sense, and yet it was so.

When he tried to pull away she anxiously pulled him back to her, at that moment unable to imagine her mouth without his. For a second he tensed and resisted, then he yielded to her, blessedly allowing her to live just a little longer. "I'm not asking you to do it for The Mount." He pressed his words breathlessly against her lips. "I'm more selfish than that. I'm asking you to do it for me, because you're all I can think about, because I want to be with you, and this is the only way I know to make that happen."

"She'll never let me pass her task. Surely you know that."

"That's why the others are with her now." Alex's shattered the moment.

Edward released her and straightened his jacket. "They're negotiating a length of duration, the parameters for your service to Vivienne, and her treatment of you. Plus one of us will be in her apartment with you at all times."

"And can't she just say no to all this negotiation? Following the rules has never been her forte."

"Not when she's threatened with a higher authority," Alex said.

"Trust me," Edward said. "Even she won't deny them what they ask this time. I promise you."

Just then Edward's phone rang. Rita could only hear his end of the conversation, which consisted of, "I see. All right. If that's what she wants, of course I will. It doesn't matter. I'll do it."

He stuck the phone back in his pocket and sat in silence for a second.

"Well?" Alex couldn't keep the impatience out of his voice.

"She's agreed to our terms." Edward held Rita's gaze. "Now all that remains, darling, is to get you to agree to finish your initiation."

"I've already finished my initiation," she growled.

"I know you have. We all know you have, but we all want you to be a part of us, a member of The Mount. And I want that more than you can possibly imagine, Rita."

"What guarantee do I have that Vivienne'll play by the rules this time?" Rita asked. "She never has before."

"Because she doesn't want the powers that be snooping around, and because I'll be there with you all the time." She didn't miss the look he shot Alex. "We'll be her slaves together, and if she does anything to harm even the tiniest hair on your head," he lifted her chin and laid a tender kiss across her lips, "then we slaves will revolt."

Chapter Nineteen

Lorelei answered the door to Vivienne's suite when they arrived. Rita was still struggling to keep from bolting, but Edward and Alex flanked her. In all truth, they were actually supporting her in her weak-kneed effort to enter the lair of the bitch who would soon be her mistress. "Keep your eyes averted," Alex whispered between clenched teeth. "You won't be a pet here, sorry to say."

At last Vivienne came into the room, wearing an ice-blue kimono, and looking as though she were expecting either sex, or to torture someone. Rita wondered if there was really any difference between the two with her. She was certain Vivienne would make Aurora look like an amateur in the dungeon. Vivienne smiled like a child at Christmas. "Ah, my new slave has arrived." Her smile was suddenly swallowed up in a frown. "And certainly overdressed for her station. Lorelei, get her out of those clothes. She won't be needing them."

It was amazingly hard to keep from crying as the cool blond began to undress her, one by one removing the garments that had made her feel like a goddess only a few short hours ago. They were replaced with a shift of plain white cotton cut low enough in the front for her breasts to be exposed and slit to the waist in front and behind. Once she was dressed, Vivienne moved to inspect her, running a hand over her breasts. "You're a slave now, girl. You have nothing to hide and everything to offer your superiors." She pinched Rita's nipple causing her to flinch.

Alex grabbed Edward by the arm to keep him from coming to Rita's aid, but it was too late. Vivienne turned with lightning speed and gave Edward a resounding slap across the face. "You will wait quietly or face the consequences. When I'm finished with this slave, then I'll attend to you. Alex, you may leave. I've no room for a third slave in my house right now."

Alex glared at her, but did not disobey.

When he was gone, she turned her attention back to Rita. She ran her hand inside the front slit of the slave garment and shoved a finger into Rita's cunt, then chuckled knowingly. "Ever at the ready, aren't you, girl? That's good because you'll service any of my guests who request it, though I personally can't imagine why anyone would. Nonetheless, you'll provide whatever form of pleasure or service is required in this household while you're here. Is that clear?"

Rita nodded. "Speak up, girl. You're not in the Zoo now. Is that clear?"

"Yes."

"Yes what?"

"Yes, mistress?"

"That's better. May, come here." She turned to the Asian woman who was now standing quietly behind them dressed in nothing but black garter belts and spiderweb stockings that disappeared into heavy biker boots. "Take Edward to my room. I'll deal with him there."

The Asian nodded and escorted Edward out of the room, but not before he managed one parting glance at Rita.

When they had gone, Vivienne turned her attention back to Rita. "You'll wait here until I've dealt with Edward." She opened the robe and stepped out of it to reveal a matching corset. "That may take awhile," she added breathlessly. Then she followed May and Edward into another part of the house, leaving Rita standing alone in the middle of the reception room for what seemed like ages.

In spite of her best efforts, she was unable to keep her thoughts away from what must be going on in Vivienne's room, and whatever it was, it sounded like a helluva lot more fun than she was having. The groans and grunts of pleasure were unbridled. Anger burned in the pit of her stomach, made hotter by the overwhelming sense of helplessness. It was only Lorelei sitting on the sofa in front of her that kept her from walking out. So this was how Edward was going to protect her, by fucking Vivienne? Somehow his slavery didn't seem nearly as onerous as hers did.

It was research, she reminded herself. It didn't matter. It was only for a story, nothing more, but somehow that didn't make the sounds of pleasure coming from the bedroom any easier to bear.

When Vivienne returned, at last, she was dressed like Athena in a white toga and crested helmet with a horsetail plume. Belted at her waist was a vicious-looking flogger, among other strange whip-like objects that made Rita's skin prickle. "Come along, girl. I need your help in the dungeon."

Rita felt ice in her stomach as she followed Vivienne into the same hallway where Alex had brought her to Edward's suite, then down a long flight of stairs, as though they were going to the Presence Chamber. But when they arrived at the bottom, there was no mistaking that this was the dungeon. The smell of leather and metal and old candle wax filled the air, along with the more human smells of sweat and sex, and maybe even blood. Rita shivered.

"This is Aurora's favorite place," Vivienne breathed. "But Aurora won't be with us tonight. It'll just be you and me meting out the punishment." She nodded to a man chained between two supporting pillars, his shadow casting spectral images in the flickering candle light.

"As you may know, punishment is hard work, and as much as I enjoy watching it and supervising, I really only like to get sweaty for sex." She took off her helmet and shook loose her hair, then she handed one of the whips from her belt to Rita. "That being the

case. You'll be doing the punishing, getting him ready for me." She
chuckled softly. "Then when he's all pink-bottomed and gagging for
it, you may watch me fuck him."

A masked guard dressed in black leather from head to toe
brought in a sturdy wooden chair for Vivienne. She motioned him
to move it close to the chained man.

As they approached, Rita could see that the man in chains was
swathed from head to toe in body-hugging black PVC, the very sight
of which made her skin crawl.

"This one," Vivienne said, nodding to the prisoner, "took unfair
advantage of our customers. As the manager of such a fine establish-
ment, I can't allow such bad behavior." She heaved a sigh. "So pretty
boy here must be punished. Oh don't look at me like that, Rita. I do
know where the bread comes from. The place wouldn't run nearly so
smoothly and have such a reputation if I wasn't good at what I do."

"But if he likes to be punished, won't he just be encouraged to
do it again so he can get punished again?"

"I didn't say he likes being punished, did I?" She waved a dis-
missing hand before Rita could protest. "Oh don't worry, it's completely consensual. Besides, his punishment is a one-off, guaranteed
to teach him a lesson." She pulled his head up, but the man saw
nothing. The only openings in the mask were small breathing holes
at the nose and securely closed zippers over his eyes and his mouth.
Damn, this lot was fond of zippers, Rita thought. And sure enough,
even as the thought crossed her mind, Vivienne opened a trap door
zipper that exposed the whole of the man's arse.

Almost without thinking, Rita reached out and touched the
exposed buttocks, which clenched beneath her fingertips. A muffled
moan came from inside the suit.

"Nice, isn't it?" Vivienne said. "And wait till you see it all pink
and throbbing." She nodded to the whip, but Rita instinctively took
a step back.

"Girl, I brought you here to serve me. Slaves can be punished, you know, and believe me, I won't be as gentle as Aurora is. Granted I don't expect you to know the intricacies of the dungeon, but even you ought to be able to handle a two-tail. Pay attention." She grabbed the whip from Rita's hands and with a fast, efficient whoosh, laid a trail of pink across the man's arse, making him flinch and moan, then she grabbed Rita's hand and yanked her down until she could lay her palm against the bulge in the PVC at the man's crotch. She brought the two-tail down across his bum again. Rita gasped at the feel of the man's cock surging against her palm and was immediately reminded of the pleasure she felt when Aurora had spanked her.

"There. You see. He can endure it just fine." She handed the two-tail back to Rita. "And when he can't, then I'll fuck him."

The first smack against the exposed bottom made Rita's stomach churn, and for the tiniest of seconds, she thought she might be sick, but instead something amazing happened. Her pussy trembled, and a surge of power moved up through her chest, shoving at her nipples. She brought the two-tail down again and heard Vivienne sigh. "That's right, give him what he deserves. Imagine what a cunt he is to take advantage like that, to betray my trust."

Rita found herself thinking of Vivienne's chastity belt, of Edward standing by not even trying to stop her, of Edward who got her into this mess in the first place, of Edward who only minutes ago had his cock buried to the hilt in Vivienne's cunt. And the two-tail came down with such venom that the man uttered a muffled cry inside his suit. Instinctively she reached to feel his crotch. Apparently the pain had not taken away from the pleasure. The man felt as though his cock would burst through the PVC. Vivienne positively squirmed with delight. Then to Rita's surprise, she lifted her toga, exposing her bare pussy. The dungeon guard who had brought her the chair helped her to her feet and into a mean-looking strap-on.

Rita's heart was in her throat as Vivienne shed the toga

completely and moved into position wearing nothing but the strap-on. The man's tight nether hole clenched and unclenched almost as if he anticipated what would come next. "Well?" Vivienne stroked the strap-on. "Lubricate it for me."

Rita dropped to her knees and began to deep throat the appendage, but stopped abruptly when Vivienne clouted her across the top of the head. "Not the strap-on, you stupid cow, him. Get his arse ready for me."

The man's bottom was now bright red. Though he couldn't speak, he must surely be able to hear, and it seemed to Rita as though he were suddenly straining backward, thrusting his butt out toward her. But then it was easy enough to imagine all sorts of weird things under the circumstances. There was no imagining the clenching and unclenching of his lovely back hole. She suckled two fingers until they were dripping saliva, then spat against his anus and began to massage around it, teasing it open ever so slightly at first with alternating finger tips. The man moaned and clenched his crimson arse cheeks, which she took for encouragement and thrust her middle finger home. There was definitely moaning now. As she stretched him and massaged him, he wriggled and thrust back against her hand.

The two-tail came down hard against the man's ass, causing Rita to jump back and catch her breath. "You keep quiet, you twat," Vivienne ordered the man. "You're being punished, and you know you deserve it." She smacked him again and nodded for Rita to continue.

Rita had just inserted a second finger and was scissoring back and forth inside his anus when there was yet another loud zipping sound. Vivienne pulled the whole bottom half of the man's suit down around his ankles, and his erection popped free as though it were spring loaded. Then she handed Rita the two-tail, pushed her aside and bore into the man's anus with the strap-on. He bucked, grunted, and gasped. With one hand, she clamped down on the underside of his penis with her thumb and growled. "You'll come when I give you permission and not before." Then she nodded to the two-tail. "Use it on his balls. He's a bad boy. He deserves his punishment."

Rita did as she was told, very gently at first until Vivienne cuffed the back of her head again, making her teeth rattle. The next time she smacked him harder and his penis got even bigger, if that were possible.

"That's a girl. Smack those distended full sacks. Make them even more uncomfortable." Vivienne grunted between thrusts. "Make him pay for what he's done. Make him hold it till it hurts. Smack him again, now suck his cock. That's right, take him in your mouth, all the way, torture him. Make him pay."

The whole situation was insane. Vivienne was fucking some poor schmuck up the arse with a strap-on—the arse Rita had just fluffed, and she was whipping his balls and sucking his cock. And even more insane, with her other hand, she was finger fucking herself like there was no tomorrow.

Vivienne's laughter wormed its way into her head. "That's right. Punishment makes your pussy wet whether you're taking it or giving it, doesn't it girl?"

The man was in a frenzy, grunting and thrusting and half howling his frustration like some muffled, strangled animal trapped inside the PVC suit. And the more he wanted it, the more turned on Rita was.

"You want him to fuck your little hot pussy, don't you, Rita? Don't you?"

"Yes," Rita gasped pulling away from his cock. "Yes I want him to fuck me."

Vivienne's laughter rang through the dungeon and echoed off the walls. "That's too bad, girl, because he's not for you." She pulled out with such force that the man howled frustration or pain. It wasn't clear which. She ripped the strap-on free, then in a well-practiced move, she undid the man's shackles and shoved him back into the chair where he landed on his wounded bottom with a hard grunt and a sharp intake of breath. "No, he's definitely not for you, Rita. As I said, you may punish him. In fact, I have no doubt that he deserves punishment from you. But I'm the one who fucks him. He's all mine. Aren't you Edward?" She turned her back on Rita and straddled the gasping Edward, easing herself down onto his cock with a breathy whimper. "But you can watch while he makes me come. Then you can watch while he comes, would you like that, dear?"

Rita saw everything through a cold red haze that made it feel like her head would explode. But in spite of the anger and humiliation, the watching still made her pussy ache to be satisfied. Vivienne hammered and ground against Edward with angry grunts that sounded more like rage than pleasure. And after her first orgasm, she unzipped Edward's eye slots, and giggled almost girlishly. "You can come now Edward."

And he did come, lifting Vivienne from the chair, wrapping her legs around him, and hammering her against the wall with so much force that Rita feared he'd break her spine, and yet she came, and kept coming until Edward was spent and dropped to the floor on his knees. And then Rita came, her orgasm racking her like some strange burning torture, all of which she experienced through a mist of angry tears.

Chapter Twenty

RECOGNITION DIDN'T COME NEARLY as often as Owen would have liked, but occasionally it came just at the right time, and today happened to be one of those times. "Thanks luv. You're a lifesaver." He gave the house cleaner of the flat complex where Rita lived just enough of a kiss on the cheek to make her think she was the only woman in the world. "I'll let myself out when I'm done. Here, this is for your help. Rita will be so relieved that the story will now be in the next issue, thanks to you." He handed her twenty quid, after all, he could afford it. Then he added, "She might even mention you in the story, you know, a little thank you at the end. Would you like that, honey?"

He wasn't sure how much English the woman understood, but she understood twenty quid, and she understood he was hot and paying attention to her. That was enough. It was usually enough. Besides, the woman had nice tits.

Inside Rita's flat, he pulled the door to behind him. He didn't know how much time he had. The last time she called him it was to say that the information she had got in Kent was paying off and she'd be out of the office for a while. Frankly he didn't care where the hell she was. He didn't need her any more.

He slipped off his shoes and dug in his pocket for latex gloves. He wasn't about to leave fingerprints. Who knew what could happen? In the lounge next to the window he booted the computer and waited impatiently for it to come up. He had checked her PC at the office, but not with much hope, since she was never there these days. He didn't know what difference it made, since Vivienne had basically already written the story. He wished she would give it to him. He didn't have a good feeling about putting something in the magazine without time to go over it and add his personal touches, but in the end it wouldn't matter. The money was in his account, and he was willing to let Vivienne put whatever she wanted into *Talkabout*. After all, it wasn't his magazine. Any story on The Mount would be a coup for him. Besides, hadn't Lorelei promised it would be an award-winning exposé? It was win-win the way he saw it. Add to that getting to fuck Lorelei a couple of times a week and life couldn't get much better. Who knew, maybe Vivienne would be so grateful that he might even get inside her sexy little cunt. His cock felt heavy at the thought.

He was surprised to find nothing on Rita's computer was encrypted. There were no passwords, no secret files, no nothing. It was amazingly generic really, other than all the basic research on The Mount, the same information he already had. She had recently accessed several vintage porn sites. He quickly keyed the sites into his Blackberry chuckling to himself. He would have never figured Miss All-Work-and-No-Play for an Internet porn fan.

After an hour of searching, his frustration levels were peaking, and if he had been at home, he would have thrown something. He knew a fair amount about computers, and he had expected that whatever he found would be encrypted. Vivienne didn't seem interested in what he found as long as he found something. And he hated the thought of disappointing Vivienne.

But it was beginning to look like disappoint Vivienne he would, because wherever Rita kept the information she had gathered about The Mount, it wasn't here or in the office. He was just getting ready to close down when he noticed an incoming email. He hadn't thought about emails! Quickly he pulled up the new message. It was from Rita's mother.

Rita,

This has got to stop. Why are you keeping me away? How long will you punish me for the past? I'm your mother, no matter how much you pretend otherwise, and I love you. Please at least email. We can work this out.

A quick look down through Rita's emails revealed a good half of them were from her mother, and none of them answered. He wondered what had happened that would keep a girl from her mother, especially a girl that he grudgingly had to admit, had so much potential. But that wouldn't interest Vivienne.

He reached down to shut off the computer, and his Blackberry slipped from its case onto the floor. As he bent to pick it up, he noticed a memory stick lying on the under frame of the computer table, completely hidden from sight. His heart skipped a beat, as he fumbled it and dropped it beneath the table. On his hands and knees, he dug it out, then stuck it into the port. And there it was! Pages and pages of notes on The Mount, all written by date, almost as though it were a journal. He read with his pulse racing.

Leo never fucks his pets, in fact he treats them all with the greatest of kindness, but he chooses which pets can fuck which, and he watches. Having him watch while Brutus fucked me was almost as arousing as the sex itself. I don't know what any of these people do when they aren't pets. Pets don't talk, so we only know what we can communicate with our bodies.

Owen unzipped his trousers to give his engorging cock a little breathing room. Jesus! Who'd have thought Little Miss Pert Tits had such a wild streak? He read on, stroking his lengthening penis with a latexed hand.

I don't fully understand what initiation into The Mount involves. So far it seems to involve lots of sex, good sex, sometimes scary sex. But there's so much more. I know there is, but I can't seem to get anyone to talk to me. The vintage porn sites seem to indicate that The Mount may have been around for a very long time. Not the restaurant, but the society, or cult or whatever it is.

A secret sex cult? Well, everyone in London had heard those rumors, but could they possibly be true? And was it possible that Vivienne would give him anything as juicy as this to publish.

At first I was afraid, hand-cuffed to the handlebars of the Harley, alone in the dark with both my holes filled. But when I calmed down a bit, I realized I could not only come easily in this predicament, but I could come repeatedly, and every orgasm built on the last, stronger than the one before. It was like I was on some incredible drug, the more I orgasmed, the more powerful I felt, and the more powerful I felt, the more mind-blowing the orgasm. I don't know where I was when Morgan returned, but it wasn't anywhere on this planet. When he returned, he took out the dildo and fucked me, and I think he must have felt what I was feeling. He came so hard I thought he'd break bones, and he kept coming. The sex was wild and feral. His leopard tattoo seemed amazingly appropriate under the circumstances.

Owen downloaded the files with one hand, while the other worked his cock. He had just put everything back in its place and was about to shut down, when he had an idea. He went back to the emails from Rita's mother and copied them, still stroking his cock.

When he shut down the computer, he could hear the cleaning woman just outside the door. He did his best to stuff himself back in his trousers, then opened the door and motioned her inside.

She liked the kissing. She definitely had the tongue for it. She didn't seem to notice the latex gloves, or maybe she thought it was just kinky. At first she protested when he pushed her back against the door and kneaded her tits. But it wasn't much of a protest, and when he sucked and nipped her through her white T-shirt until her nipples swelled like they'd drill through the fabric, she whimpered softly and reached for his fly. With slight of hand in which he prided himself, he slipped a condom over his cock. After all, he didn't know where this chick was from.

Under her skirt, beneath practical cotton knickers, her pussy was shaved smooth and slick. It gripped at his fingers like a sucking mouth. When he shoved aside the crotch and pushed into her, her eyelids fluttered and she gasped some gibberish he didn't recognize before she wrapped her legs around him and braced herself against the door frame.

He thrust so hard, he feared he might break the door, but he couldn't help it, not after what he'd just read. The cleaner's lovely tits bounced and bounced with each thrust, and she kept saying, "Is good, so good. Is good, so good."

After he came, he disposed of the condom and the gloves in the cleaner's rubbish bin, kissed her on the cheek and, feeling rather generous, he slipped her another twenty quid.

Once he was out of Rita's flat and back in his car, he called Lorelei on the designated mobile and arranged a meeting at the Ritz, giving himself enough time to get back to his flat for a shower and a freshen-up. After what he had just found, he figured he was guaranteed a very good fuck from Lorelei. Things just kept getting better and better.

Chapter Twenty-One

SLEEP NEVER CAME EASILY for Rita lying on the thick carpeted floor at the foot of Vivienne's enormous bed. Perhaps it was knowing that Edward was always in that bed with the bitch. But then so were several other people. It was humiliating on the bad days to lie there listening to the wet sounds of sex, and instead of being outraged by her obvious ostracizing, being so horny that there was no rest until she came on her fingers, often more than once. In spite of Vivienne's instructions that she was to allow herself to be fucked by whoever wanted her, Vivienne had angrily refused all those who had asked for her company and made her watch without touching herself while she offered them any of her other servants to satisfy their needs. Some of them got off on being watched by Rita. Most didn't care as long as they got fucked.

Edward, for the most part, ignored her, hidden behind his golden mask and often trussed up in whatever costume suited Vivienne's fancy at the moment.

It was the first peaceful night in Vivienne's flat since Rita became the woman's slave. Vivienne had spent the evening at The Mount, making an appearance and doing her normal working duties. She returned to her apartment complaining of a headache, for which she took two sleeping pills and a glass of fizz. Then she shooed every-one out of her room except for Edward, making venomous threats toward anyone stupid enough to disturb her. A few had headed off to various guest rooms in the flat. Most had sought out other more hospitable accommodations. Rita had found a place on the floor of the lounge in a pile of pillows—slaves were not allowed on the furniture unless they were invited. It was the most comfortable bed she had had since her arrival, and still she couldn't sleep.

Try though she might she couldn't shut out thoughts of Edward cozied up with Vivienne. Every little night sound caught her imagination. Was Edward fucking her quietly, secretly, folded around her in a spoon position, his hands cupping her exquisite breasts? Or maybe his face was buried between her legs; maybe he was licking fizz from Vivienne's girlie cup as he had done to her.

Whatever he was doing, he would be without a mask. The thought twisted her insides to some weird hybrid of pain and arousal. Had she not endured all this just for a glimpse of his face? That was stupid! She thrashed amid the pillows trying to get comfortable. Of course she had endured all this for the story, and whatever feelings she might have had for Edward, he certainly didn't return. She was a game, nothing more. Just like Vivienne had said.

She rose and tiptoed into the kitchen for a glass of water. She was all about getting her exposé, she reminded herself. What better time to do a little research than when Vivienne was in a drugged sleep.

The flat was enormous, but she had been there long enough to know her way around. She tiptoed down the hallway to the study, which was on the river side of the flat, and a long way from Vivienne's room. Even without sleeping pills and fizz, one could have an orgy in the study and Vivienne would never hear. Rita had massaged Vivienne's feet there once while the woman took care of paperwork. She had promised herself she'd come back to check things out first chance she got.

Quietly she squeezed between double doors made of some exotic wood with a swirling pattern in the grain, pulling them shut behind her. The study was almost as big as Leo's, but much less masculine. The city was never really dark and streetlights bathed the room in silver glow, so much so that she could almost read by it. In spite of the fact that the building had been renovated when The Mount sprang into existence, the study had the feel of a place untouched by time, and that intrigued Rita. The antique wooden file cabinets were locked, and so was the big oak desk. She craned her neck to take in all the shelves of books. It was like looking for a needle in a haystack even if she knew what she was looking for, and she didn't.

In the pale light, her attention was drawn to the marble sculpture that rose like a bas relief from floor to ceiling against the back section of wall. It was the familiar motif of Venus and Mars wrapped around each other in a conjugal embrace. Mars's armor and weapons were strewn across a woodland glade. He wore nothing but a beautiful erection, which he was about to thrust between Venus's open thighs. The thin fabric of Venus's gown had been pushed up over her hips to reveal the sculpted details of her vulva exquisitely open and ready for penetration.

With one hand, Mars fondled her full breasts, which had tumbled free from the top of her gown, while the other supported her bottom in his efforts to lift her onto him. The sculpture had the fine attention to detail Rita had seen in the works of Bernini. Mars's fingertips seemed to press into the soft flesh of Venus's breasts and buttocks. Rita could almost see the moisture dewing between Venus's labia. The work had the patina of old marble, and the power to elicit arousal, like everything else at The Mount.

Rita couldn't resist touching the sculpture, knowing that she would be well punished for it if she were caught. She ran her hand up over Venus's flank, traced the shape of her open vulva, then turned her attention to Mars, running her fingers down the flat of his stomach, catching her breath at the exquisite detail of his pubic curls. She couldn't resist. She slid her hand down and closed it around the shaft of his penis, moving her fingers over the cool marble until her thumb came to stroke the curved rim just below the head.

There was a click that sounded unbelievably loud in the silence. She jumped back and caught her breath, just as the whole panel on which the sculpture was mounted swung open to reveal a small, wooden chamber lit by the flicker of gas light.

When she was in control of her racing heart again, she cautiously stepped inside. The room was not much wider than her bathroom at home, but longer, both sides lined with leather-bound volumes. She leaned close and squinted at one of them. The gold gothic lettering read, *The Laws and Statutes of the Covens of The Mount, London Coven*. It was dated 1898. From what she could tell, the earliest volumes dated back to the late 16th century. A careful glance inside revealed that the older volumes were all in Latin. As she walked slowly down the length of the room perusing the shelves, the books became histories, again the earlier ones in Latin. There were volumes upon volumes, all labeled *The History of The Mount, London Coven*, followed by dates.

Her pulse was like a drum roll in her ears, and her lungs struggled to get enough oxygen. This was exactly the break she had been looking for, and yet, how could it possibly be?

She tiptoed to the back of the room, where there was an oak chair and table on which one of the volumes lay open next to a bottle of ink and a nibbed pen. Scarcely trusting herself, she squinted down at the open page to find handwritten in italic script:

> *In spite of all that Vivienne demands of her, the initiate, Rita Ellison Holly, continues to conduct herself in a manner that none can question. The rest of the council grow tired of her prolonged suffering, and yet there is nothing we can do other than bring the matter before the Elders and risk everything we've worked so hard for. Rome still considers us little more than a backwater coven, primitive and barbaric, hardly worthy to be considered a*

coven at all. And if we were to make our situation known,
perhaps we would only confirm their opinion of us. But
then again, perhaps they are right.

Beneath was a pen and ink drawing of a sleeping woman
stretched on her side. The shift she wore had fallen away to expose
her full breasts, nipples tight—perhaps from something in the dream
world. The hem of the garment was scrunched around her hips just
high enough to intimate what lay at the juncture of her thighs. With
a start, Rita realized she was looking at a drawing of herself curled at
the foot of Vivienne's bed.

It was signed, *Edward Darcy Ellison.*

"What are you doing here?" Edward's voice came from behind
her, but before she could do more than jump, he commanded,
"Don't turn around. Stay put, and close your eyes."

She did as he said. There was a click and the sound of the
panel closing.

"Sit down." She obeyed, not sure how much longer she could
have stood anyway.

He approached her from behind and slipped a black silk
handkerchief over her eyes, tying it securely against the back of
her head. "I'm not masked," he said, "so you'll have to be. It'll be
like old times."

For a long moment there was silence, so much so that she wasn't
sure he was still in the room with her. Then at last he spoke with a
heavy sigh. "It's true then, you are planning to do an exposé, and this
whole thing has all been about your story."

Before she could make an excuse, he continued. "Oh, I don't
blame you. I would do the same if I were you, especially after all
that's happened. But I had hoped..." His voice drifted off, and once
again she wasn't sure he was still there in the room.

"Hoped what?"

He forced a laugh that sounded almost painful. "Surely you must know what I hope."

"No, I don't. I have no idea what you hope. I just assumed you were all bored and I was the entertainment, then behind closed doors while you fuck each other, you and Vivienne have a good laugh at my expense."

His hand came down so hard on the table next to her that she could feel the breeze it generated. She yelped and practically fell out of the chair. "You can't possibly believe that, Rita." Suddenly he was kneeling in front of her, grasping her hands in his. "You can't honestly believe that I would rather be with her, that I would—"

Her laugh soured at the back of her mouth. "What am I supposed to believe, Edward? Vivienne couldn't wait to get you off to her bedroom to fuck her when we first got here, even before you two tricked me in the dungeon. It all seems pretty clear to me."

"Jesus, Rita! What are you talking about? I was hauled off to the dungeon and prepared for her little joke as soon as I was turned over to May. Whoever it was in the bedroom with her, it sure as hell wasn't me." She felt him move and figured he had sat down on the floor next to her. "As for the dungeon," he continued, "I had no choice. My part in this deal in order to stay close to you, is that I am to fuck her when she wants it, and that I am to show my appreciation for her kind condescension by coming when I'm expected to.

"And in the meantime," his voice trembled with anger, "just in case I decide I might want to sneak off with you, she's taken care of that too." He stood quickly and she heard the swish of clothing, then he guided her hand to his bare belly. There was a sharp intake of breath as he guided her fingers to rest, first against the hard leather and metal belted low around his waist, then still lower to the tight-fitting metal that caged his penis and balls unyieldingly.

With a groan that sounded feral and desperate, she tried to pull away, but he held her hand against the cage of the chastity belt.

"This is my punishment for wanting you." Then he pulled her hand to his lips and kissed it. She could hear his heart beat in the raging of his breath. "This is my punishment for loving you."

He gave his words no time to sink in, no time to find that place inside her that usually did a fair job of separating reality from fantasy. Once again he was on his knees, this time pushing her thighs open, exposing the tender inner flesh to the efforts of his insistent mouth, sucking and nipping and kissing a path toward her pussy.

"No Edward." She tried to push him away. "Don't do this. I can't reciprocate and you won't be able to come and—"

"Shshsh." He rose from his explorations and silenced her protests with a kiss. "I can cope with the chastity belt. I've done it before." He slipped a hand down over her pubis, pushed the slave gown aside and entered her with his middle finger. Her pussy grasped hungrily at him and she shifted her hips back and forth against him almost involuntarily.

"There, you see?" He whispered against her nape. "I can feel how badly you need it after all these nights when you've had to lie there alone on the floor with no one to hold you." He slipped his other hand inside the yielding top of the gown and cupped her breasts in turn, stroking her nipples with the pad of his thumb. "With no one to help you orgasm. And when I have to come with Vivienne," he nuzzled his way down to her breasts and suckled, then ran his tongue around her areolae, "I think of you lying there on the floor masturbating, and I imagine pushing my cock into your pussy and emptying all my pent-up desire into you." He inserted another finger into her cunt and stroked her clit in tight circles with his thumb, causing her to gasp and squirm beneath his touch. "I'm not sure the whole world could contain my desire for you, Rita Holly."

As he kissed and fondled his way down over her belly, his grunts and groans were the sounds of pleasure and not the frustration she had expected. "My God," he whispered as he lowered his face to nuzzle in between her legs. "I've dreams about the way you smell, the way you taste, oh such lovely dreams." His tongue flicked over her distended clit and she whimpered and lifted her arse off the chair, offering him her cunt like some animal in heat, and he responded in kind, licking and nipping at her swollen labia until her lips pouted their full invitation to his advances. Then he lifted her feet onto his shoulders so she could bear down on him, positioning her bottom exactly where he wanted it. Then he ate her like a feast, his own little grunts and gasps defying the restraints of the chastity belt as she humped his mouth shamelessly until there was no breath left in her, no strength, no thought that didn't involve his mouth on her pussy. But instead of backing off when her cunt began to shudder with orgasm, he pressed in closer, opening his mouth wide, as though he would devour her vulva whole, raking across the folds and valleys of her with his teeth. He wriggled his tongue deeper into her, and drew his lips tight around the hard rise of her clit, keeping her whole body at a plateau where orgasm thrummed nearly continually over her distended clit and up her spine.

He moaned as though the pleasure were his own, cupping her buttocks in his hands, drawing her still closer, stroking her anus with an insistent finger, which became bolder in its pressings until it fucked her nether hole like a penis while the waves of pleasure washed over her again and again.

—◦◦◦—

Sometime later, she didn't know how long, but when the world calmed around her again, she lay on the wooden floor wrapped in his arms, the hard press of his chastity belt against her thigh. She struggled to move, but he pulled her back to him.

"She'll find us."

"She can't come in here. Only I have access. And it's still early. She never rises before noon, especially not after she's taken sleeping pills." He kissed her ear and cupped her breast. "We can stay just a little while longer."

"You wrote that, and did the sketch?" She nodded to where she assumed the table was, but it could have just as easily been toward the door.

"Yes. The sketch, well I come from a long line of artsy folk. As for the rest, I'm the historian of the London Coven."

"Then you're witches?"

"Of course not. When we chose to call ourselves covens it was an act of defiance really, a way of thumbing our noses at the church, at the powers that be, at the powers that wanted to control what a person believes, what a person does with his or her body, who a person makes love with." He chuckled softly. "Of course no one knew any of this but us. We were a secret society, and still are after all these years."

"How many years?"

"Lots. Possibly even more than any of us know."

"And this isn't the only coven."

"There are others, all organized the same, all overseen by a high council. "Then there are members who aren't on the council?"

"Yes, people from all walks of life, bankers, scientists, house-wives, lorry drivers."

She took a second to let the thought of a housewife domi-natrix sink in before she spoke. "Vivienne called me Rita Ellison Holly. Why?"

"Because I recruited you, you share my name. It's always been that way with The Mount. I can give you a basic overview of the history and how we work if you'd like. You'll get all that when you're finished with the initiation, but if you're not planning to hang around, then you might as well know now."

"I don't understand. I've researched everyone here at The Mount, and granted I couldn't find much, but I found a little something on everyone. Everyone but you. For you, I found nothing. It's like you don't exist."

"I don't. At least not right now." He forced a pained laugh. "But I keep hoping that will change soon."

"That makes no sense. How can you not exist? You're right here, next to me in my arms, and—"

"And you've never seen my face."

His words unsettled her, made muscles that had nothing to do with sex knot. She remembered Vivienne referring to him as the monster behind the mask, and in spite of the warmth of the room, she felt cold.

He placed his fingers against her mouth. "We won't speak of this, not now. But I hope the time will come when we can."

She snuggled back against him, reveling in the shape of his body, wondering what it would be like to be with him without the chastity belt, to stay wrapped in his arms all night. "Why are you telling me all this if you know I'm going to write an exposé?"

She felt him shrug against her. "Maybe it's time we were exposed. Maybe we deserve nothing better."

She didn't know what to say, so she said nothing.

"And just so you know, you were never only the entertainment. Everyone who has been with you loves you. We all love you. We want you to be a part of us."

She struggled to breathe. "If you love me, then why don't you just be with me? Why do you let her do this to you?"

"I can't tell you that yet, but I promise if you finish the initiation, she'll no longer hold sway, and then we can be together. I know that sounds like an excuse, believe me, I know, but it's the best I can give you right now." He placed a soft kiss on the back of her neck. "Please trust me. Please just try to hang on just a little longer."

"And the exposé?"

His sigh was warm against her neck. "Darling, nothing you

could do would make me love you less, but consider this: I'm not the only one who will be hurt by this exposé, and the person who will probably be hurt by it the least is Vivienne."

He helped her to her feet and walked her back to her pallet of pillows on the floor. "Get some sleep, my love, and I promise you, we'll get through this."

———

It was nearly three days before they had the chance to speak again, and that only fleetingly, but it was enough. Vivienne was checking out the wine cellar for a special vintage for some VIP arriving unexpectedly, and Lorelei was called away on business. May, who was supposed to be keeping an eye on her, was in the shower. Rita caught Edward on his way to the history vault. With trembling fingers, she passed him the flash card, anxious to be rid of it. "This is for you. Alex dropped by the house and picked it up for me."

For a second he stared down at the tiny piece of plastic and metal before closing his fingers around it in a grip so tight his knuckles shown white in the afternoon light. "Are you sure?"

"I'm sure." She swallowed the lump in her throat. "All I ever really wanted was to see your face, and I don't want the first look I see on it to be disappointment."

He scooped her into his arms and kissed her, whispering in a breathless gasp against her ear, "I love you, Rita Holly."

Then they heard the front door open and Vivienne complaining about the mess the wine cellar was in, and they both fled their separate ways, Rita seeking the far corner of the flat, hoping Vivienne wouldn't holler for her until she had her emotions under control again.

Chapter Twenty-Two

"No one will believe this story was written by any of the *Talkabout* staff," Owen said. It took him a second to realize that the harsh rasping sound was his breath, and he was now wishing like hell that he'd given the steak and kidney pie a miss at lunch. Indigestion was the last thing he had expected when he arrived at the hotel room that had become the venue for his regular rendezvous with Lorelei.

He sat stiffly at the table staring at the monitor of his laptop, but no matter how long he glared at the words of the document, they didn't set any better with his internal editor. His cock, which until minutes ago had been ready and anxious to play, was now unusually limp. He forced his attention back to Lorelei, but even her outrageous curves swathed in mauve silk couldn't make the story on the monitor look any better.

She was saying, "The magazine will, of course, be given a chance to retract the story and offer an apology to The Mount. I'm sure they won't want to take us on in court."

"I don't understand. Why are you giving me this story if you're then going to turn around and sue *Talkabout* for printing it?"

"It's not for you to understand, Owen. All you need to know is that it serves our purpose."

He shoved a sweaty hand through his hair and bit his lip until it hurt. "This will end my career, you know that?"

"Oh come on, darling, don't pout." She fondled his tie, tugging on it until it reminded him disturbingly of a noose, then she giggled softly. "You've been well compensated, in lots of ways." She nodded to his crotch, which suddenly felt extremely vulnerable. Then she added, "You've made sure Rita Holly gets the credit for the story?"

"Yes." He pulled the tie away from her and tugged at his collar, which seemed unusually tight. "Just like you asked, but I'm her editor, no editor with half a brain would print this story."

Lorelei rolled her eyes. "Oh please, Owen, like you care about the magazine's reputation. We know how much you hate your boss, how much you think this job is beneath someone of your talent. What better way to get even with the bastard? Don't you see the beauty of the plan?" She opened the chic leather briefcase on the dressing table and rummaged through it. "It's nothing personal, and anyway it won't be you that we'll be threatening, will it?"

"Well, Rita Holly sure as hell doesn't have any money. She's a nobody."

"That's right, she's a nobody. She's irrelevant. She's just serving a purpose."

"Like I am."

"Yes. Like you are. Only she doesn't know it. You do. You've known it from the beginning." She pulled a file folder from the case and handed it to him.

"What's this?"

"The lease to your villa in Majorca. Yours to enjoy as long as you live. A bonus for your full cooperation. You do like Majorca, don't you? I took the liberty of including a few photos."

And she had. There was a pool, a view of the sea. There was a master bedroom bigger than the whole *Talkabout* office suite. And in spite of the situation in which he found himself, he suddenly had a hard-on.

She handed him a first-class plane ticket. "You fly tomorrow, before the magazine hits the streets. Your accounts here have been closed and the money transferred." She handed him a sealed envelope. "Here are your bank documents."

For a second, he could do nothing but stare down at the new life

The Mount has so effortlessly, and efficiently, arranged for him. At last, he managed a breathy half-whisper. "How did you do this? How did you get my information?"

"That's not your concern, but you would do well to remember just how easily it was all taken care of." She closed the briefcase with a resounding snap. "What is your concern is this. That you never set foot on British soil again."

Before the shock of her words could even knot his stomach, she unzipped the silk dress and stepped out of it. "You are never to speak to anyone about anything that has gone on between us." She waved a dismissive hand before kneeling on the floor in front of him and unzipping his trousers. "Oh, it's all right if you mention the time you came to The Mount with Rita. People saw you there, after all." She eased his cock out of his trousers and gave it a deep-throated suck that made the whole encounter seem even more surreal than it already was.

Then she pulled away with an ice cream cone lick to the length of him, and slipped out of her bra. "You are never to mention to anyone where you got the money. Is that clear?"

He nodded. He'd didn't much like bossy women, but God, she was so exquisite, and such a delicious fuck, even when she was manipulating his life like it was some sort of computer game. He forced his attention back to her lecture. "Good. As far as the rest of the world is concerned, your long-lost auntie died and left you her fortune." She cupped her heavy tits around his cock, and in a mix of horror and arousal, not quite sure if his luck was good or bad, he began to thrust. How could he help himself?

She chuckled softly. "There, you see? The whole arrangement is growing on you, isn't it?" As if to emphasize her words, she began to tongue the head of his cock, creating a seesaw of irresistible sensations each time he thrust.

"I have…" Lick, thrust, "family here…" Lick, thrust, suck. "Friends," he grunted, cupping the sides of her tits to tighten their grip, feeling like his balls would burst from the weight of their load, and wondering how he could be aroused when his world was crumbling around him…sort of.

"Your friends can come to you." Lick. Lick. Thrust. "Remember," suck, thrust, "you can afford to fly them to your villa whenever you want." She stood and slid out of her knickers in a move that was as business-like as her handling of the contents of the briefcase, and Jesus, it was such a turn-on! The woman was destroying his career, and she would, no doubt make him come, in the process, and he would absolutely not resist. Was that sick, or what?

"Vivienne's given you a win-win situation." He returned his attention to the mouth that had been sucking his cock and tried to concentrate on her words. "Surely you can see that, Owen? She even arranged to have your belongings shipped to you. And my cunt." With her long mauve nails, she opened her slit, making certain he got a good look at the juicy pink swell of her, then she rubbed her thumb rhythmically over the growing nub of her clit. "My very horny cunt is all yours until the limo comes to take you to the airport." With that she positioned her pout above his cock and wriggled down onto him, squeezing and kneading with her girlie muscles until he couldn't think straight, until it was all he could do to hold his wad.

"But remember, Owen dear," she leaned forward and bit his earlobe almost causing pain, "if you break any of these simple rules Vivienne has set for you," her voice became a humid whisper, "you'll lose it all as quickly as you gained it." She chuckled softly. "The Mount giveth, and The Mount taketh away." She ground her bottom into his lap and gripped him so tightly that he cried out, unable to breathe, as he shot his load in gut-wrenching spurts.

When he was done, she grabbed his hair and pulled him into a deep, dangerous kiss, her tongue snaking inside his mouth like she owned it. Then she pulled away and wiped mauve lipstick from his parched lips. "There. You see, Owen? Money, sex, a story that will rock London. All your dreams are coming true, just like you always wanted."

Chapter Twenty-Three

"GET DRESSED." MAY SPOKE like she was talking to a naughty child. She handed Rita jeans and a T-shirt and a hooded jacket along with some plain-Jane underwear, then she left, pulling the door shut behind her. Rita heard the key turn in the lock.

She had been changing Vivienne's bed, a task the woman delighted in giving her on the mornings after the orgy had been particularly good, in spite of the fact that there was a full cleaning staff. It was only then that Rita noticed the silence, and her skin crawled up her spine. Vivienne's flat was never silent, usually not even in the middle of the night. She wasn't certain, but it felt like she was alone in the house. She had never been locked in before. There was no need. She knew well enough that if she left, the initiation was over, and she had failed. Vivienne would have loved nothing more, but if she had endured this much, she wasn't about to give the bitch the satisfaction.

Feeling a rising sense of unease in her chest, she stripped out of her slave dress and put on the street clothes, which felt oddly confining after the days in nothing but the loose cotton shift. She folded the shift neatly and continued with her work. When the bed was changed and the room tidied, she sat down on the floor at the foot of the bed and waited.

The shadows were lengthening when the lock turned in the door, and to her surprise two guards, whom she had never seen before, came into the room.

"Rita Holly?" the big one said in a resonant voice that reminded her of a street preacher.

"Yes?"

"You are to come with us."

With one behind and one in front of her, they marched her down the back stairway to the level of the main restaurant, then past the kitchen and down the long stairs to the Presence Chamber. With each step the knot in her stomach grew colder and tighter. Something was wrong. It couldn't be more obvious if it were written all over the walls in big red letters.

Inside the room, all chairs on the dais were occupied. No one was dressed for the occasion. In fact they all looked as though someone had grabbed them in the middle of whatever it was they were doing. Alex was in sweats with a towel around his neck, looking as though he had had a work-out but no shower. Leo was in khakis with grass stains on both knees. Both Aurora and Morgan looked as though they had just dropped in from the banking district. Lorelei and Vivienne looked like they were dressed for a day of shopping. And Edward looked especially incongruous in the dapper golden mask and jeans with an untucked cotton shirt. No one spoke. No one smiled.

With a wave from Vivienne, the two guards stepped back, and Rita was left alone in the middle of the big room. "I'm guessing you know what this is about," Vivienne said. It was only then that Rita noticed the copy of *Talkabout* magazine resting open across her lap, and the knot in her stomach clenched still tighter.

Vivienne stood and came to pace in front of her, magazine in hand. "Personally, I would have thought you'd at least have the decency to leave before this, this piece of rubbish hit the stand. But then you've never had any shame, have you?" She came to stand in front of Rita and began to read from the magazine.

Drugs, sex cult, white slavery, endangered species gourmet, we've all heard the wild rumors and the gossip about that enigmatic dance club and restaurant, The Mount. And who is to say what's actually true, since reservations are rarer than hen's teeth, and a night out at The Mount would set most people back a couple months' salary.

She waved her hand. "But never mind any of that, let's skip over to the good part, shall we?" She ruffled through the pages and began to read again.

There in front of the High Council, I was stripped and two of the bouncers were ordered to "make me come."

Suddenly Rita felt light-headed, and her face felt as though it would burst into flames.

"Oh it gets better, much better." Vivienne began to pace again and read as though she were auditioning for a role on the West End.

There were at least a dozen of us, all naked, all wearing collars, all forbidden to speak. Then Leo, the bearded one they call The Zoo Keeper, singled me out along with one of the male pets, whom he called Aralias and ordered him to have intercourse with me while he observed and masturbated. He always watched when—

"Stop it." Rita's voice sounded breathless, like she'd been running. "I didn't write that. I've written better than that since I was twelve."

Vivienne turned on her and slapped her so hard she nearly lost her balance. The two guards came to her aid as she struggled to right herself and to hold back the tears that were as much from rage and frustration as they were from the sting of the slap.

"Of course you wrote this," Vivienne roared. "How stupid do you think we are? Who else would have known these things? Who?" She shook the mangled magazine in Rita's face, then calmed herself and offered a smile that would have sweetened honey. "Of course The Mount will demand a retraction and an apology. You, well, you're hardly worth suing, are you?" She heaved a sigh. "The worst I can do to you is banish you from The Mount and end this travesty of your initiation. If everyone had listened to me in the first place none of this would have happened."

"She didn't write it, Vivienne." The room was suddenly silent, and Edward got to his feet, holding up the flash card Rita had given him. "She gave me this almost a week ago."

"Oh for fuck's sake, Edward, how stupid can you be?" Vivienne snapped her fingers and Lorelei stood, rattling several sheets of paper. "Read it," Vivienne ordered.

Lorelei cleared her throat and began to read as though she were reading a poem.

At first I was afraid, hand-cuffed to the handlebars of the Harley, alone in the dark with both my holes filled. But when I calmed down a bit, I realized I could not only come easily in this predicament, but I could come repeatedly, and every orgasm built on the last, every orgasm was stronger than the one before.

Vivienne raised a hand to stop her. "I'm not without my resources, Rita. Surely you didn't think I would trust a journalist into the flock without doing a little research of my own."

"If you'd done a little research, you'd have known breaking and entering is illegal, but I'm sure you didn't do it yourself, did you?"

There was another hard slap across the face, and this time Rita tasted blood.

"You stupid, vile bitch!" Rita lunged, but the guards grabbed her arms and held her tight.

Out of the corner of her eye, Rita saw two more guards move to flank Edward, who nearly catapulted off the dais to get to her, roaring her name like a lion protecting his pride. Vivienne ignored him.

Rita forced a deep breath, straightened herself, and shrugged free of the guards. "You know I didn't write that." She held Vivienne's gaze. "If I had written it your arse would have been nailed to the wall where it belongs." She turned her attention to the rest of the council. "I don't understand any of you. You outnumber her. Why do you let her push you around like a bunch of goddamned sheep? You know she's lying. Surely you know she's lying."

Vivienne tossed the magazine at Rita's feet and returned to her chair on the dais as though she were queen of the universe. "You've all read the evidence. It's time to vote. Shall we?" She sounded like she had just asked the local ladies' club if they wanted tea or coffee. "Leo?"

The big man looked tired and drawn. His gaze was on the space behind Rita. His face was neutral. "Banish her."

Aurora bit her lip and shook her head. "Banish her."

Alex cursed under his breath, his eyes locked on her, then he nodded almost painfully. "Banish her."

And so it went, with each vote feeling like a nail in her coffin, until a sense of betrayal sizzled along her nerve endings, and the knot in her stomach became a clenched fist. Only Edward did not vote. He wasn't given a vote because she was his recruit. She had no doubt he would be well punished after she left. "I'm sorry, Rita," he said very softly. "I'm so, so sorry."

She managed only a step forward before the guards flanked her again. "If you're so sorry, Edward, then vote with your feet. Come with me. Don't let that bitch tell you who you can and can't be with. You can do what you want. You don't have to—"

"Edward? Do what he wants?" Vivienne laughed as though she had just heard the best joke ever. "Afraid not, girl. He's not free to go with you anywhere. I warned you that you would never be able to understand the relationship Edward and I share. But I'll try to boil it down for your simple mind. Edward belongs to me, and he knows it, don't you darling?" With her hand on his shoulder, she pushed him back down in the chair next to her.

And he stayed.

For the first time, Rita felt like the bottom had dropped out of her world. She turned on her heels and fled up the steps, stumbling through a haze of tears. The guards hurried after her until she pushed through the back exit, then she was alone. Out on the street, it was raining, and night was settling on the water-pocked Thames. There was a limo waiting to take her home, but she ignored it. She wanted nothing else to do with The Mount. Ever again.

She had sacrificed her job, her heart, everything, and for what? She had enough money for next month's rent, then after that? Well, she didn't know what after that. At the moment, living rough sounded better than hearing her mother's I told you so when she showed up home broke and miserable.

It was only after she left The Mount that she realized her mobile had been returned to the inside zipper pocket of the jacket, along with her wallet. In her state, she would not have noticed if the mobile hadn't signaled an incoming text. For a second, her spirits lifted. Perhaps it was Edward texting to make things right. She jerked it from her pocket, practically dropping it on the wet pavement. It wasn't Edward. It wasn't a number she recognized. It simply read:

F U try 2 contact Edward or any1 at TM again, your mum will b told evry detail of the past few wks.

She shoved the offending phone back in her pocket and walked on in the rain, letting the tears fall uncontrolled. Surely the mysterious texter must know that she couldn't find Edward even if she wanted to. He didn't exist. Hadn't he told her that himself? Hadn't her efforts to research him proven that? She didn't understand it, but the thought still gave her a chill. Damn it, she should have at least stormed the dais and unmasked him. Surely she deserved to see the face of the man who her ruined her life. Perhaps Vivienne was right. Perhaps he really was a monster after all.

She wasn't sure how long she walked, but at some point she got tired of being wet and cold and caught a taxi.

As she stumbled up the stairs to her flat, she bumped into Lidia, the cleaning woman, and tried to force an apologetic smile.

"Oh, Ms. Holly. Hi. You are so wet. You'll catch cold."

"I'm fine, Lidia," she lied. Who knew, maybe next week she'd be needing Lidia to put in a good word for her with the house cleaning agency she worked for. "What about you? Do you have an umbrella?" The girl always seemed so under-dressed for the London weather.

"My cousin, he is driving taxi. He will come for me." She smiled. "Did Mr. Owen get your memory stick to you? He said you needed it real bad for the important story."

"Pardon?" Rita stopped in her tracks and stood dripping on the carpet. "Owen was here?"

"Oh yes. It is almost two weeks ago now. I let him in. He said it would be OK. Ms. Holly? Are you all right?"

Rita suddenly remembered to breathe. "Ms. Holly, you must go inside now. You'll catch cold." Rita nodded and stumbled up the stairs as though she were sleep-walking. The slimy bastard betrayed her. She should have known when he offered to help with the story that he had something up his sleeve. Damn it! She knew she shouldn't trust him, but she would have never expected him to pull a stunt like this. He must have been working in cahoots with

Vivienne. Surely it couldn't be a coincidence that he wrote her story and Vivienne ended up with a copy of her private journals. She'd kill him. Next time she saw him she'd rip his throat out and make him eat it. Fat lot of good that would do. The damage was done, and all she could think about was that now she would never get to see Edward's face.

She slinked up the last flight of stairs barely able to put one soggy foot in front of the other, aching in places she didn't know existed until tonight, wondering how she'd ever face tomorrow. There was a bottle of malbec in the pantry. She'd start with that, then she'd worry about what to do next. She turned the key in the lock, shoved open the door with gargantuan effort, and found herself face to face with her mother.

Chapter Twenty-Four

THE CHICK'S PARENTS WOULD shit themselves if they knew their little angel was taking it up both holes and begging the two biker blokes to fuck her harder. Gavin couldn't remember her family's title, but they probably owned half of some small county somewhere. And anyway he thought these were the same two bikers who were giving the chick's father a ride last month. She was just another one of those rich twentysomethings with no prospects, no ambition, but lots of mum and dad's money to blow. Like he gave a shit. Rich people could afford to get creative with their sex fantasies. He might be just a glorified bouncer, but what he saw on the job beat the best porn he had ever watched, and he got paid well for his efforts.

Like an unhappy stray cat, the chick suddenly shoved the bikers aside. "Get away from me," she huffed. "You're rubbish, both of you." As she crawled from between them and heaved herself off the big bike, the two blokes shrugged and went to work on each other. The chick's eyes were locked on Gavin. Both hands cupped her half-lemon tits, pinching enormous nipples as she moved toward him. "I want a real man."

Before he could give her the usual employees don't fraternize spiel, her tongue was halfway down his throat and she was undoing his fly.

She offered a breathy giggle, at the discovery of his hard-on. "I thought you might be enjoying the show." She guided his fingers over her smoothly shaved puss. "I like to be watched."

He pulled his hand away and struggled to disengage her. "You are being watched." He nodded to the cameras strategically positioned around the room. "So am I, and I'm not a part of your little fantasy." He'd already been reprimanded once for taking improper liberties with members, but Vivienne could hardly punish him when every time he turned around she wanted him to fuck her while she pretended to be Rita Holly. And she had literally ordered him to make that bird come, so how could she say anything?

"Come on," the chick pouted. "I know you want me." She nodded to the two bikers. One was now buried to the hilt in the arse of the other, who was stroking his cock with a vengeance. "They won't miss me." She pulled his hand back to her pussy, opening her legs just enough for him to get a good feel of her slippery pout. His cock jerked against his half-open fly. She sighed. "There, you see? I bet your balls are so full." She guided his hand deeper and gyrated her naked hips like a belly dancer, riding his fingers as they thrust and stroked almost of their own volition.

She undid his fly and shoved trousers and boxers down, groping his arse as she did so. He pulled away long enough to shrug out of his jacket. "Mmm," she sighed as she released his erection into her hand. "I want it in me." Her slit quivered and gripped at his fingers, and the smell of hot pussy bloomed from under the clean sanitized smell of wealth.

"You're not in Surrey any more, bitch. If you want that," he nodded to his stiff cock, "you do what I tell you."

"Oooh," she breathed. "Tell me what to do."

"That's better," he whispered, glancing up at the cameras, hoping that Vivienne was watching. Pretty stupid to think such a thing, he knew, but he couldn't help himself." He could feel the rich chick— what was her name, Eliza? Jemima?—straining against his hand, her whole body tightening as she tugged at her tits with one hand and yanked on his cock with the other. Oh, she was close. So close.

He pulled away, and she howled her frustration. He grabbed her by the hair and pulled her to him. "You come when I say, bitch, so hold your cunt." He shoved her to her knees and guided his cock into her mouth, imagining what it would look like to Vivienne, hoping it would make her jealous and hot for him.

The chick moaned and gagged as he thrust into her gob, but she kept sucking like she couldn't get enough. He slapped her hand away when she tried to finger fuck herself, and she whimpered.

Butt-fucking Biker Bloke grunted, "I'm coming, holy fuck, I'm coming!" just as the bloke being fucked shot a fountain of semen onto the shiny chrome of the big bike. Gavin was afraid Rich Chick would pinch her swollen nipples right off as she tongued the underside of his cock to the rhythm of her thrusting hips.

"Stand up," he ordered. She had little choice with his hand still twisted in her hair. He half dragged her to the seat of the bike and shoved her up onto it while the two biker blokes looked on stroking their cocks. There, he forced her legs wide apart. Her cunt was all dark and swollen and pulsating. And slippery. God, it was so slippery. She whined and whimpered like a sprog begging for sweeties, lifting her tight little arse off the seat, flashing her clenching bum hole at him. And bloody hell, he had to have her. He felt so full. His need to come was spurred on by the thought of Vivienne watching all wet and horny.

He shoved into the bird's tight cunt, and she wrapped her legs around him like she would break his ribs. He grabbed her arse and pulled her to him, bending to bite her fat, begging nipples as he did.

"I'm coming, I'm coming," came her humid gasp against his ear. And she gripped him like a tight fist. He held back as long as he could. He didn't want Vivienne thinking he couldn't hold his wad. But the chick's slit was so tight and so wet, and she just kept thrusting against him until it was inevitable. One last hard shove, and he spurted massively, grunting and jerking until it almost hurt, but oh God, such a relief. Such a relief.

Chapter Twenty-Five

THE THOUGHT OF TURNING and running back down the stairs barely had time to register before her mother scooped her into her arms, oblivious to the rain soaking through the front of her very expensive silk blouse. "I'm so sorry, my darling, so sorry," she whispered against Rita's shoulder.

Rita could only respond by sobbing. At times like this, maybe a girl just needed her mother. Maybe the unpleasant scene she had been dreading between the two of them could wait, at least for a little while. She had already had enough unpleasantness for one day.

With the front of her blouse wet from the rain and her shoulder wet from Rita snuffling, Coraline Martelli helped her daughter out of her wet clothes and made her a warm cup of cocoa. When the catharsis was over and Rita was swathed in her favorite terry robe and tucked up in her bed, her mother pulled the chair to her bedside and held her hand as she had done when Rita was as a small child. Back then, Rita had thought her mother was a dark-haired angel with pretty red lips that always smiled and strong arms that kept her safe from the monsters under the bed. With a sudden tightness in her throat, Rita realized not that much had changed, except the monsters were now real, and they wanted to destroy her.

Her mother studied her for a long moment in the amber light of the bedside lamp, then she reached out and pushed a damp lock of hair away from her face. "You look thin, Ree. I knew that without Rosa to cook for you, you wouldn't eat well."

"Mama, please. I'm eating fine. I've just been…" Her voice drifted off, and in spite of herself, she felt tears welling again.

"My poor baby. I'm so sorry. I never intended it to be this way. I searched and searched for you. I thought maybe you'd try to find your father. I never imagined you'd leave the States. Then I sent Paulo to London on business, and he discovered these amazing articles by some freelance journalist named Rita Holly."

Rita stared down into her cocoa. "Using my middle name was a give-away. I should have known better."

"It wouldn't have mattered if you had called yourself Queen Elizabeth, I would have still known it was you. Remember, you used to read all your stories to me when you were a little girl? How could I not recognize the voice of my own daughter all grown up and taking London by storm."

"Hardly by storm, Mama. In fact I imagine you're the only one who noticed."

Her mother waved away the self deprecation. "Anyway, finding you was easy once I realized you had left Seattle and transformed yourself into a London journalist. When I realized what was going on, I knew I had to act. Your friend Kate let me into your flat once she knew how worried I was."

And just like that the mother-daughter bliss popped like a soap bubble, and the old issues surfaced again. Rita pulled her hand away from her mother's grip. "So you had me tailed like a petty criminal and bribed my best friend to break you into my flat?"

"It wasn't a bribe. She was worried too."

"Mama, this is exactly why I left in the first place." The venting of her frustration, once begun, was like a runaway train. Defying Coraline Martelli took courage. Best get it all over with before the courage failed her. "I needed space. I needed a life of my own, and

Martelli isn't it. I'm not like you. I'm not a born businesswoman. I have no nose for it, no feel for it, and I saw what it did to us, to you, and I just couldn't—"

"Paulo's taking over Martelli."

"I just couldn't spend my life doing something I have no love for. I mean it's hard enough…" She stopped suddenly and caught her breath as her mother's words finally soaked in. "What?"

"I said Paulo's taking over Martelli."

"Paulo?" Rita barely trusted her own voice. "Taking over? Really?"

Coraline Martelli held her daughter's gaze. "He has the nose. There's never been a more loyal employee. Why not? Why shouldn't he do what he loves? Why shouldn't you both do what you love?"

Rita held her breath, unable to believe what she was hearing. Paulo had always been like a big brother to her ever since her mother hired him to work in the stockroom in the evenings after school. "And you're OK with that, Mama?"

Her mother nodded. "If you'd only told me you wanted to be a journalist instead of running off to England, I would have—"

"You would have bought me my own magazine, yes I know, Mama, that's why I didn't tell you." She smoothed the duvet over her lap. "I wanted… I needed to do it myself."

Her mother chuckled softly "Only a small magazine, darling. You would have to prove yourself before I bought you a big one." She waved away her remark. "I would never have pressured you to take over Martelli Fragrance. I remember too well what it was like when your grandfather did that to me." She gave a heroic shrug. "Fortunately for Martelli, I did have the nose, and the business sense. That's why I had to find you. That's what I wanted to tell you."

She reached out and took Rita's hand again. "I sacrificed a lot for the business, but the one thing I won't sacrifice is you. So if you're angry at me for hiring a private detective and deceiving your best friend, well, I can only add those to the long list of things I need to ask your forgiveness for."

Into the emotionally charged moment, the phone rang. It was her mother's mobile, ringing from inside her bag.

Coraline Martelli groaned and rolled her eyes. "I told Paulo not to call me here." The ensuing conversation was in animated Italian.

Rita closed her eyes, and the sound of her mother's voice washed over her as it had done when she was a child. She heard her mother open her briefcase and heard her spreading files and bits of paper all over the foot of the bed. It was a good thing her mother had the brains and the nose because she couldn't organize her way out of a paper bag.

The conversation got louder and Rita opened her eyes as her mother rifled through papers and hand-written notes on Martelli stationery. If it was raining water outside, it was raining bits of paper inside. Rita caught a piece of expensive company stationery before it could float off the edge of the bed, and her heart did a flip-flop.

Suddenly it was as if the room were full of beating wings. She shoved aside the duvet and shuffled to the lounge, plopping down in the chair in front of the desk to boot the computer. Her mother followed, still half-shouting in Italian, hands flying through the air like she was conducting an orchestra. Rita could see her reflection in the monitor as she pulled up the vintage erotica sites one by one, until she came to the one she was looking for.

And there it was, the elegant copperplate script surrounded by the same erotic drawing. How could she not have remembered? She looked down at the words in Latin written beneath a tiny, simplified version of Venus and Mars embracing on the Martelli stationery. In Latin it said, *The depths of our animal nature and the highest mount of our divinity.* She had seen it all her life and never paid any attention to it. It was just words in Latin. Neither it nor the drawing had meant anything until now.

Her mother had stopped talking, and the phone hung loosely in her hand. Paulo's confused voice carried on at the other end until she cut him off, and mother and daughter were engulfed in charged silence.

"You're a member of The Mount." It wasn't a question.

"Yes. Roman Coven. I'm the head of the High Council there." Her mother gave a self-deprecating smile. "We aren't as barbaric as Vivienne and her lot. We alternate every three years. But I know coven law better than anyone else, so the job falls to me a little more often than I'd like." She nodded to the monitor. "Those drawings are from my collection. Edward's great-great-grandfather did them."

Rita felt as though all the air had gone out of her lungs. "You know about Vivienne and Edward?"

Coraline Martelli took her daughter's hands and pulled her away from the computer. "I know about everything, dear. In fact, I know more than Vivienne knows. Much more."

Her mother led her back to the bed and tucked her in, then sat down next to her. For a long moment neither woman spoke, then Rita found her voice. "You know everything? How?"

"Rome is the oldest coven of The Mount. The original. Not much escapes our notice, and even less escapes the head of the High Council."

"Especially when the head of the High Council is my mother." The thought suddenly made Rita's head spin. Had her mother gone through what she had gone through?

"Was my father a member of The Mount then?" Rita asked.

Her mother shook her head. "He was a rock musician, like I said. An American. He wasn't anybody famous. It was a one-night stand," she reassured her daughter. "He didn't know who I was, and I never even knew his last name, but it wouldn't have mattered. You would have still been a Martelli. I wanted a daughter, and he didn't think it a hardship to give me what I wanted." She chuckled. "Of course he didn't actually know what I wanted."

After her mother had given her time to absorb her little bomb-shell, she continued. "I love the business, and I'm good at it, but if you scratch the surface, it's The Mount that's shaped me more than anything else, and it's always been my hope that the time would come when I could share it with you."

She stood and moved to the window at the foot of Rita's bed and looked out onto the rainy night. "No daughter wants to think about her mother doing what she's done, especially when it involves initiation into The Mount. That's why you were invited to join the London Coven. It's always that way with children of members. Not all children undergo initiation when they're grown." She turned away from the window and offered Rita a smile. "But those who choose to, do so in a coven other than that of their parents."

Suddenly the room felt tight and airless. "You knew about this? You knew about Edward?"

Her mother nodded, holding her gaze. "I told you, I know everything. That's why I didn't come to you sooner."

"Since you know everything, then I'm assuming you know that I've been banished for writing an exposé for *Talkabout*." No matter how casual she tried to be about what had happened only a few hours earlier, her face still burned with the shame of it.

"Rubbish! Anyone with half a brain would know you didn't write that article, and since no one in the London Coven knows who you are—well almost no one—then I can't believe you'd be privy to any special secrets."

"Like what?"

Her mother raised a well-arched eyebrow. "Have you not read the article?"

Rita shook her head. "I've only heard the choice bits that Vivienne took great pleasure in regaling the High Council with." As an afterthought, she asked, "Who there knows who I am?"

Her mother ignored the question.

"Mama? I know that look. What are you up to?"

Suddenly the woman was rummaging through her briefcase

again until she extricated from the detritus the offending copy of *Talkabout*, which she shook triumphantly at her daughter. "Rita, darling, you just leave this to me. When I get through with Vivienne, I promise you, she'll regret the day she messed with my daughter."

"No, mama! There you go again interfering. It's always been this way. I get a B in Latin, my mother sorts the teacher out, and I end up with an A. I don't get the job I apply for, my mother comes and buys the position for me."

"You earned that A, and you know it. Your Latin was better than the teacher's. And it was hardly necessary to buy you the position when I owned the company." She gave a shrug that made her look like she was wearing heavy shoulder pads. "Technically that means that you owned the company, right?"

"That's not the point. I left because I wanted to fight my own battles, and sometimes that means losing."

Her mother studied her for a long moment then took a deep breath. "Do you want to lose this battle?"

"No! Of course I don't. I loved my experience of The Mount. I guess I only realized how much after I'd lost it, but I love Leo and Morgan and Alex and Aurora, and I—"

"And you especially love Edward, yes I know my darling." Once again she gave her daughter the long hard stare. Then she looked down at the magazine in her hand and cocked her head. "If you don't want to lose this battle, then you'll have to let me tutor you a little bit in coven law. That wouldn't be considered interfering, would it?"

Suddenly Rita's heart was in her throat. "You'd do that?"

"It's the only way you'll be able to take on Vivienne head to head. But before that, there are three things you need to do. First, don't under any circumstances, read the *Talkabout* article. Your not knowing is the key to getting you back in. Secondly, call Kate. She's worried sick." She looked down at her watch. "And finally, get some rest. Nothing's going to happen tonight."

Chapter Twenty-Six

VIVIENNE SAT NAKED IN front of the vanity while Lorelei bent over her, careful not to obscure her view in the mirror as she applied her mascara for her. She never dressed until every other part of her morning ritual was finished. She enjoyed being naked, and even more, she enjoyed looking at herself naked.

Vivienne was in a foul mood. Whatever happened between her and Edward after Rita Holly's banishment must have been ugly. It was the logical reason for such a mood after Vivienne's triumph over the High Council last night. It didn't matter that none of it was Lorelei's fault, she just happened to be in the line of fire.

She finished the mascara and stepped back while Vivienne studied the final result with a pout. Through the mirror her gaze fell on Lorelei standing behind her, and the pout became something more threatening. "Are you impatient, Lorelei, darling? Do you, perhaps, have something more important to do?"

"No. Of course not," Lorelei lied. "I have nothing that can't wait." She had sacrificed a lot to be Vivienne's confidant. She knew none of the other council members trusted her or even believed she had a right to be here, but it didn't matter. She was close to the power, right where she'd always wanted to be. Worth the sacrifice, she thought. But now, for the first time, she was having doubts. The whole incident with Owen Frank bothered her. While he was rewarded for being an arsehole, Rita Holly was punished for doing everything right. A large part of the blame was hers. But it had always been her job to help Vivienne get what she wanted. This was no time to develop a conscience.

She quickly returned her attention to Vivienne, who was once again admiring her own reflection. With a wave of her hand, she ordered, "Get me the blue corset, the one with the Spanish lace."

It was a corset she wore only for Edward. Strange how she punished him and schemed to hurt him, then almost in the next breath tried to please him. When Lorelei opened the corset drawer, there, on top of the expensive bespoke finery, washed, repaired, and neatly folded, was the tatty sweat suit Vivienne had worn in the alley to fuck Gavin. She had just had him fired for shagging a member. Lorelei wondered if she had fucked him in the hoodie first.

"Would you hurry up? I'd like to get dressed sometime today if you don't mind."

Lorelei jumped to find Vivienne suddenly standing so close that her bare breasts nearly brushed her arm. "I'm sorry, but this was in the wrong drawer." She nodded at the sweat suit.

"It's not in the wrong drawer. It's exactly where I want it." Vivienne released a warm breath against the back of Lorelei's neck and whispered, "Be a dear. Put it on for me."

As she unfolded the hoodie and held it out for Vivienne to slip into, Vivienne knocked it away. "Not me, you stupid cow. You. Go on. I want to see you in it."

While Vivienne watched, Lorelei stripped, trying to ignore the twinge of guilt that came from something so silly as putting on clothes that reminded her of Rita Holly. At last, she stood in nothing but her underwear, feeling as though the moment she put on the sweat suit Rita would somehow know it was her who had betrayed her—under Vivienne's orders, she reminded herself.

Vivienne gave her a smack to the back of the head. "Take off the bra and panties too. It won't look right if you don't."

Lorelei swallowed her irritation and did as she was told. And when she was completely naked, she slid into the yoga pants and hoodie trying not to think about what they represented. From somewhere, Vivienne produced the hideous pink flip-flop shoes. "And these. Put these on."

They were too big for her, but Lorelei put them on and offered a weak smile, which was rewarded with a slap across the face. She yelped, from the shock more than the pain, but Vivienne grabbed her by the hair and pulled her close. "She would never smile at me, would she?"

Glaring at Vivienne was such an unusually honest sensation that for a second Lorelei felt a flood of relief. But it was short-lived. Vivienne jerked down the zipper of the hoodie and grabbed her breasts, squeezing and kneading, pinching her nipples, shoving her backward with every pinch. "You stupid little slut," she breathed. "I warned you that Edward would never be yours, didn't I?" There was another resounding slap, this time across Lorelei's breasts. Lorelei stumbled backward and her left foot slipped out of the loose-fitting flip-flop.

She barely caught her balance before Vivienne grabbed her face and kissed her as though she were trying to climb right inside her, tongue first, pushing her back until she was in danger of falling onto the bed behind her. "I told you. He's mine. He never really wanted you. He just likes easy sluts. And you were the easiest, the way you flaunt your bouncy tits with your nipples all pointy and hard." She shoved a hand inside the sweat bottoms and jammed a finger into Lorelei's pussy, making her jump. "You're always slippery, always pouting, like a bitch in heat."

She kissed her once more, even harder, and bit her lip as she came up gasping. "Fight back, damn it! She would. You know she would." She slapped Lorelei again, hard enough to make her ears ring, hard enough to ignite the explosion that was long overdue.

"You vile bitch!" The words burst from Lorelei's throat with more ease, and much more pleasure, than she would have thought possible. She stepped aside and shoved Vivienne face-first on to the bed, then wedged her arm behind her back none too gently. "You may own Edward, but you don't own me." She picked up the flip-flop that had fallen off her foot and brought it down with a hard thwack against Vivienne's bare bottom.

Vivienne yelped and bucked on the bed, uttering muffled curses into the mattress, but Lorelei held her fast as she brought the shoe down again and again, until Vivienne's lovely bottom was bright pink. She uttered a chesty moan as she squirmed, and Lorelei got an exquisite view of her swollen pussy, pouting open, begging wet.

With a surge of power that went straight to her own pussy, Lorelei smacked her bottom again, then jammed two rough fingers inside her pout and began to scissor. "Sooner or later when you fuck with people, they're gonna fuck back." Lorelei found herself doing a poor imitation of Rita's American accent. She leaned over and whispered into Vivienne's ear, "You fucked with me, you bitch, now I'm gonna return the favor." She rammed a third finger into Vivienne's cunt and Vivienne nearly bounced them both off the bed as her first orgasm hit. Bloody hell! How many times had Lorelei seen Vivienne come—even made Vivienne come, but she'd never seen the woman like this. She pulled her fingers out and licked them, making Vivienne watch.

Still quivering all over, Vivienne lifted her bottom higher, opening her legs until the pillowed slick swell of her trembled like an invitation.

"You want your hole filled, don't you?" Lorelei chuckled. "It would be my pleasure." She grabbed up her panties from the floor and bound Vivienne's hands behind her back. Then she left her, writhing bottom up, while she rummaged through the drawer of the bedside table for her strap-on. The crotch of the sweat bottoms was already wet and slippery. She'd always heard that power was an aphrodisiac, but she hadn't imagined it would be anything this hot.

She made Vivienne watch while she stroked the damp pout of her lips through the crotch of the sweats. That alone would have been enough to make her come, but she had better things in mind. She stepped out of the bottoms and slipped into the strap-on. Once it was secure, she manhandled Vivienne onto her knees in front of her cock. "Suck me, bitch, suck me the way you did Edward that first night in front of the council." She grabbed her by the hair and forced her lips toward the cock. With a little whine so out of character for the head of the High Council, Vivienne did as she was told, leaving bright smears of expensive lippy all along the length of the shaft.

Vivienne deep-throated the strap-on like it was the tastiest cock she'd ever had, and Lorelei's pussy got even slicker at the sight. With each thrust of the strap-on, she clenched her pussy muscles, and the harder she clenched, the deeper Vivienne took her in. "Please," Vivienne gasped, when she came up for air. "Please, Rita, put it in me. I need it in me."

It was a bit unsettling to be called Rita, but Lorelei had done her fair share of role playing, like everyone else at The Mount. And in some small twisted way, she felt she was making up for some of what she had done to Rita. She chuckled. "Certainly. You are head of the High Council after all. I hear and obey." She looked around the room and saw that the dressing table was just about the right height. She shoved a makeup bag, perfume bottles, brushes, and a curling iron off onto the floor with a loud crash, then pushed Vivienne over the top of the table until her bare bottom was at exactly the right height. With one knee, she shoved her legs apart until her snatch pouted like an open mouth begging to be satisfied. Vivienne ground her pubis against the table and her desperate whimpers sounded more animal than human.

But she deserved to suffer. Lorelei slapped each of her arse cheeks in turn with the stiff cock, then brought it up between her legs and slapped her begging pussy until Vivienne was in a frenzy, her cunt gripping and grasping blindly for the cock each time it slapped her. Her whimpers became sobs of frustration as Lorelei teased her lips open with the tip of the cock just enough to hint at how good it would feel buried deep in her pussy. "Please," Vivienne begged. "Please, Rita, don't torture me so. I can't stand it. Please put it in me."

"Oh I'll put it in you, you bitch. I'll put it in you like you've never had it." With her hand, Lorelei gave the strap-on an extra coating of her own saliva, then bending quickly, she spat against Vivienne's anus, and before there was time for protests, Lorelei spread the woman's tender buttocks like two halves of a peach and shoved the cock into the pulsing O of her pucker.

The scream that ripped at Vivienne's throat, was pain and pleasure well balanced, and Lorelei grabbed her hips to keep from being catapulted across the room by the aftershock of another orgasm. The force of Vivienne grinding back against her made her come too and they both shuddered together until at last Vivienne collapsed over the dressing table with a sigh.

Lorelei spoke next to her ear. "So you don't just want to be me, you want to be fucked by me. Who knew?" She gave her one last hard poke up the back hole with the strap-on, then pulled out. "Consider yourself lucky, bitch. Edward has to fuck you, but I don't." Lorelei felt it the minute she'd said it, the shifting of power brought on by one sentence too many. She stood back still struggling to catch her breath, but she was well aware that the racing of her heart now had nothing to do with sex.

"Untie me." Vivienne's voice was icy enough that Lorelei needed no further convincing that the game was over. She did as she was told. Vivienne stood rubbing her wrists, her gaze never leaving Lorelei. Quickly, she slipped into the kimono that lay draped over the chair of the dressing table and yanked the sash tight as though it had done something offensive. "Get out." Her voice was beyond anger. Lorelei knew the tone. Vivienne didn't have to show anger when the punishment she was, no doubt, already devising in her head would show it so much more effectively. And as sure as night would bring darkness, Lorelei knew with a cold clench in her gut that her punishment for knowing what she shouldn't know, for doing only what she was told, would be ugly indeed.

Chapter Twenty-Seven

WHEN RITA WOKE IT was early afternoon. She hadn't realized just how tired she'd been. Her mother wasn't kidding about the crash course in coven law. For two solid days they had pored over the volumes. Her room was piled with the books her mother had managed to conjure out of nowhere, one of the benefits of being head of the High Council, she had said.

At present, Coraline Martelli was nowhere to be found. But her belongings were strewn all over the front room, and for two days Kate had been bouncing off the walls with excitement over the dance lessons the woman had arranged for her to have with Alex. Yes, Coraline Martelli was definitely in town.

Rita had just got out of the shower when the doorbell rang. She slipped into her robe and found Lidia, standing shyly in front of her. The ponytail high on the back of her head was losing the battle to contain her wispy blond hair, and her pale goose-fleshed arms were folded protectively around her body as though she were cold. Her smile out-brightened her tired appearance.

"Ms. Holly, I'm sorry to bother, but I wanted you to know that I will no longer work here after first of the month. I have cousin who works at the Ritz. She found me a better job there in the kitchen." The girl blushed pink to the roots of her hair. "I am good cook."

"That's wonderful, Lidia. Good luck. We'll miss you, but the Ritz is a nice hotel."

"Your boss, Mr. Owen, he goes there. My cousin, she delivers room service. She says he has a suite, and there he meets some beauti-ful woman with a very strange name, I don't know, maybe Loral Hie or something. You know this woman?"

Lidia suddenly had Rita's undivided attention. "Mr. Owen say to my cousin this Loral Hie works at The Mount. You know The Mount?"

"Oh yes. I know The Mount. I don't suppose Mr. Owen told your cousin what he and this Loral Hie were doing there at the Ritz?"

Lidia stepped closer and glanced about to make sure no one was listening. Then she spoke in a near whisper. "Men like Mr. Owen, they always have pretty woman, you know? He's good-looking man, yes?

He's a slimy bastard, Rita thought, but she smiled encouragingly at Lidia. Bless her heart, she had no idea what a big help she was being.

The woman continued. "My cousin says they were having, how you say, a nooner, you know?" Lidia demonstrated by poking the index finger of her right hand in and out of the circle formed by the thumb and index finger of her other hand. "They have lots of nooners there at the Ritz, my cousin says. But Mr. Owen, he tells my cousin that is very important business they were doing."

Rita nodded sagely. "Oh very important, I have no doubt."

She wished Lidia well, then went to the kitchen in search of coffee and something to eat. Suddenly she had an appetite. She had just buttered her toast when her mother blew in heavily laden with shopping bags.

"You wouldn't believe the latest news." She hoisted the shop-ping onto the already buried sofa. "*Talkabout* is in an uproar. Seems your dear Owen Frank is unavailable for comment on the controver-sial exposé." She plopped a bulging bag of pastries from the bakery around the corner down onto the table and turned up her nose at the instant coffee jar sitting on the counter. "At the moment, the response from The Mount is to laugh. They're saying the whole thing is too ridiculous to even consider, and they wonder why Owen Frank would let such a story into his magazine." She rummaged through the cupboard until she found the mocha maker. "And, get this, they're claiming never to have heard of a Rita Holly. Can you imagine?" Her mother sighed as though she had just heard the best news ever, then she went about the business of making real coffee. "Rita, dear, I may just buy you your own magazine yet. You'd be great as owner of *Talkabout*."

Over good Italian espresso and fresh *pain au chocolat* Rita told her mother about her conversation with Lidia. They were like teenagers gossiping and giggling, and Rita realized how much she had missed that since she'd left Seattle. Perhaps it if had happened more often, she wouldn't have left home. Her mother stood to put on another pot of espresso. "I know I promised to let you handle this, Rita, but what I wouldn't give to be a fly on the wall when Vivienne gets what's coming to her."

Rita wasn't as certain as her mother. Vivienne always had an ace up her sleeve, and she couldn't fight the niggle at the back of her mind that once again her mother had come to the rescue. "Mama?"

"Yes dear."

"If I'm able to override Vivienne's banishment and all is forgiven, and if I'm made a full-fledged member of The Mount, am I getting in because of you?"

Her mother plopped down in the chair next to her. "No one gets into The Mount because of anyone else." She held Rita in her intense dark gaze. "No matter how many generations their family has been in The Mount, each person must pass the initiation entirely on their own." She offered a bright smile. "And from what I've heard, you already passed the initiation with flying colors. Even Vivienne can't fault your service to her. That's why she had to cheat to get rid of you."

Most of the shopping had been for Rita, and her mother knew

almost as much about fashion as she did about perfume. The dress was midnight blue, off the shoulder. It slinked and clung to Rita's curves like a second skin. In fact, it fitted like it had been made for her, and Rita figured it probably was. The jewelry was simple pearls. The dress needed nothing else. Her mother had flown her own hairdresser in to do Rita's hair and make-up. Standing in front of the mirror gazing at the finished product, Rita had to admit, she looked stunning. "But how will I get in?" she asked. "I've been banished, remember?"

Her mother affectionately smoothed a strand of her hair that didn't really need smoothing and offered a happy sigh. "You're going in through the front door, of course, like the Martelli heiress should, that is if you don't mind condescending to use the Martelli name again. You have reservations. Rita Holly may have been banished, but Rita Martelli has not. Oh, by the way," she added as an afterthought, "you'll be joined for drinks by the club owner."

"The club's owner? I've been trying for weeks to find the club's owner. Who is it?"

Her mother offered a Mona Lisa smile. "Rita, dear, you were looking in the wrong places. All you ever had to do was call me. I would have told you everything. But for now, let's just make it a surprise. And remember, it's *not* knowing what that bloody exposé says that's the key to defeating Vivienne."

Before Rita could question further, her mother's mobile signaled a text. As she read it, the smile returned to her face. "Sorry about that dear, just some business I had to take care of. A foreclosure on a villa in Majorca. Seems Vivienne hasn't been careful about who it was leased to." She sighed happily. "If you want something done right, you have to do it yourself."

Just then the doorbell rang. "That will be the limo, darling," her mother said. "A Martelli limo this time." She slipped her arm around her daughter's waist and walked her to the door. "A couple of reporters saw you going into The Mount with Leo the other night and, well darling, they're not stupid. They already suspect they've found the lost Martelli heiress. Cat's almost out of the bag anyway, why not give them something to talk about?" She gave her now speechless daughter a wink and sent her out the door.

Chapter Twenty-Eight

FOR THE SECOND TIME in less than two weeks, there was a feeling of déjà vu, as the limo pulled up in front of The Mount. Rita might be relying on the Martelli name to get her in the door, but in the end, she knew she would still be 100 percent reliant on plain old Rita Holly when it came to facing down Vivienne and proving her innocence.

The driver helped her out of the car. "Ms. Martelli, shall I escort you to the door?"

Ms. Martelli. Suddenly that name didn't seem nearly so onerous to her. "That won't be necessary, John. I'll manage from here."

There were whispers around her as she stepped on to the carpet and under the awning. She heard the Martelli name mentioned several times. Her mother was right. It was time to give them something to talk about.

The door man opened the door and as she entered, she was certain all eyes were on her. Mostly, Lorelei's eyes were on her, her jaw dropped nearly to the desk where the reservations book lay open. Rita had never felt more proud of her heritage.

"You have a reservation for Martelli. Rita Martelli."

Lorelei gave several fish gasps before she regained control. "But I thought—"

"You thought the reservation was for my mother. A forgivable mistake." Rita held Lorelei's shocked gaze. "I'm told I'll be joined by the club's owner. I can't tell you how much I'm looking forward to that meeting."

Lorelei led her back to the private dining room, the same one where she had met Edward what seemed like a hundred years ago now. There, in a booth not terribly far from the one where Edward had shown her the best way to drink champagne, Lorelei seated her. Then she stood shifting from foot to foot, in her expensive shoes, as though she were waiting for Rita's attention.

After what she deemed an appropriate amount of time to let the woman squirm, Rita asked, "Is there something else?"

"I just wanted to say…"

"Yes?"

"I didn't know. Honestly I didn't."

Rita smiled sweetly up at the woman, who suddenly seemed to be sweating through her peach taffeta. "That's OK, Lorelei. I'm pretty sure before the night's over you'll have a chance to make up for it, a chance I'm thinking you'll want to take full advantage of. Now go get the owner, would you?"

Lorelei practically ran out of the dining room.

Rita didn't have to wait long before Aurora came to her table with a bottle of Moët et Chandon on ice and two glasses. "Compliments of the owner," she said, the corner of her mouth almost twitching with what might have been a smile. "He apologizes for making you wait, and will be joining you very shortly." She poured the champagne and left.

Rita barely had time to take in the smells and sounds of the lovely dining room and to sip the delicate champagne before a familiar voice came from behind her. "Sorry I'm late. But I had to go back to my suite for my mask." Edward slid into the booth next to her and pressed a warm kiss against her lips. "Welcome back, my darling, back to where you belong."

She suddenly felt light-headed as though she had just finished the whole bottle of fizz. "You're the owner of The Mount?"

"I am, well the club, at least. And thanks to you and your mother, I'll soon be regaining the control I've lost."

She felt an unpleasant tightening in her chest, as though the next breath might not be guaranteed. "Is that why you didn't come with me? Because my mother made you an offer you couldn't refuse? She said she wouldn't interfere, she said—"

He interrupted her. "Your mother hasn't told you about me, then?"

"Told me what?"

He moved a little closer and took her hands. "A long time ago, I made a very foolish mistake." Even though she couldn't see his face, there was no missing the tightness in his voice, the quickening of his breath. "I gambled away what was mine. I owned The Mount, and like you, my family has a long history with The Mount. People looked up to me because of my abilities, because of my position, then I let them down. Then I lost it all."

"To Vivienne?"

He nodded. "I was young and naïve and in love with her at the time. I thought she loved me too. I thought it was just a friendly game. I thought…" He forced a humorless chuckle. "Well, what I thought hardly matters now, does it?"

"So Vivienne owns you?" Rita breathed. "How can that be?"

He cleared his throat as though it would rid him of threatening emotions. "I lost control of The Mount and became her slave. Slaves take on the identity of their masters, so you see, effectively I don't exist. Not as long as I'm her slave." As he paused for a sip of champagne, she noticed his knuckles were white around the delicate stem of the glass. "Nothing like that in the history of The Mount had ever happened before. The Council of Elders decided, even though, constitutionally, Vivienne's wager was on shaky ground, to let the bet stand, to teach me a lesson. They hadn't figured on Vivienne being such a tyrant, or on her knowing coven law well enough to capitalize on her position and maintain it."

He raised a hand before she could respond. "You have to

understand, if it were just Vivienne, I would have run away with you, and never looked back. You can't imagine how badly I wanted to do just that. But everyone here suffers because of what I did. I owe them all, some of them I can never repay. And besides, you shouldn't have to run away from your rightful heritage."

"So my mother orchestrated the whole thing?"

"Your mother orchestrated our meeting. I agreed to persuade you to undergo initiation. The rest you did on your own. And when Vivienne had you banished, staying was the only way I could assure you'd be able to fight another day. Then the London Coven will finally be free of Vivienne, and I can take back what's mine," he squeezed her hand and raised it to his lips, "hopefully all of what's mine."

"And I was a part of the deal?"

"No." He released her hand. "You weren't."

"But you just said my mother used you to bring me into the fold."

"Oh, she did. She absolutely used me to bring you into the fold. But my falling in love with you was never a part of the deal. There are things that even someone as powerful as your mother can't control."

His words left her breathless, unable to speak. She hardly knew what to say. He loved her? Did he really? She'd secretly hoped, but hopes were barely more than fantasies and not to be trusted.

Into the breach of expectant silence, he tugged at his jacket and cleared his throat again, suddenly unable to meet her gaze. "Lorelei has gathered the High Council in the Presence Chamber. If you're ready, I think it's time you take your rightful place in The Mount." He offered her his arm and escorted her away from the table, then down the hallway behind the kitchen toward the stairs, a route she felt quite familiar with now.

At the bottom, she stopped, suddenly unable to move, suddenly feeling weak all over.

Edward took her in his arms. "Don't be afraid, my love. You are Rita Holly Martelli. You come from a long line of members of

The Mount, longer than anyone in that room." He nodded to the doors. "And you've done everything right. You've made your family proud. You've made me proud. When you've done what has to be done in there, then this is yours to remove." He guided her hand to the cheek of the golden mask. "And what's beneath is yours to keep, if you still want it."

She lifted her mouth to his and kissed him, forcing words around the tight knot of emotion in her chest. "You know that I do. More than I've ever wanted anything." He offered her his arm, and together they pushed through the double doors into the familiar bedroom light of the Presence Chamber.

Chapter Twenty-Nine

ELLEN DANIELS WAS THE estate agent who gave Owen the keys to his new villa. Then she'd stayed on for drinks and dinner and sex. Lots of sex. Clearly she found him fascinating, and she was just his type. She had big tits, a pussy with a cast-iron grip, and she loved to suck cock. He wasn't into exclusivity by any means, but, with him just settling in, Ellen offered lots of hot, kinky tail, and she looked fabulous on his arm whenever he went out.

She stood before him dressed to the nines with her arm around the shoulder of a gorgeous brunette, hand resting in a slight cup against the woman's lovely bra-less breast. "Owen, darling." Ellen's throaty contralto always sounded like she was gagging for it. "This is Vicki." She gave the brunette's tit a little squeeze, and he couldn't help noticing those lovely high tits were barely covered by the tiny black dress that looked more like a nightie. "She wants to come with us. That is all right, isn't it?"

One look at the chick's straining nipples and her nicely rounded bottom was enough to convince him that the only thing better than showing up at The Club with one gorgeous woman on his arm was showing up with two gorgeous women on his arm. "Of course you can come, love."

The woman shot a confused glance at Ellen, who smiled back at her reassuringly and nodded. Then she turned her attention back to Owen. "Vicki doesn't speak English."

He'd paid a fortune to get reservations for himself and Ellen at the exclusive grand opening of The Club Restaurant. He was pretty sure the place was just a Mount wannabe, but there had been rumors that Vivienne herself might show up, and he wanted to be in the right place just in case.

In her excitement at the news, Vicki gave Ellen an enthusiastic tongue kiss. When she finally came up for air, Ellen smiled apologetically at Owen. "Vicki's very affectionate, and very grateful." While he watched, she scrunched the skirt of the brunette's dress up until her black lace knickers were visible. "She has such a yummy pussy. Would you like to taste?"

She shoved aside the crotch of her friend's panties, and the chick's eyelids fluttered. She sucked her bottom lip and caught her breath as Ellen parted her cunt lips and slipped a finger into her distended snatch. Owen was already hard enough to strain the expensive fabric of his trousers as he watched Ellen thumb the nub of her friend's clit, before bringing her juicy fingers to his lips for a taste.

"Mmmmph. Good," he groaned, licking and slurping.

Ellen nuzzled the top of the brunette's dress open until her dark nipples were forced upward free of the bodice. She pulled Owen, first to her own mouth for a deep-throated kiss, then she guided him down to Vicki's peek-a-boo nipples. "Aren't they nice," she crooned as he suckled and kneaded the brunette.

"And look." She shoved him away long enough to turn Vicki around and bend her over the arm of the couch. There she pushed the dress up and slid the crumpled panties down until the chick's nicely tanned bottom was completely exposed. "Her little bum hole is so nice, don't you think?"

Owen could barely hold his wad as Ellen parted her friend's raised buttocks and began to tongue-fuck her pulsating dark pucker.

The brunette groaned and thrust her arse back into Ellen's face. She grunted some expletive he didn't understand. Dirty talk he figured, and he nearly ripped out his fly in his effort to free his cock. Desperate for relief, he fingered and poked until he had spread the brunette's slippery pout. With such a raging hard-on he could hardly walk, let alone make it to The Club. That was all right. They'd show up fashionably late and well fucked, the way he figured most wealthy people did. As he shoved into Vicki's tight snatch, Ellen hopped on to the leather couch, mindless of her stilettos, and positioned herself over Vicki's mouth, pulling aside her own thong for a good pussy licking.

Owen wondered if it got any better than this, fucking one chick senseless while she ate another chick's sopping pussy. Just a quickie before dinner, then, after an expensive meal, eaten while being seen and admired at The Club, the three of them would continue the party here at his villa. Unless Vivienne had better plans for him. That thought, along with the brunette's tightly gripping pussy, was enough to make him jizz.

<center>~~~</center>

Owen felt nauseated as the restaurant manager handed him back his bank card. "I'm sorry, Mr. Frank, but the charge has been declined."

The meal they had just eaten would have set him back a month's salary at *Talkabout*. He forced a smile, trying to remain calm, trying to keep the expensive dinner from coming back up. "There has to be a mistake. Try again."

The manager shook his head. "I've tried it three times, sir."

"Then try a fourth time" Owen growled. "I know how much I have in my account. What's the matter with you stupid people?"

Out of nowhere, a very large man in charcoal suit moved to stand protectively next to the manager. People at the tables around them began to whisper among themselves. Ellen heaved a busty sigh and produced a credit card from her bag. The manager studied it for a moment, then looked up at her wide-eyed. "You work for Coraline Martelli?"

She nodded to Vicki. "We both do. And we'll take care of the bill."

"But I thought you were an estate agent," Owen sputtered.

"I am if Ms. Martelli wants me to be." She ran a finger down the side of his sweating face. "You don't look well, Owen, darling. But at least you've been well fucked tonight, and I can't think of anyone more deserving. Now why don't you go on home and take some rest."

Confusion and panic rose at the back of his throat. Normally he would feel good about being on the radar of someone as important as Coraline Martelli. Instead, he felt like he'd just swallowed a fish bone.

The drive home seemed interminable. How could a night that started out so well end up so shit? The closer he got to home, the tighter the knot in his stomach got. He thought of Lorelei's warning, but he'd done nothing wrong. He'd kept every rule. The whole incident with his bank card had to be some mistake. He'd iron it all out in the morning. He reminded himself things always looked better in daylight. Then he saw the heavy chain and padlock across the gate to his villa with the two uniformed men standing in front, and he knew this time that wouldn't be the case.

"Owen Frank?" The bigger of the two spoke with a heavy Spanish accent.

"Yes?"

"We are to escort you to pack your belongings. You are trespassing on Martelli property."

The nausea returned with a vengeance and, for a second, he thought he'd either throw up or pass out. Instead, he choked out his protest. "There has to be a mistake. The place was leased to me. How can it belong to Coraline Martelli?"

"Oh, it doesn't belong to Coraline Martelli anymore. She has deeded it over as a gift to her daughter."

"Her daughter?"

"That's right. She says you know her daughter."

"How the hell would I know her daughter?"

The big man unlocked the padlock and stepped aside for Owen to enter. "Rita Holly Martelli?" He shrugged. "Strange, Ms. Martelli said that you would understand."

Chapter Thirty

THERE WAS NO DENYING the stirring and fluttering of expensive clothing on the dais as Rita entered the Presence Chamber on Edward's arm. Only Vivienne sat as still and pale as the bas relief of Venus in the library.

"What's the meaning of this?" Vivienne's voice was barely controlled anger.

Rita stepped forward with more confidence than she would have thought possible. "I petition the High Council of The Mount, London Coven, to reconsider my initiation and my acceptance into said coven and to hear my defense in the case raised against me."

"I second the petition," Leo spoke up.

"And I," Aurora added. She still wore her waitress uniform, and so tight was the tension in the room that she looked as though she were about to catapult from her seat.

"This is ludicrous," Vivienne snapped. "Get her out of here, and stop wasting my time."

"She has the right to defend herself, Vivienne," Morgan spoke up. "You know the law."

Vivienne adjusted herself on her chair like a queen on her throne and forced a chuckle. "All right then. If you all insist on humoring her, who am I to disagree." She scrutinized Rita with a disdainful eye. "At least she had the decency to dress for the occasion this time. Which of you put up the money for her little dress?" Vivienne's scorching gaze moved from Rita over to Edward. "I can't imagine how she got in."

"She came in through the front door," Aurora said. "She had a reservation."

"Is this true?" Vivienne turned her attention to Lorelei." Lorelei nodded. "You gave her a reservation?"

"I did."

There was ice in Vivienne's voice. "We'll discuss this later." She turned her attention to Edward. "Come take your place." She patted the seat next to her. "Let's get this little charade over with."

Edward didn't move. "This is my place, Vivienne. This is where I belong."

There was a collective shifting among the High Council. Even from where Rita stood, she could see the color rise along Vivienne's cheek bones. If this didn't end tonight, she had no doubt Edward would pay dearly for his insolence.

Edward turned to Leo and nodded.

The Zoo Keeper pulled a copy of *Talkabout* from inside his jacket and opened it to the offending exposé. When he spoke, he sounded unusually formal. "Ms. Holly, could you please tell the council what is involved in the Crossing Over ceremony?"

Rita shrugged. "When someone dies, they're said to cross over to the other side. I don't know. What does that have to do with the initiation?"

There was a murmuring among the High Council. Leo raised his hand to silence everyone. "What about the Blessing of Five?"

"I don't know."

"The Making of the History?"

"No idea."

Leo frowned down at the magazine open in his hands. "And yet is your name on this article, the article which explains all of these secret parts of the final initiation rite."

"Oh for heaven sake," Vivienne exploded. "Can't you see she's lying? Of course she's going to tell you she knows nothing about it. What else is she going to say? She's a journalist, in case you've forgotten."

"That's right. I am a journalist, and I'm a good one." Rita took another step forward. "One who would never write a story without backing it up with her sources, one who would never leave important questions unanswered. For instance, perhaps you could tell us why Lorelei was meeting secretly with the editor of *Talkabout* at the Ritz?"

Vivienne spoke as though she were humoring an impertinent child. "First of all, girl, I don't answer to you. Second, I don't keep track of what Lorelei does on her own time."

"Perhaps, in the interest of good journalism, I should ask Lorelei then."

All pretense of tolerance vanished. Vivienne stood and stomped her foot. "I already told you, I don't answer to you, and neither do my people. Who do you think you are waltzing in here taking control? Guards, get this woman out of my sight," she yelled.

But as the guards approached, Edward raised a hand, and they both stopped in their tracks. "Who does she think she is, indeed." He took a step forward and laced his arm through Rita's. "Shall I tell you who she is, Vivienne? She is Rita Holly Martelli, and she has as much right to be here as you do. More actually."

The color drained from Vivienne's face, and she swayed, grabbing the arm of her chair before she collected herself and squared her shoulders. "I don't care if she's God. Her own mother would agree with me that she's betrayed The Mount and is not worthy to be a part of it."

"My mother, and everyone in this room, knows I didn't write that tosh. But we all have a pretty good idea of who did. One person here knows for certain who wrote it, two actually, isn't that right, Lorelei?"

It was as Rita suspected, the Martelli name held a powerful sway over the woman's shifting loyalties. Lorelei nodded. "I know. Yes." She looked at Vivienne.

"I said get her out of here," Vivienne shouted to the guards.

They didn't move. No one moved. No one breathed. At last Edward spoke. "All those who are convinced that the initiation of Rita Holly has come to a successful conclusion and that she is worthy of membership into The Mount, London Coven, please stand up now."

Lorelei was the first to stand, followed quickly by everyone else except Vivienne, who dropped into her chair as though her strength were gone.

Edward took Rita's hand and led her onto the dais. "Members of The Mount, London Coven, may I present to you Rita Ellison Holly Martelli, our new companion in freedom."

Instead of waiting for each member to come forward and welcome her, as was tradition, Rita moved to stand in front of Vivienne. There was a collective gasp among the High Council, and Edward grabbed her arm, but she gently shrugged him off.

"Vivienne Arlington Page, your life is mine to do with as I choose."

The council gasp became a shocked murmur, which Rita ignored.

"It's within my power to banish you without any coven support and leave you to survive in the world as you've not had to do since you were accepted into The Mount." She nodded at the look of surprise on Vivienne's face. "Yes, my mother tutored me well on coven law, and I'm a fast learner."

The murmur died away and the room was swathed in wire-tight silence.

Rita continued. "Coven law states that your position is forfeit to the one you've wronged. I think it's safe to say that includes just about everyone in this room, no one more so than Edward." She turned to face the council. "As in accordance with the law, who among you wishes to take up this woman's position and fulfill the duties she has forfeited?"

The silence in the room felt like a tightly held breath. At last Leo took a step forward and spoke. "Is as you have stated,

Vivienne Arlington Page now belongs to you. Since it is you who have broken her power, then I say that it is to you her power and position should go."

Around the room, there were nods of agreement. Leo continued. "Are there any who would object to this?"

No one did.

In spite of her fantasies about this moment, the sudden urge to run from such responsibility was visceral, but Rita squared her shoulders, swallowed the fear and was amazed by the steadiness of her own voice. "If this is the decision of the council, then I will abide by it. I take my rightful place as head of the High Council and reinstate the three-year rotation of that position of power."

She turned her attention back to Vivienne, who slumped in her chair, gaze locked on the floor. "I have no wish for revenge upon you, Vivienne, so I offer you a choice. You may take the punishment I deem suitable for your actions, then serve as my slave until I see fit to release you. If this is unacceptable to you, then you may be banished from The Mount forever. I leave you the choice."

Again there was the collective gasp, and from no one louder than Vivienne. "I don't understand," she breathed.

"It's simple. I don't want your job as manager of The Mount Club. You do it well and you have a presence. I have other interests. If you choose to take my offer, you'll stay in your apartments, doing your job, serving me."

Rita ignored the murmurs on the dais. "If you serve me well, I'll treat you with the respect any member of The Mount deserves, and I'll give you the right to earn your freedom. But if you cross me, even once, my mother tells me there's a zookeeper in the Argentine Coven who would love to have you for a pet. I hear she's not nearly so gentle as our Leo." She reached out her hand to Vivienne.

The whole council seemed frozen in time, silent, breathless, waiting. Then, with a sigh and a whisper of silk, Vivienne slid from the chair on to her knees and pressed Rita's hand to her lips. "Do with me what you will, Mistress."

Barely aware of the surprised mumblings on the dais, Rita helped her to her feet and motioned for Aurora. "Slaves don't wear such finery."

Morgan came to Aurora's aid. They removed jewelry, gown, sexy lingerie, everything, until Vivienne stood in her stunning nakedness, too exquisite for Rita to resist. The woman's eyelids fluttered, and a serrated gasp escaped her throat as Rita brushed her breasts with her fingertips. Her nipples were instantly erect.

"You like that?" Rita hoped she didn't sound as surprised as she felt. "Yes, Mistress." Vivienne's response was breathless, her words clipped. "I like it a lot." Without clothes it was easy to see the tensing muscles in Vivienne's tummy and the subtle rocking of her hips.

How could Rita's touch be that exciting to one who hated her so badly? Cautiously Rita leaned close and kissed her. Vivienne's mouth was responsive, lips parted, tongue welcoming. Her breath grew heavier as the kiss deepened. Rita caressed the slender waist and the swell of her bottom, until now an act done only in her fantasies.

"Please, Mistress," Vivienne breathed.

Arousal overcame shock as Rita insinuated her hand between Vivienne's thighs, pressing her middle finger against surprisingly slippery folds to thrust upward. The sense of power was almost as arousing as the hot grip of pussy. Vivienne shuddered at her penetration and uttered a kitten-like cry.

She shifted and rocked, and her whole body grew tight as Rita thumbed hard-pressed circles around her new slave's distended clit. With two, then three, fingers, she thrust and scissored the sucking grasp of her cunt. Vivienne went feral, humping her hand, gabbling and grunting like some sex-crazed pet from Leo's zoo.

Rita felt her own pussy tremble in empathy. "Is this what you wanted?"

Vivienne managed only a nod before she shuddered so violently that she fell back into the chair, writhing and gasping, gathering herself into a convulsing foetal hug while the council watched in shock.

When, at last, Vivienne's orgasm had eased to little quivers, Rita found her voice. "If you wanted me to make you come, all you had to do was ask. You had complete control over me." She helped her to her feet. "And now I have control over you." Holding Vivienne in a hard gaze, Rita motioned for the guards. "Take my slave to the dungeon. Let her think about her bad behavior and anticipate her punishment. I'll attend to her personally, but first"—she turned to Edward—"I have a more urgent matter."

Chapter Thirty-One

As the High Council watched, Aurora helped Vivienne into a slave shift, then the guards led her away to the dungeon. Even in the clothing of a slave, Vivienne still looked like the queen of the universe. No doubt she knew better than most how much worse it could have been for her. Rita didn't want her broken, she just wanted her a little more submissive, and she was looking forward to teaching her all about submission.

When the doors closed behind Vivienne, Rita pulled Edward into a blood-boiling kiss that left him gasping for oxygen. "If there are no further objections," she addressed the council, "then I want what's been promised me."

There was a mutual nodding of heads, and Leo stepped forward. "What has been promised you, you have rightfully earned. The ritual is prepared."

Edward offered her a pussy-creaming smile and caressed her breasts through the clingy fabric of her gown. "Expensive dress?"

She chuckled softly and cupped his hands tighter to her. "Very. Will you have Aurora cut it off me?"

He traced the swell of her nipples with his thumbs, then dropped a humid kiss onto each one. "I think we might manage without that this time." He nodded to Alex, who moved behind her, sending shivers up her spine as he nibbled her nape. Then he unzipped her dress and slipped it off her shoulders, lingering to slide his hands over her exposed breasts.

Morgan and Leo moved forward to support her while she stepped out of the gown. Then Edward knelt in front of her and undid her stockings from blue lace garter belts, placing a kiss high on the inside of each thigh, nuzzling in close until she could feel the hard edge of his mask and the heat of his breath against the damp crotch of her panties.

Aurora and Lorelei knelt on either side and removed her stilettos and stockings. The delicious sensation of tongue and teeth on her instep generated tremors that snaked up her legs straight to her pussy. As Aurora began to nibble and suck her toes, she squirmed with such pleasure that Morgan and Leo's support became essential.

While Aurora fellated Rita's toes, Lorelei nipped and licked the muscular bulge of her calf blazing a trail up the back of her thigh ever closer to the tightening muscles of her bottom. Meanwhile, Alex made his approach from the north, teasing and nipping his way down her spine to the small of her back.

As Edward removed her garter belt and eased down her panties, Morgan and Leo tongue-bathed her arms and shoulders, working their way over the ticklish flesh of her armpits to the outer swell of her breasts where they lingered to caress and suckle. Every sensation was stronger than the last culminating in Edward flicking his tongue in ravenous slurps over the tip of her heavy clitoris straining at the apex of her cunt.

Then, just when she was about to come, he stood and moved aside for Leo, who took her mouth with none of the reserve he had shown toward her when she was his pet. He slid his hand between her legs to stroke her slippery pout with his palm. His voice vibrated next to her ear. "Rita Ellison Holly Martelli, you are now changed."

She struggled to concentrate on his words and not the pleasure his hand generated against her thrumming cunt.

He continued. "You are no longer as you were, and who you have become is one made new. You now belong to us and we to you. You have crossed over to this family who have claimed you as their own."

Without losing the rhythm of his stroking, he turned his attention to Edward. "This woman takes upon herself your name. Is therefore you who must guide her across." As he stepped away, Edward lifted her into his arms and carried her down another flight of stairs hidden behind the dais. The others followed. At the bottom, they entered a round stone chamber lit with sconced candles. It smelled strongly of herbs and old candle wax. There, in the middle, Edward lowered her onto a large stone slab unadorned and unhewn. The others moved to circle her rocky bed.

From somewhere, Lorelei produced a vial of oil that smelled of evergreen and sage and placed a drop of it on her forehead. "I anoint your head that you might always act wisely as you sojourn in The Mount."

She bent and gave Rita a lingering kiss as she handed the oil to Alex, who continued the ritual. "I anoint your heart that compassion might always imbue your actions." Once done, his straying hands and mouth detoured from her heart to her breasts, while Lorelei continued her explorations of her willing mouth.

Aurora was saying something about anointing her womb and her becoming a creative force in The Mount, but it was hard to concentrate when the enforcer's palm was curled over Rita's pubis with her middle finger circling and stroking the node of her clit.

Morgan anointed her knees, something about humility in all she did, but it wasn't her knees he was kissing. Instead, he was working his way up the inside of her thighs. When the vial was finally passed to Leo, Rita was so lost in the physicality of the High Council's blessing that she feared she might come and ruin their lovely ceremony.

"I anoint your feet," Leo was saying, "that you may never stray from the path you have chosen." As he bathed her ankle and heels with his tongue, she was beginning to hope they'd just keep on anointing, at least until she came.

From her aroused haze, she could see Edward standing at her feet, his golden mask shimmering in the candle light. He spoke. "This is the history of Rita Ellison Holly Martelli, fledgling member of The Mount, London Coven nominated for initiation by Edward Darcy Ellison.

Alex pulled away from her breasts and spoke. "A worthy dance partner and one loyal from the beginning."

"Punished for disobedience by me." Aurora pulled away and took over the history.

And it went on and on, with each council member droning through the whole history of her time at The Mount, which seemed pretty silly considering that it couldn't have been more than a few weeks. Besides, she already knew her history, and she was horny and desperate to get to Edward.

"I know of no one who wore the cat suit better," Morgan was saying.

She was just about to voice her impatience when Edward moved to stroke her pubic curls and caress her folds. "Hold on just a little longer, darling." His voice was tight, and he seemed to be struggling to breathe. "I know how badly you need to come. We both do, but it'll be so worth it, just like I promised."

Everything seemed haloed in golden light and her whole body buzzed not unlike it had the night she was chained to the Harley. For a second she drifted away, lost in the drone of her own history and Edward's yummy caresses.

"We now offer up the gift that was promised," Leo was saying. Suddenly the world was back in sharp focus. From his pocket, the Zoo Keeper took a silver key on a chain and placed it around her neck.

Aurora and Alex helped her to sit. "Take what's rightfully yours." Aurora nodded to Edward.

With her body still thrumming, Rita rose on her knees and moved toward the man who had inhabited all her fantasies since that first night on the Eurostar. Her heart raced in her chest. Her hands trembled.

Edward caressed her neck and bent to kiss the spot where her pulse hammered against her throat, as though by doing so he might calm its shuddering. Then he straightened and searched her face. "I'm yours, Rita Holly, body and soul. Let what has been promised be fulfilled."

Holding her breath, she reached behind his head, and with unsteady fingers, untied the black velvet ribbon that held the mask in place, then she carefully pulled it away.

There was a collective sigh of approval from the council.

It was neither the face of a monster nor of an angel she uncovered. Edward unmasked was rough-edged and completely lacking that expensive pretty-boy patina that Rita assumed would have appealed to Vivienne. His cheekbones were high and well defined. His nose was slightly crooked, as though it might have been broken at one time. Just above his left temple a thin white scar skirted his eye and stopped at the rise of his cheekbone. It was a small imperfection that made him look like he was not someone to be trifled with. That thought made her insides quiver with anticipation.

It was then she noticed the tight line of his lips, the slight wrinkling of his high forehead. "Well?" he said.

She offered him a smile and a hiccup of a laugh. "You'll do, Edward Ellison. You'll do."

He pulled her into a hard embrace, forcing the breath from her. "I can't tell you how glad I am to hear that." The words were smothered against her shoulder.

She could have stayed there forever, laced in his arms, but Edward extricated himself and stepped back, giving the others room to unzip and unbutton and kiss and caress until he stood before her in only his boxers. Aurora knelt to slip them over his hips, lingering long enough to tongue his navel and the light path of auburn hair trailing down to his penis. To that, she had no access. It was firmly caged in the confinement of Vivienne's chastity belt.

Before Rita could voice her protest, Edward nodded to the silver key hanging around her neck. "I'm yours now, darling. My face is not all you have access to."

"It's like Christmas." Morgan offered a wet sigh that sounded nothing like it came from a man who rode a Hog. "Go on, luv. Open it."

"We haven't had a new member in a while," Aurora added.

Rita took the key from around her neck, careful not to drop it in the mix of nerves and arousal coursing through her body. Edward joined her on the altar slab, straddling her on his knees, presenting the metal prison of the chastity belt before her. Then he took her hand and guided the key to the lock.

The whole council held its breath in anticipation, as the key turned. With a chink of metal, the belt opened, and Edward gasped almost painfully as his penis sprang free from its bonds and immediately into Rita's waiting hand. She nearly lost patience as Lorelei and Leo removed the belt from around Edward's waist. She'd waited so damned long for this. When they were done, she threw the key as far as she could. It landed with a metallic clink in a dark corner.

Once freed from his prison, Edward sprang like a leopard, pushing her back onto the slab and shoving her legs open with his knees. With very little maneuvering, he pushed into her with a grunt that ended in a sharp gasp as she tightened her grip around him, tightened it as though she would never let him go, and in truth, now that she finally had him, she didn't plan to. With each driving thrust, he raked her clit with his pubic bone, making it raw and demanding. She wrapped her legs around him and arched upward to meet him, not wanting to linger, not wanting to make it last, just wanting relief from the long wait.

He curled his fingers in her hair and pulled her closer, his breath coming in great gasps. "The ceremony's officially over when we come, then everyone else can come, and we can leave," he panted. "Then I can have you all to myself." The tension that made his whole body feel like tight, warm leather drew her to the brink right next to him, growling and pushing and bearing down. Each thrust built upon the one before, engulfing Rita in the same altered state she had experienced on the Harley only magnified by the emotions that raged through her.

When her orgasm came, she howled like an untamed pet in Leo's zoo, like the scream of the Harley under Morgan's expert control. With one last thrust, Edward exploded inside her, grunting and shuddering, holding her to him so tightly that she feared he might break her, as he emptied himself in her. "I love you, Rita Holly," he gasped as he collapsed on top of her. "And now I have you right where you belong."

Then the room erupted in frenetic sex. Morgan and Leo were both on their knees between Lorelei's legs, one in front, one behind, their tongues at work on both her holes. But it felt like they were doing it to Rita. As she watched, her pussy clenched around Edward's penis, still erect inside her. Strangely, she also felt what Leo and Morgan were feeling too, balls heavy, cocks arching toward receptive orifices.

"Do you understand now?" Edward began to thrust again as they caught a glimpse of Alex slipping his thick cock into Aurora's swollen pout. The enforcer had shed her waitress uniform down to her fishnet stockings and garter belts. Alex had forced her pert breasts upward out of the leather bra to suck and bite her nipples until they looked like maraschino cherries on mounds of pale ice cream.

"It feels like me." Rita choked on the emotion of the words. "Like I'm doing it, like I'm feeling it all."

"Like all of us, like we're all feeling it," Edward replied. And suddenly it was as though everyone had piled onto the stone altar next to them.

Flesh pounded flesh. The smells of candle wax and herbs were subsumed in the smells of hot, urgent fucking. Whimpers and thrusts and growls crescendoed to a group orgasm that rocked the chamber, which suddenly felt big enough to contain the whole universe. Then it shrank back around them, shrank until it felt like a womb about to give birth. Indeed, it was about to give birth to Rita Ellison Holly Martelli, who saw herself for the first time through the eyes of her new family. It was a family she was proud to be a part of, a family she was very much looking forward to getting to know better.

Acknowledgments

Big, gigantic, enormous thanks! Thank you, Renee and Joanna and all the lovely Ladiez at Sh! Women's Erotic Emporium for being my boundless source of information and inspiration during the writing of *The Initiation of Ms. Holly*. Ladiez, you're great! Thank you, Adam Nevill, for all your encouragement and invaluable insights into writing erotica. Thank you, Miranda Forbes, and all the great folks at Xcite Books and Accent Press. You're the best! Thanks and appreciation to the T Party Genre Writing Group for all the encouragement and support. Thank you, Raymond, for believing in me and being proud of me. *Volim te mnogo*!

About the Author

K D Grace believes Freud was right: in the end, it really IS all about sex—well, sex and love. And nobody's happier about that than she, because otherwise, what would she write about? She lives in South England with her husband and the growing gang of hooligan birds who frequent their bird feeders. When K D isn't busy writing, she's busy digging in her ever-expanding veg garden or taking long walks in the British countryside. She finds inspiration outdoors in nature, and most of her best story ideas come to her while she's walking or gardening.